CW00549293

Eight Weeks Later

A Novel

G.T. London

MAVITAE
Publishing

Copyright © 2024 by G.T. London

All rights reserved.

No part of this publication may be reproduced, distributed, or transmitted in any form or by any means, including photocopying, recording, or other electronic or mechanical methods, without the publisher's prior written permission, except as permitted by U.S. copyright law. For permission requests, contact Mavitae Publishing or G.T. London.

Much of this story takes place in Hawai'i, with some changes to locations and towns for the author's artistic license.

The story, all names, characters, organizations, and incidents portrayed in this production are fictitious. No identification with actual persons (living or deceased), places, buildings, and products is intended or should be inferred.

Dedicated to my husband, Jason—my partner-in-adventure, always my first reader, as well as my inspiration and guide.

Contents

A few words sprinkled across the pages

Aloha: A word embodying love, kindness, and connection in Hawaiian culture. Used to greet and bid farewell, it reflects a warm, welcoming demeanor.

Aumakua: Ancestral spirits believed to protect and guide families. They can manifest in various forms, connecting past generations to the present.

Braddah: A friendly term, similar to "brother" in English, used to address a close friend or acquaintance with warmth and familiarity.

Da family: An informal term for "the family," reflecting a sense of closeness and familiarity.

Hala tree: A tropical tree with long, narrow leaves and aerial roots. Found in the Pacific Islands and Southeast Asia.

Honu: The sea turtle, a symbol of good luck, endurance, and longevity in Hawaiian culture.

Humuhumunukunukuāpua'a: a Hawaiian triggerfish with vibrant colors.

Keiki: A term for children, emphasizing their importance and cherished status in the family and community.

Koa tree: A native Hawaiian tree known for its strength and durability. Symbolically, it represents integrity and bravery.

Lanai: A porch or balcony, often an outdoor space where people gather, relax, and enjoy the tropical surroundings.

Mahalo: Thank you. It reflects appreciation and thankfulness in Hawaiian culture.

Malasada: A delectable pastry, deep-fried and generously coated in sugar. A popular treat enjoyed during festivals and special occasions.

Ohana: The Hawaiian term for family. It extends beyond blood relations, emphasizing the idea that nobody gets left behind or forgotten.

Poke: A delicious Hawaiian dish featuring raw fish, usually tuna, seasoned with various flavorful ingredients.

Poi: A staple food in Hawaiian cuisine made from taro root. It holds cultural significance and is often associated with abundance.

Pū: A conch shell horn.

Slippa: Casual footwear, usually referring to flip-flops. Perfect for the laid-back island lifestyle.

Waʻa canoe: A traditional Hawaiian canoe, symbolizing the connection between the islands and the sea, as well as the seafaring heritage of the Hawaiian people.

Prologue

Water, water everywhere. I crane my neck slightly, but I still see water. My gaze darts around, only to be met with the relentless continuity of water. I'm lying on a small black rock surrounded by rippling blue vastness.

My eyes act like a 33 mm camera lens, scanning the area frantically. Still nothing but water. Ah, there's the sun, vanishing into the horizon and blending with the water.

I let out a sigh of exasperation. So, I really did jump off of that cliff.

A crab with beady eyes is scuttling toward me.

Looking around, the shore is over there, and the path is in that direction as well. This rock stands in the middle of the ocean. Oh, man. I can't swim, and there's so much water around me.

Something brushes past my neck, and I give a little

shriek. Looking down, I realize it's a necklace, not a creature.

Ah, it's a turtle-shaped necklace.

Why am I wearing a turtle necklace?

"Oh!" I remember suddenly.

Chapter One

As I make my way from the airport to my beach house, the loud grumbling of thunder shakes the air. The tropical storm intensifies, and I can barely see the road. Blimey, there are no other cars around.

I can't believe that I own a beach house in Hawai'i. I'd love to say that I can't wait to settle in and listen to the soothing sounds of the ocean, but the truth is, I can't wait to sell it and return to London. Fast.

"You have reached your destination," announces the GPS. The voice is female and has an American accent.

Raindrops pelt the windscreen more fiercely, completely obscuring my vision. I pull over cautiously and park the car then wrestle with the car door, pushing and grunting against the relentless force of the wind, which is just as determined to push back—it's a right tussle, I tell you.

I hear you, mate. I'm not particularly keen on being here either.

I should have arrived at 5:00 p.m., but my flight was delayed five hours. The car rental office was about to close when I finally showed up.

My first flight lasted almost thirteen hours and the second was six hours. I crossed North America and two large oceans. Yet it's still the same day here in Hawai'i. Tomorrow has already started in London.

My London. It's my hustling and bustling city. My home.

I should have listened to my brother, Luke. He encouraged me to book a hotel for the first few days. He's always been the logical one.

I finally push open the car door and then run to a large gate crowded by wild bushes. There's no number on it. Noticing another gate on the left, I run to it, getting soaked in just a few steps.

Number 234. Nope, not my house.

Mine must be the one with no number.

I run back to the other gate, which has seen better days. I reach for the rusted latch, but it refuses to yield. The rain pounds endlessly, drumming my face, weighing down my eyelashes.

I push with all my might and the gate creaks open a fraction, only to grind to a stubborn halt.

As frustration bubbles up, I square my shoulders and, with newfound resolve, push against the gate with my right shoulder. The old wood groans. The gate opens a tiny bit more and stops. My vision blurs as rainwater streams down my face. With one final Herculean effort, I give an all-out shove. I stumble forward as the gate moves.

"Whoa, whoa."

I'm faced with a weathered single-story house crouched in the dark. I dash across the lawn but misjudge my steps and stumble, nearly taking a disastrous fall. There's dense vegetation all around the house.

I finally reach the covered porch. Thoroughly soaked but not shivering. This rain is different from what I'm used to in London—more like a warm touch from Mother Nature than a chilly hug.

I wipe away the rain from my face and observe my surroundings, illuminated by the soft light of my phone.

The first order of business is finding the key to the house. I've been told it's underneath the porch, on the right.

But it's so dark, and the rain is even more intense now. And the right side of the porch is covered in vines. I sigh then sprint back down the stairs. The ground is muddy.

I push the leaves aside.

"There you are!"

The rock. I lean in to grab it but slip, landing on my knees. A large leaf covers my face.

"Argh!" I shout, while I remove the rock, still on my knees.

A small hollow in the ground has been revealed, and within it is a small metal box with a secured combination lock. I snatch the box and run back to the shelter of the porch.

I punch in the combination that the lawyer included in his email: 0808. It seems like a dream now, but it was only a week ago that he called me at my coffee shop with life-changing news.

"You've inherited a beach house from your grandparents in Hawai'i."

I chuckled. "I can guarantee you've got the wrong person. I don't have grandparents in Hawai'i. I don't have any grandparents."

"Our research verifies that you're the only successor of the Williamson family. The documents confirm it."

"Mr. Moore, I'm sorry, but there's no relation between me and anyone from Hawai'i. My family is from Bristol. I don't even know who the Williamson family is."

"I'm aware of your adoptive family in Bristol, but I'm referring to your biological family."

"Ah, I see. My biological father lost his family in the war in Europe. And my mom . . ."

I trailed off momentarily. I barely knew anything about her. All I knew was she was from America.

"The house was your maternal grandparents' home." The lawyer's voice was tender and almost sad.

After a moment of silence, I asked, "This Williamson family, do you know them?"

"Yes, they were close friends of mine."

"Give me a few moments, please."

I made my way to the small office behind the front

counter of my coffee shop. After exhaling and taking a sip of water, I said to the lawyer, "Okay, I'm all ears."

And now, here I am on the opposite side of the globe, drenched to the bone and standing on the porch of my beach house on an island in the Pacific Ocean where it's summer all year round.

It's kind of ironic because my whole life, I've been dreaming about traveling. And just last week, I was ready to make my dreams a reality. I was all set to travel the world for six months. But Hawai'i? Nope, it wasn't on the agenda.

The rain roars.

"How much rain can this place take?" Shaking my head, I take the key out of the box.

The golden key slides right in, but the door makes a loud, high-pitched screech as I open it. The rusted hinges groan.

"Hello," I murmur.

The old wooden floors creak under my weight, sounding as if they're about to give way. Dust scatters across the floor. I walk down a short and wide hallway that curves into a large living area on the left. There are some other rooms on the right.

It feels as if the house is alive and watching me with intense presence. My footsteps echo as I look for light switches.

Nope, no electricity. Not tonight.

I use my phone as a torch, take small steps, and look around. There's a sharp and loud crack. I freeze in place, my heart racing. A moment later, I realize that it was just an old floorboard.

The furniture in the living room seems to be frozen in time. My gaze lands on an ancient sofa with flowery cushions. I move toward it and touch its worn fabric with my fingertips. The sofa groans as I lower myself onto the cushions.

I can see a long, narrow kitchen opposite the sofa. There are large windows between the couch and the kitchen, but I can see only dark beyond the glass.

Like curtains, my heavy eyelids are slowly drawing themselves closed, though without my consent. I'm exhausted.

"Nope, not just yet," I exclaim loudly, over the thunder and rain that sounds like a percussion band. "Let's see the rest of the house."

The wind howls as I open the door to a large bedroom. It seems everything's alive in this house.

There are two smaller bedrooms across the hall. The bathroom is surprisingly spacious for a home this size. I'm still curious, but the battery on my phone is running low and I need to conserve it.

I return to the creaking couch, lean back into it, switch off my phone, and plunge into darkness. My eyelids close. While drifting off, I promise myself that everything will be better when I wake up to the calming rhythm of the ocean.

But that's not what I wake up to. Instead, I wake to the sensation of fur on my legs. I utter a curse and then hear a hissing sound—maybe a wild boar snuck into the house? A shadowy figure darts toward the kitchen. I grab my phone in case I need to call 911, forgetting I turned it off.

I urge the phone to boot up. "Come on, come on."

Once I have light from my phone again, I scan the room and spot a cat in the corner of the kitchen. I collapse back on the sofa in relief.

"Come on, kitty cat, I didn't know I had a roommate here."

With a whoosh, the cat rushes from the kitchen into one of the bedrooms, and I hear a loud crash. I wince. "Blimey, what now?"

It sounded like a fragile vase, but I'm not about to try to figure it out in the pitch dark.

Chapter Two

I try to drift off again, but it's not happening. It's 2:00 a.m., and my phone is at fifteen percent.

It's dark. There's no electricity.

Suddenly, I recall the lawyer mentioning a fuse box. And here I've spent hours in total darkness. "The fuse," I say to myself. "There's a fuse, dude."

I grab my phone and look for the bedroom with the fuse box behind its door. Door one opens into a small room with a single bed. There's no fuse box there. Door two opens to another small bedroom. No fuse there. I find it hiding behind the door of the larger bedroom. There are many switches, but I see the main switch at the top, sitting on OFF. I flip it to the right, but nothing happens.

I shake my head. "It ain't happening tonight," I utter, as I walk back to the sofa. The rain rumbles with the storm, and I can hear leaves brushing against the house. Thankfully, I manage to fall asleep again.

When I wake, it's 7:00 a.m. and my neck is stiff.

"Congrats, Mr. Drama," I say aloud, holding my neck and looking around at my surroundings—an extreme change from London. Nothing seems to be mellow in my life. It's been drama from the moment I was born.

There's a lot I don't know about my past, but I know I was born in London and that my mother was hit by a car a few weeks before my first birthday. Five years after I lost my mother, I was put in foster care. I didn't understand why I had to leave my home, my bedroom, my only world. I kicked and screamed, trying to hold on to anything—my bed frame, the door handle. I reached for my stepmother, begging her to hold me, but she just stood by the kitchen door and didn't say a single word. My father wasn't around. As usual, he was away, working.

"Roy, let's get into the car now," a smiley lady said. I learned later that she was a social worker. "You'll have a nice home, new toys, and lots of delicious meals."

"But I want my daddy," I said, sobbing. I had a home. I didn't understand what was happening. A man with the smiley lady hoisted me into his arms. I stopped screaming but continued to cry. The woman opened the car door, and the man lowered me next to her in the back seat.

This is your new home!

Meet your new family!

Here's your new bedroom!

These memories still make me uncomfortable. I shake them off and rise from the couch, put my hand on my chest, and take a few deep breaths. I'm thirty-four and don't want another new home, just like I didn't want a new home at age six. Luckily, I was eventually adopted by a loving mom and dad. But I'm still haunted by the memory of being forced out of my home and into a new one that I didn't want.

I look around. *This isn't a new home*, I remind myself. It's just an inherited house. I had no idea I had grandparents here, and I have no idea why they chose to stay strangers to me. Why would they do such a thing? But then, I'm done trying to use logic and reasoning when it comes to parents—or grandparents. I am curious, though: How did my mother end up on the other side of the world, in London? Why wasn't I told earlier about her Hawaiian roots?

My eyes drift around the living room. The electricity is on, but the abundance of natural light coming into the house overpowers the interior lights. I'm relieved that the fuse wasn't broken after all. My gaze eventually settles on a striking pair of light-green eyes in the far corner.

"Hello, roommate," I whisper. For the first time since leaving London, I feel warmth spread through my chest. I grew up with a couple of cats.

The cat runs into the hallway.

"Nice meeting you too."

It's quiet. No thunder or rain. I turn around and find myself staring through the large windows.

I gasp at the sight of the ocean beyond the garden. "Whoa! Whoa." It's like an enormous blue magnet. The blue is so intense, it's almost overwhelming—the sky, the

13

ocean. Between the expansive windows stands a door with a key hanging from it.

I move around and take in the other details that I missed last night. The kitchen cabinets are small and constructed of light-colored wood. In the corner of the living room stands a big wooden dinner table with wobbly legs. I suspect that it was once the focal point in this family home. The thought of my blood relatives gathered together makes me painfully aware of how they abandoned me.

"Nope, no new home, man," I mutter. "Not on my watch." I shake my head and snatch my hand back from the mahogany tabletop. I'm getting rid of this house. Sell. Fast. This time around, it's my choice. I'll leave in a week and continue with my around-the-world travel plans.

I can't wait to get on that plane next Wednesday. I have seven days to get everything in order so that the lawyer can handle the sale for me.

Stepping onto the back porch, I take in the scenery. The ocean. A golden beach. Rows of swaying palm trees.

"Wow," I whisper. "That's a view."

It's a lovely morning with a gorgeous sky and a warm temperature. Hard to believe it's February 2.

I look up at the enormous house to my left. A woman is standing in front of the second-floor window. She steps back before I can smile and wave. Perhaps people aren't as friendly as they say around here.

I gingerly step onto the grass and walk around. The garden is larger than the house; I walk around the side and back of the house. There's so much vegetation. I then make my way to a small wooden gate separating the grass from the beach. I step onto the warm sand—the golden sand!

Inhaling deeply, I let the salty breeze fill my lungs, taking in the scent of the ocean. Gentle waves crash against the shore, and the sound calms my mind. Did I just stroll from my living room to the beach barefoot? Ha! This is a new twist in life.

I sit on the sand, which is scattered with black rocks. They're the remnants of ancient lava flows that cooled once they met the ocean long ago—knowledge gleaned from the magazine on the flight.

I slowly close my eyes, basking in the serenity of the moment. *I'm in Hawai'i.* I let out a sigh.

Then something solid and wet collides with my cheek, shocking me out of my peaceful moment. "Son of a b—"

I stop midcurse, my hand flying to my face. Excruciating pain explodes on my left cheek.

A small bundle of black curls darts in front of me, followed closely by a woman who is clearly out of breath.

"I'm so sorry!" she says, stopping, panting heavily. "I didn't mean to throw the ball this far. He's usually pretty good at catching the ball. Are you okay?"

"Yeah, I'll live," I mutter, rubbing my sore cheek.

"It's only a small ball."

"Yeah, well, it hit me pretty hard," I grumble.

The little thing with black curls runs back to us with

the ball in its mouth, bouncing excitedly. So, the wetness is dog slobber—on my face.

"Hey, little fella," I say, trying to distract myself from the pain. I tickle his neck. A coat of curly fur cascades over his face. "You're quite a sight to behold, aren't you?"

He drops the ball and takes a few steps away, waiting for the next throw.

"Curly, here!" The woman throws it, and off he goes to retrieve it. Then she extends her hand to me. "I'm Curly's human family." I take her hand and look up at her. That's when I notice she's gorgeous. Her smile is stunning, revealing perfect teeth that shine like pearls. She also has adorable dimples and striking green eyes. Another sight to behold.

"Wow," I say, glancing away as I stand up. "Nice meeting you, Curly's human family. I'm Roy."

"Oh, you're a Brit."

I smile and tighten my grip on her hand. "I'm Roy, a Brit."

Our hands stay locked in a firm grip for a long two seconds.

"Nice meeting you too." She smiles and points at the small bundle of curls in the distance, sniffing some beach bags. "I've got to run. I'm so sorry again." She takes off after the dog.

"No worries," I murmur, holding my face and watching them disappear. I didn't get her name. *Oh well, I'll be out of here in a few days anyway.*

Walking back to the house, I sense someone watching

me. I turn back hoping to see Curly's gorgeous human family, but I can't see her.

Then I look up. The neighbor is standing in front of the window again. It's hard to tell if her short hair is blond or gray. I pause a beat and then smile and wave, but just as before, she steps back and recedes into her house.

That house. Goodness gracious, the size of that thing! It looks as if it's trying to occupy the entire coast. And the aesthetics, dear me. Whoever designed that house clearly had an aversion to subtlety.

I can only imagine the conversations among the locals. "You can't miss it, mate. Just look for the house that could double as a navigational landmark for lost sailors!"

I return to my little beach house; the contrast is overwhelming. My face is still burning. It's not even 8:00 a.m.

Chapter Three

Coffee. No matter what the day throws my way, there's always coffee. Kitchens calm me. Cooking grounds me. When I turn the kitchen tap nothing comes out for a few seconds. Then a rush of air escapes and water trickles out.

I assemble the coffee maker, securing the top chamber of the moka pot onto the bottom. Then I place it on the electric stove and watch the pressure build. As the coffee brews, so does my bitterness and pain. I think of the family meals I didn't share in this kitchen. The pain might also have something to do with my throbbing face.

I spot the cat sitting by the hallway.

"Hey, roomie, do you have some ice by any chance?"

No response.

"How do you get in and out of the house anyway?"

The cat disappears, but I still don't see a cat door anywhere.

The water starts to boil. It passes through the coffee grounds, and the rich, dark liquid seeps into the upper chamber. The aroma intensifies, and once the last of the liquid has sputtered out, I remove the moka pot from the stove.

"Here is how to transform sadness," I say to the cat. "All it takes is the delicious scent of coffee." I pour myself a cup.

I own a small café in a historic brick plaza in Central London. In the corner of Pages and Beans Café is a stack of books, and I've positioned a couple of upholstered armchairs below a vintage-looking PAGES sign. I take great pleasure in delighting commuters, welcoming them with a smile, and remembering their names or drink preferences. I watch as they march off to their high-rise offices in the city skyline feeling grateful that I'm no longer part of that corporate crowd.

My café fuels my passion: serving food with a touch of happiness. But my real joy is cooking for family and friends. When I was young, I never had a proper family meal due to my stepmother's lack of care and my father's constant absence. My biological father never noticed how thin I was getting when he came back from his work trips. It was my teachers who filed a report with social services. At six years old, I was unkempt, too thin, and had no lunches. And no friends. I was undernourished until I met my first foster family. Then I had food, but I was still a scared child.

My mind slips back to our family kitchen in Bristol. I

met my adoptive family when I was ten years old. For the first few months, I would stand by the door listening to the rhythmic sounds of dinner preparation and enjoying the inviting aromas. Then one Sunday morning, my adoptive mother asked me if I wanted to help with the Sunday roast preparation. "You can take care of the vegetables," she suggested. I sprinted up to her, nodding.

Even the simplest dish has the power to heal and nourish the soul. That's what happened to me.

Chapter Four

Sipping my coffee, I give myself a proper tour of the house. All doors are open. The larger bedroom also has a large window, which frames a view of the sky, ocean, and beach.

"Nice one," I say.

It's unbelievable that my grandmother lived here until six months ago, and that I was utterly oblivious! Life's a right whirlwind of surprises, I'll say that much.

Her room is tidy, and it looks as if she spent time in here recently. The bed has a worn-out but nice bedspread with a Hawaiian motif. The wood flooring seems darker in one corner, and there's a faint scent of something rotting. I find puddles forming around the bed. Looking up, I see the damp ceiling. I could investigate that; there's a ladder outside at the back. If it seems easy to fix, I might give it a go.

No grandmother, whether alive or not, should have water dripping down from their bedroom ceiling.

Walking into another bedroom, I'm greeted by a simple sight. A single bed with a delicate green bedspread sits against the wall. The window looks out to the front yard, which contains bushes and a couple of tropical-looking trees with long, narrow leaves.

Gotcha, you! I say, noticing the slightly open window with branches reaching toward it. I make a mental note not to close this bedroom door; otherwise, my roommate won't be able to get into the rest of the house.

I look out. The roots of the tree make me smile—I've never seen anything like them. Many are above the ground, reaching from the trunk outwards and downwards. It's as though the tree has many legs. I chuckle at the thought. Was this my mom's bedroom? Did she grow up here?

I feel a memory trying to surface as soon as I step into the bathroom, the last door on the left side of the hallway. It's a deep recollection, and it takes a while for me to make sense of it.

I was possibly five years old and in my run-down bedroom at my father and stepmother's house. Its white walls, once bright, were faded, and there were patches of peeling paint. My small bed was pushed against one of the walls. There was a high window, so I could see the sky only from a particular angle while lying in bed.

I had to pee, so I slowly opened the door and slipped out.

"I told you to play in your room." My stepmother shuffled me back into the bedroom, shutting the door in my face.

I waited for a while then quietly opened the door again to sneak into the toilet.

"What did I tell ya?"

I stopped and pointed to the toilet, not looking at her.

"Go on then, how many times a day must you pee?"

I ran toward the bathroom at the end of a narrow corridor in our London flat.

Her hair, usually unkempt, was often held in place with rollers, and she was always cold and distant. But that always changed when my father was at home. He was a welder who did railway maintenance, so he was away a lot.

Another memory takes me into that bathroom of my childhood.

My skin felt as if it were being ripped off my back with each frantic scrub.

"It hurts," I yelled.

As my stepmother poured shampoo over my head, I screamed. It burned my eyes until tears ran down my face.

I knew that a painful bath meant my father would be home soon. It also meant that I could leave my small bedroom and eat with them.

Not long after, the man and the smiley woman turned up. They took me away from my home and drove me to some stranger's house.

My first foster family was a couple who had big smiles

25

and filled my lunch box with nice things. But I didn't want nice things for lunch. I wanted my father to come and get me.

He never did.

After a while, I started liking my new life. But one night, I woke up to screams and shouts and rushed to hide under the bed. Glass shattered.

I must have done something wrong, I thought, as I was the one who was always upsetting the adults. But no one came into my room.

After that, the terrifying nightmares started. The more the couple argued, the more I woke up drenched in sweat.

"You'll wake him up—stop shouting," I heard her say one night. She was crying. When she checked on me, I pretended that I was sleeping.

After some time, things took a turn for the worse. I woke up one morning and my bed was wet. But it wasn't sweat. I could smell it. I tried to hide it by pouring water on the sheets.

"It's only water," I told her, when she saw my bed.

"It's okay, sweetie," she responded, giving me a hug. "Let's have a bath."

I cringed.

"Remember, you liked playing in the bath last time. You held the showerhead."

I nodded; I really liked her. After my bath, I saw her walking into my bedroom. I quietly moved closer to the door, careful not to make a sound. I watched her quickly change my bedsheets.

Then the same man and smiley woman from before arrived. They told me that I was leaving this home too and that they had already arranged another nice new home for me. The couple in this home was getting something called a divorce. At that moment, they assured me it had nothing to do with me, but I sensed it was about my presence. It upset people.

This time, I didn't kick or scream.

When I was leaving, the nice woman hugged me and said, "I love you, Roy. I'm sorry this didn't work out."

I walked into the car, my head down, holding my toy.

It was the first time I'd heard "I love you, Roy."

And it was also my first heartbreak.

Chapter Five

My curiosity pulls me back to what I assume was my grandmother's bedroom. A small golden hinge on a box flashes when I pull open the drawer next to her bed. The lid is engraved with hibiscus flowers. The hinge and its clasp look new, not a sign of rust on them.

Sitting on the bed, I gently open the lid.

Inside I find photos of people who must be my family. As I look through them, I come across a portrait of my grandparents—Hina and Ben Williamson, along with two young children. He has a proud smile, holding his family close. My fingers trace the image of my mother; she must be around five years old. I have a few photos from her childhood. I know those eyes. I see a very happy child. This makes me happy, too. She gets her looks from her father: deep-blue eyes, light-brown wavy hair.

The girl sitting beside her must be her friend. Dad told

me that I didn't have any aunts or uncles because neither he nor Mom had siblings. Perhaps a Hawaiian friend? She has dark-brown wavy hair and a gently curved nose. She looks a bit younger than my mom. The two friends beam happily.

Feeling a strange sensation, I look out the window. My mother used to play on this beach when she was a child. I ponder how her life was, growing up here. At long last, it's time for me to find out more about her.

Last week, after receiving the call from the lawyer in Hawai'i, I called my father, who still lives in London.

I usually call him a few times a year—on Christmas or for his birthday—so he was surprised to hear from me. He now lives alone, and he's my sole connection to my mother. Speaking to him makes me feel a little bit closer to her.

"Did you know my mother was from Hawai'i?" I asked him.

"Was she? I never knew."

"So you didn't know about her family?"

"No, I didn't."

"But how is it that you can marry someone and not know anything about her background?"

"You asked me this before, and I told you."

Yes, I had asked, and he had told me. But I suspected that he wasn't telling me everything. He'd said that they got married a few months after being introduced. My father hadn't delved into her background or history, as he didn't talk much about his past. He'd arrived in London without any family, having fled the Balkans due to the conflict. They'd agreed to leave their pasts behind.

"Things were different for us," he said again. "We wanted to start a new life here without dwelling on painful pasts. It worked for us."

I looked at his face on my phone screen. I noticed a vein on his forehead. His once-strong cheekbones had softened, and his jet-black hair had turned silver and thinned.

After a stretched few seconds, he looked away, as if he'd been thinking of saying something but had changed his mind.

"Is there something else?" I asked.

"No," he said, but he blinked several times.

Now, I pick up another photo, this one of a baby's first birthday. Is this my mom? The hair is darker, but babies change. *Kalani's 1st birthday, 0808*, is written on the back of the photo.

Who is Kalani? My mother's name was Leilani, though she went by Lena.

Lena, Leilani, and Kalani—things are starting to get a bit confusing here, Mom. Is Kalani your nickname?

I pull out a photo of the same baby with a toddler next to her. The toddler is clearly my mother. And as I shuffle through the stack of photos, I find many other photos of the same two girls with my grandparents. I flip over one of the photos.

"*Leilani and Kalani,*" I read aloud, the names crashing into one another like billiard balls on a table.

31

Leilani and Kalani.

"Leilani and Kalani," I mutter, hoping that the repetition will help my whirling mind.

Did my mother have a sister?

What now? Still holding the photo, I stand up and try to ease the tension in my neck by pushing on my back muscles.

Mi-aw

I turn my head abruptly toward the door and pain shoots through my neck. "There you are, roomie! You do have a voice."

Mi-aw

"Did you just respond to me, kitty?" I say with a chuckle, releasing my grip on the photo. The cat takes a few steps toward me.

No one told me about a sister.

"I think I have an aunt, kitty cat."

With a nonchalant air, her tail trailing lazily behind her as if she has no particular purpose in her journey, she turns and leaves.

"Yeah, I'd walk off if I could. Too blimey confusing."

Her birthday must be August 8—0808. For crying out loud, what else will I discover in this house?

My thumb remains on Kalani's cheek for a beat. I have an aunt.

"Nice meeting you, Aunt Kalani."

A chill races down my back as a thought hits me. Oh, man, the fact that I'm inheriting this house implies that Kalani has passed. My breath catches in my throat. I'll never get to know this person. It seems as if I lose my family members as quickly as I find them.

I sit down again and a Polaroid photo catches my eye. Happy teenagers. "*Leilani, Kalani, and Kimo*" is written on the back.

Kimo.

In the photo, Kimo is a youthful man with a sun-kissed complexion, brown hair, and chestnut-colored eyes. Who is this Kimo? There are more photos of Kalani and Leilani in their teenage years, and Kimo is in most of them. Maybe he's a cousin? A close friend, maybe a neighbor kid. I wonder if he still resides here in Nalu, a small town on the south shore of the island, or if he ever did.

I conclude that since he knew my mother and aunt, finding him would be a worthwhile quest. I must ask the lawyer.

I set three goals to achieve before my return to London, just six days away: Meet with the lawyer. See if I can repair the roof. Find this guy, Kimo.

But first, I need groceries.

Chapter Six

As I drive to the local supermarket, windows down, I take in the warm February sun, the Pacific Ocean, and the stretches of beautiful beaches. The town snuggles against the foothills of a mountain on the right, with the vast ocean stretching to my left. Unbelievably, this mountain is no ordinary one—it's a dormant volcano! How mind-blowing is that?

People stroll along both sides of the road, which is lined with palm trees and lush tropical plants. There's something about the swaying palm trees that makes me smile. I wonder why they have a "happiness" effect on people. I drive slowly, as does everyone else. No one appears to be in a hurry. This must be the laid-back Hawaiian lifestyle I've heard about.

I note the expansive grassy areas between the road and the ocean and see a large gathering—perhaps a family get-together. There's even an enormous bouncy castle in the middle of the grass.

"Wow, that's cool," I say with a chuckle. I wonder if bouncy castles were here when my mother and aunt were growing up.

As I approach the central part of Nalu, the roads and restaurants, cafés, and shops get busier. Still, the notion of "busy" here differs from what I'm accustomed to back home. There's so much to absorb navigating this town— the natural beauty, joyful families, couples strolling hand in hand, playful children. It feels like a different kind of life than the one I live in London.

At the local store, I select some groceries and also look for cat food. This morning my roomie enjoyed a small piece of cheddar from the sandwich I received on the plane. She's shy, but she watches me eagerly. I also go to a hardware store to purchase a few items to fix the roof leak —at least temporarily. In Nalu, everyone seems to be either wearing a smile or just about to break into one. I feel as if I've said "Good morning" to more people in the last hour than I do in the mornings at my coffee shop in London.

When I return, I reach out to touch the gate I shouldered when I arrived. My fingers brush against the rough grain of the wood, and I apply a bit of upward pressure, just enough to ease the latch out of its well-worn groove.

With a subtle creak, the gate responds as if acknowledging my effort. It seems to know that I'm now willing to take the time to understand it, to work with it rather than trying to force it open with impatience. As I continue to lift, the gate glides smoothly on its hinges, revealing the beach house.

"Kitty cat, hey, kitty cat. Here's some food for you." I place it on a small plate in the kitchen. Nope, she isn't interested.

"Do you prefer cheese?" I know I shouldn't feed the cat cheese, but sometimes, building bridges requires doing extraordinary things. "Here's a small piece for you."

Here she comes. I grin at this small orange being with a white neck ruff. It's as if she's wearing a white scarf.

She is curious as she checks out the cat food after gulping down the nibble of cheddar.

I'm nervous about meeting the lawyer today. I should've asked for a morning meeting as I'm feeling impatient and want to get the process started. The plan is to arrange meetings with a few local real estate agents so I can sell the property as quickly as possible.

The lawyer, Frank Moore, is flying in from O'ahu. Since he was a friend of my grandparents, I'm hoping that he'll enlighten me about why they never made an effort to contact me.

In the afternoon, the crunching of pebbles signals his arrival, and a car comes to a stop just beyond the gate. When he effortlessly swings open the wooden gate, I'm already waiting on the front porch.

"Hi, I'm Roy. Nice to meet you." I extend my hand, and he shakes it. "Come on in, please."

"It's great to meet you, Roy, finally," he says with an expansive smile. He exudes warmth. "I'm Frank." He takes off his shoes.

"No, no," I say. "No need."

"I've been to this house hundreds of times, son. Never walked in with shoes on, so if it's okay, I'll take them off." He shifts his gaze down to my shoes.

"Uh-hmm, okay. Sure." I remove my trainers, leaving them next to his shoes outside the door.

"Not much has changed here," he says. He must be in his seventies. He has a light tan and neatly groomed short gray hair. He is wearing a blue short-sleeved linen shirt and beige trousers. We sit at the kitchen table.

I stare at my grandparents' friend for a few beats and then, with a deep breath, say, "I have no plans to stick around, so I won't change anything. How did you locate me? Your call caught me completely off guard."

Mr. Moore puts on his reading glasses and opens his brown briefcase. "Okay, you want to get straight to the point, and I don't blame you."

"I'm sorry, how rude of me. Can I offer you a drink?"

He smiles. "Thank you. A glass of water, please." He studies me for a few seconds. "You have her eyes and smile. Your grandma."

I've my grandma's eyes. No kidding! I shake my head slightly and pour him water while he takes files from his briefcase.

"As you know, I'm a friend of your grandparents. Your grandpa departed a few years back, and your grandma joined him six months ago. They were true soulmates." He swallows hard. "Your grandma is Hawaiian, and her family owned this land. Many generations of her family."

I'm getting an uneasy feeling listening to him. I inhale subtly but deeply.

"I'm the executor of the estate and their will. They didn't know that they had a grandson. Both their daughters left home when they were young."

"Both daughters." I shake my head.

"Yes, both daughters. They knew that Leilani, your mother, died in a road accident a few years after she left Hawai'i, but as far as they knew, she was living alone in London. She told them that she had a surprise for them and was planning to visit in a few months."

"A surprise baby." I exhale. "I wonder why she didn't tell them about her marriage, her pregnancy, and everything else. I was almost one when she passed away. Isn't that peculiar?"

"Indeed, it is. There's more to this than meets the eye."

"For sure. So, how did you find me? And what do you know about Kalani?"

"So you know about Kalani."

"Only since this morning," I reply, my tone sharper than I intended.

Frank adjusts his reading glasses. "I hired a genealogy company to search for your aunt. Hina, your grandmother, insisted that Kalani was in Ireland, but your grandpa requested a death certificate for her before he passed. Your grandma never accepted that she was dead, so I hired investigators—this was her dying wish."

"Sorry, I need water too." I rise from my chair. It feels as if the house is sinking around me.

"I know this is a lot to process."

"I'm feeling ever so furious, you know?" I say, getting a glass out of the kitchen cupboard. "Why did no one have the foggiest clue about my existence? Why did my own mother keep me hidden away like some deep, dark secret? Growing up, I felt like I had no roots. And now I'm finding out about generations of family. My biological father never showed an ounce of interest in me," I say with a scoff. "When we had to sketch family trees at school, mine always ended after the first branch. Now I learn that my mother is half Hawaiian, and I apparently have an aunt as well as a Hawaiian heritage stretching back through the ages." I take a sip of water to calm myself. "Mr. Moore, none of this makes any sense."

"Call me Frank."

"Okay, Frank. How do we quickly sell this place?"

He points at the documents. "Come and look at these."

I pull my chair up next to his.

"Your family could have sold this house for millions, but they didn't."

"Well, I want to sell as soon as possible."

My chest feels tight. I admit it's hard not to like what I've seen of this town, but the child within screams at me to disregard this family, this home, and this life they led without me. I feel abandoned and hurt.

"If that's your decision, you'll need to access the death certificate of your aunt. But, just to let you know, your grandma never accepted that Kalani was dead. She said she felt it when Leilani, your mother, passed, and she never changed her mind about Kalani being alive."

"Kalani," I whisper, with a long and slow blink. There's a slight chance that she could be alive. As fast as I lost her, I could find her again.

"Yes, and people here knew your mother, Leilani, as Lani."

I nod. "You explained over the phone that my mother applied to change her name to Lena as soon as she arrived in the UK."

"Yes, that was part of the investigation findings from the Royal Courts of Justice."

"Why did my grandpa proceed with the request for Kalani's death certificate against my grandma's wishes?"

"Because he didn't think she was alive. He wanted the estate to go to the local community and environmental causes. But his wife opposed it strongly. She said she knew she had family out there somewhere, and she was right. I found you."

"She meant her daughter, not me."

"No, son, she always said 'Da family,' as we say here. You're her family."

My family. I repeat a few times in my mind trying to grasp their significance. *My family.* The words settling on my chest—heavy.

After seconds of nerve-racking silence and stillness, I

41

say, "Tell me more about 'da family,' Frank. Please start with my grandma and grandpa."

"I will, but let me ask you this first—how long are you here for?"

"A week."

"That's a short stay after such a long journey."

"I wasn't planning a vacation." I notice my bitter tone.

"Did you meet the neighbors yet?"

"Not yet. But tell me more about the grandparents, please?"

"Your grandparents had a strong standing in this community. They cherished the land and house. However, their neighbors didn't share their sentiments. Did you see that massive house?" He nods in the direction of my neighbors' place.

"It's hard to miss."

"The current owners bought the land and built the house after the original owners passed. But before they started building, they tried to buy this land too. They offered a good price, but your grandparents wouldn't consider their offer."

Frank shifts in his chair and continues. "Ben and Hina called me for legal advice because the neighbors claimed that some boundary lines didn't align with the legal property boundaries. It worried your grandparents. The Johnsons, the neighbors, wanted to build a three-story house here."

"You're telling me that they intended to construct a house bigger than the monstrosity next door? What on earth were they aiming for? A private compound or something?"

"However hard Ben tried, he couldn't stop them from building a gigantic house, but he did manage to keep it a two-story house."

"They have a huge lot as it is," I say. "Why did they want this one too?"

"I'm not sure. Some people want more and more. It stressed out your grandparents. But the good thing was, Hina learned about the building-height code, which gave your grandpa solid ground to fight the height of the new house."

"How did she learn about the height code?"

"Still a mystery to me. I asked, but she said she couldn't remember."

"I'm proud of you, Grandma!" I say.

Never in my wildest dreams did I anticipate uttering those words. Until just a week ago, I wasn't even aware of her existence. And yet, here I am, overwhelmed by pride. It's strange.

Frank continues. "They tried to intimidate your family, but just as they'd done over three decades ago, your grandparents refused to back down."

"What happened thirty years ago?"

"I don't know all the details, but a big land corporation wanted to buy this land and build a hotel. Your grandparents fought it."

"Why did they have to fight, though? It's their land and their decision."

"Well, people will use any means to get what they want. They wanted this land."

I shuffle the documents that Frank presented to me. "There's so much to take in here. One moment, please," I say, standing to fetch the photo of Mom, Kalani, and Kimo.

"Do you know a Kimo?" I say, when I return. I pass Frank the photo.

He looks at it and shakes his head. "I don't think I know this Kimo."

"*This* Kimo?" I ask.

"It's a common name here in Hawai'i. So I know a few Kimos."

Great.

Chapter Seven

It's 2:00 a.m. and I just dialed Luke's number, short of breath.

He answers immediately. Of course he does.

"Hello? Roy, are you there?"

"Yes, I am."

"Why are you even up? It's the middle of the night there."

"I'm good, it's just the time-zone shenanigans."

"It happened again, didn't it?" Luke asks.

"Huh? What are you talkin' about?"

"You know damn well what. It happened, didn't it?"

"There's nothing to worry about, old chap. I'll go back to sleep now."

"Do you have the photos with you?"

"Hardy har har."

"I'm always a phone call away."

"Enough with your nonsense," I say. "Good night."

"Good night. Call anytime."

That was silly, calling Luke because of a nightmare. And he makes me livid because he knows me better than I know myself. But he's the best brother in the world.

I met him when I was ten, while sitting on the edge of a chair. He was fifteen then. I hated him—he had a permanent home, a mother and a father who loved him. I didn't know then that life was giving me another chance: a loving family.

I take a photo out of my wallet. It's of my late mother and me when I was a baby, when her warmth and affection surrounded my frail existence. The photo is fading and has tattered edges.

I started running away from my foster families before they had a chance to send me back to social services. But I would never leave without this photograph and a simple toy —my yellow fire truck. These items were my lifeline. I'd also hold the picture tight when the night terrors woke me up.

As time passed, I started carrying a new memento—a photograph of my last foster family. The family that eventually adopted me.

In the photo, I'm seated on a bench squeezed between my mother and father. Their arms are wrapped around me. Behind me stands my brother, his arms resting on my shoulders. It's as if they form a human shield, a united front against the uncertainties of the world. When this photo appeared in my little backpack shortly after the picture was taken, I knew it was Luke who'd put it there.

The genuine smiles on their faces and the way they hold me close tell a story of acceptance and support. It's a moment frozen in time, a snapshot of a special moment in my youth. These people gave me a stable home.

Yet despite all their assurances, I couldn't shake the fear that it would all crumble, just as it had before. I was sure I'd have to leave this family and meet yet another new one. I didn't think I'd find a forever home.

How ridiculous is it that I have this photo with me? I'm thirty-four, for goodness' sake. I'll decide where my forever home is, and I don't need a photo pinned to my pj's to get my breath back after a bad dream.

I stare at both photos—my past and my present. Memories of my biological mother's love and a loving foster family's embrace.

Last week, when I was getting ready to travel to Hawai'i, Luke picked up these two framed photos in my living room and said, "I have a feeling that there might be another version of this. With your Hawaiian family."

"Nah, I highly doubt it," I retorted, my tone laced with irritation. "They didn't bother looking for me for thirty-four years. I have no intention of ever carrying their photo."

"I think you should take these photos with you to Hawai'i."

"Don't be silly," I responded. But I took them out of their frames and packed them anyway.

My thoughts drift to one of the times I ran away from

home. I was eleven years old. I'd forgotten to take the photos with me.

I crouched among the trees and winding paths of Brandon Hill Park in Bristol, my heart racing with anticipation. The trees always embraced me. I climbed one, sat on a branch, and looked around.

"I'm taller than everything!" I shouted, "I'm bigger than that house! I'm bigger than this city!"

But Luke had an uncanny ability to track me down no matter where I hid. Sure enough, as I peered through the branches, I saw him approaching with a smirk.

"Caught you again!" he exclaimed, as if we were playing hide-and-seek.

There was something strangely comforting about how he found me every time. Still, I decided to up the ante. Next time I ran away, I tucked the two photos in my small bag along with my fire truck and ventured toward the Clifton Suspension Bridge, its hidden tunnels calling me. I was certain I'd found the perfect spot, a secret and obscure place where even my foster brother wouldn't think to look.

But as I ducked beneath the bridge, a familiar voice echoed behind me. "You can't hide from me!" Luke called out, his voice filled with playful determination. I turned to face him with a mixture of surprise and admiration.

"It's like you have a sixth sense," I exclaimed, half in awe and half in jest. "How do you always manage to find me?"

He grinned mischievously. "I've been exploring this city longer than you. I know every nook and cranny.

Consider me your tour guide. I'll find hidden spots and, of course, I'll find you."

I couldn't help but laugh. I loved how he sought me out, turning my disappearances into a game. At that moment, I realized I wasn't just running away—I also wanted my brother to find me each time.

As the memory fades, I look at both photos again. I'm connected to one part of my family by birth and to the other by bonds of the heart.

I don't need a new family. I'll do whatever I need to do here and return to the UK as soon as possible. I want my life back. A few years ago, I stopped questioning why my father never cared about me. Now, I need to stop questioning why my Hawaiian family never searched for me.

"Go to sleep, man!" I demand, lowering my head to the sofa once again.

I can't bring myself to sleep in their bedrooms. The sofa is fine.

Chapter Eight

I wake up in a better mood after a good few hours of sleep. It's Friday. Frank is getting everything ready, and on Monday he'll provide the required documents for me to authorize. I'm granting him the legal authority to proceed with selling this house.

I rise from the couch and gasp as soon as I see the vast blue through the windows—the sky, the ocean. I open one of the windows and stand by it.

"Good morning, Pacific Ocean."

It's just after 8:00 a.m. Joyful beachgoers stroll along the shore, moving in both directions.

On my drive yesterday, I saw a sign advertising a Friday craft market not far from the beach house. It'll be fun to check it out. Someone there might even know Kimo.

After a refreshing shower and a cup of coffee, I walk there. The sign states that the market has been running for forty years. It's nestled within a vast expanse of grass. I meander past stalls; the salty ocean breeze dances between them. People smile and say "Aloha." There's live music too. This is more than a local craft market—it feels like a community, a place to connect.

A lady smiles at me. "Good morning, do you need some slippa? These are the best for a beach life." She's selling colorful sandals and flip-flops.

"No thanks," I say with a smile. But as I continue to walk, I notice that I'm the only person wearing closed-toe shoes.

The flip-flops pull me back. I return and buy a blue pair and put my trainers into a bag. It's a little hard to walk in them at first, but I start to get used to the feeling after a few steps.

There's a vendor selling wooden carvings shaped like surfboards and turtles. I might take some home for Mom and Dasia, Luke's fiancée.

I pick up a piece, intrigued by its unusual shape. It's smooth and polished with two curved parts that remind me of wings. I run my fingers over its surface, admiring the craftsmanship.

"Eh, aloha, that's a beautiful whale tail you're holding there," the vendor says, catching my attention. "One of the finest pieces I have."

"A whale tail?" I ask, surprised.

He laughs softly. "Yes, take another look."

I examine it again. "Very cool."

"Mahalo." His smile spreads across his face, left, right,

and center. "I make them. I can engrave anything you want."

"Good job." I examine the tails of different sizes.

"Have you seen them yet?" he asks.

I look at him blankly.

"The whales."

"Uh, the whales. Nope, no time. I'm leaving in a few days."

"Just go to the beach and you'll see them. They travel from Alaska to Hawai'i each year to give birth to their lil' babies in safer water."

"I'm not the only one away from home, then," I say with a smile.

"Well, Hawai'i is their home. They come back home. They were born here. They go up to Alaska for food and adventure between April and October."

"They do that every year?" I'm fascinated.

"Yeah, every year. I was born and raised here. We see them every year."

"Have you been at this market long?"

He smiles proudly. "Over ten years now."

"Do you know a local guy called Kimo?"

"I know many Kimos who grew up around here."

"He's a friend of my aunt's and I wanted to say hello."

"Which aunt?"

"Okay, let's start again. I'm Roy, grandson of Ben and Hina Williamson. They lived down the beach. Kimo was my mom and aunt's friend when they were teenagers." I extend my hand. "Roy Fernsby."

53

He reluctantly reaches for my hand as the warm smile disappears from his face. "I don't know of no grandson of the Williamsons."

His friendliness has shifted to curiosity—and suspicion?

"I'm with you. I had no idea I was their grandson until a few weeks ago. But I'm telling the truth."

"Uh." He tilts his head a little. "You didn't know you were their grandson. Hmm, that's no good."

I nod a few times. "Yeah, no good. I never had a chance to meet them."

"Lemme think." He looks me up and down first. "You'll find Aunt Melina on the beach. She comes for sunset every night. Not on the sand. She'll be on the grass. We prohibited her from going to the sandy part."

"You what?" I've no idea who Aunt Melina is, but I don't like what he's telling me. Prohibiting a woman from going to the beach? My face holds a big question mark.

"She kissed the ground twice, man. She's wobbly on the sand. Go and find her on the grass at the end of the beach. Ask anyone and they'll point her out to you. Aunt Melina. Sometimes, she puts a plumeria in her hair."

"Ah, I see. Thank you."

I'm eager to meet this Aunt Melina lady, but it's only ten thirty in the morning, so I head back home.

My search for Kimo starts with public school records,

which are available online. The Polaroid photo leans against my coffee mug on the kitchen table: Mom, Aunt Kalani, and Kimo, three teenagers looking bright and joyful. With a furrowed brow, I examine the photo carefully.

"Here's the clue," I exclaim. Aunt Kalani's body is angled slightly in Kimo's direction. He has his arms around both of them, but his right arm is clearly encircling Kalani more closely.

"I gotcha, people."

They were more than just friends. He must be eighteen or nineteen years old, and he has tattoos on his right arm, a pattern of some sort. He stares at the camera, and his expression seems to say, "My girl is *here*."

I look up. The ocean glitters; I've never seen this tone of blue before. I carry a small table from the living room into the garden. Sitting outside in a T-shirt on a February day feels surreal.

The wooden whale tail from the local market stands on the table. I ended up buying one only. I'm not sure what I'll do with it, but I like that I own a whale tail crafted by a local artist with an attitude.

I keep searching online; there are many Kimos in the local school records, but none match the years I'm looking for.

After a few more hours and numerous cups of coffee, I finally uncover what I've been searching for.

"There you are, Kimo Alanawai."

He's one year older than my mother and two years

older than Kalani. He'd be in his fifties today. This has to be him. Now I can search for a guy using more than four letters.

Wouldn't it be splendid if he could tell me more about my mom?

Where are you, Kimo? What do you know about these sisters? What happened to you all?

I walk to the sand barefoot again. It's as if a magnet is pulling me to the beach. It's warm, just as I've seen in those travel brochures with photos of the "toes in the warm sand" experience. Here, it's real.

A few kids are building something on the beach that looks like a turtle. Waves are gently crashing on the shore.

A couple strolls past, hand in hand. They seem to be in their late 40s or early 50s. The woman has a faintly familiar accent—perhaps a mix of British and some European. He sounds distinctly American. I couldn't resist eavesdropping on their lively conversation a little. I wonder where and how they met. This is fun. People watching.

I slowly ease closer to the sand, preparing to sit, but before I can, I spring back to my feet.

"Crikey!"

In an astonishing spectacle, a whale leaps out of the water. It makes a tremendous splash as it crashes back into the ocean.

"Now that's defying gravity," I say with a chuckle as I sit.

People are pointing, staring, and watching. And then

we're treated to another acrobatic jump and a twist in midair. People gasp, and a young boy jumps up and down with excitement, yelling, "Whale breach, whale breach." Some people clap and cheer. I smile. One whale makes so many people happy.

Feeling a pull, I join the excited crowd, and we all gasp each time the whales breach.

It's finally time to see if I can find Aunt Melina. I want to be presentable, so after my shower and shave, I put on my white linen shirt and thank Dasia in my head because she insisted I pack something nice to wear. My future sister-in-law is just incredible.

The shirt is tailored just right, accentuating my broad shoulders and chest without being too tight. I roll the sleeves up to just below my elbows, hoping to achieve a laid-back style.

I give myself one more look in the mirror and hope my charm will work on Aunt Melina. My mother's friends back home adore me.

When I arrive at the beach, I don't have to ask anyone to point me to Aunt Melina. I recognize her immediately—she's sitting under a single palm tree, leaning against the trunk, facing the ocean. There's a single flower behind her left ear.

"Hello," I say, approaching her. She keeps her eyes on the ocean.

"Aloha," I try, and she turns her head. Her expression suggests I've just stepped on her sandcastle. Her gaze is piercing. So much for my linen-shirt charm.

"Are you Melina? Aunt Melina?"

She nods.

"May I sit here, please?" I feel as if I'm standing in front of a school principal and have no idea what I've done wrong.

"Sit." She points to the ground.

Great, apparently she's the least friendly person in town.

I start introducing myself, but she raises her hand and looks back at the ocean. "After the sunset."

I've never seen a sunset like this before. It's dramatic. The sun's rays filter through a small cloud, casting hues of orange and pink across the entire sky. People are scattered around the beach and grass, captivated by the sun touching the ocean. Time, as I know it, stops. This must be what *timeless* feels like.

Chapter Nine

I don't know how long Aunt Melina and I have been staring at the sunset. The ocean is gradually enveloping the sun in a tender embrace.

I suddenly feel cooler air surrounding us. The sky is still full of color, but the light is getting dimmer. I observe Aunt Melina, who is still staring at the horizon, her lips curved upward. I hear her slow inhales, and she gives a long blink with each.

She suddenly turns and catches my gaze. "Listen up, young man! If you want to enjoy the sunset or anything of truly beautiful nature, you gotta get your breathing game on point. No huffing and puffing like a big steam engine. You almost scared the sun away." Her cheeky grin is both frightening and endearing.

"Sorry, was I huffing and puffing?"

"You still are. Close your eyes. Hear the sunset."

"Hear the sunset, okay, I see, I'll try." I close my eyes

but hear only the waves. I gotta say, it feels plain silly, but I keep my eyes closed.

"Stop overthinking everything. I can practically see a million thoughts through your eyelids."

"I'm a little preoccupied. But the sunset was amazing."

"It still is."

I open my eyes. The sky is now shades of deep oranges and reds. It's getting cooler by the minute. I look at Aunt Melina again. She exhales peacefully, her face a picture of calm.

She has to be much older than my mom, my adoptive mother, Elizabeth, but though she appears weathered, she's also radiant. She has fair skin, and her eyes are framed by deep lines; a wooden hair clip keeps her long gray hair out of her face.

"Gettin' a little chilly. Time to get home."

She slowly stands. Her sharp gaze silently commands me not to utter one word.

She grabs her bag. "I've got a feelin' that I might see you around."

"You might," I say dryly, watching her step away from me. My chance at finding Kimo moves away with Aunt Melina's steady and slow steps.

My eyelids part when I hear raindrops drumming on the windowpane. Another night of tossing and turning.

The view outside the window is magnificent. Palm

trees sway and dance in the strong wind, the ocean is wild and unapologetic, and the savory aroma of salt fills my nose as I watch the foamy whitecaps rolling across the surface of the water. Like fluffy pancakes, they appear. I enjoy the beautiful nature.

I wonder what Curly and his human family with a strong arm do on rainy days like this.

"This is staying-in-and-resting weather," I murmur while making coffee. Until Monday, I don't have much to do. I had hoped to speak with Aunt Melina this evening, whether she wanted to or not, but with this much rain, there won't be a sunset.

"The ceiling!" I yell, and run to the large bedroom. There's water pouring in. I push the bed aside and place a small bucket underneath the stream. By the time the rain stops it's four in the afternoon and I've already emptied the bucket twice.

I decide to go to the beach, just in case, and I'm surprised to see Aunt Melina. This time, she's sitting on a chair beside the palm tree. There are still thick clouds in the sky.

"Hello," I say.

"Hello," she says with a smile. "I can still hear your heartbeats from a mile away. You might wanna turn down the volume a bit."

"How do I do that?" I ask.

She takes out a small beach towel from her bag. "Here, sit on this. The ground is still wet."

"Thank you," I say while lowering myself beside her.

"Take a deep breath and exhale slowly. Watch the ocean and allow your mind to wander with the waves. Water is in our nature, in our bodies. It'll come naturally. Allow your heart and mind to sync with the rhythm of the ocean."

My heartbeats have been a little bizarre since last week; the nightmares have returned, and with them, the feeling of an elephant trampling my chest, similar to how I felt during my young years. It all began when I overheard the adults speaking in hushed tones about "the elephant in the room."

As a kid I also had a vision of a massive lava rock on my chest, and in the vision my only companion was an unfriendly and grumpy iguana. The iguana's long tail and intense eyes continue to linger in my thoughts to this day.

I turn my attention to the sunset. "There are so many clouds this evening," I say, attempting to connect with what matters to Aunt Melina.

"Sometimes, we need clouds to see the most stunning sunset."

Minutes later, the dark clouds take on an orange shade as the sun reaches the ocean, transforming everything around us. It's indeed a magnificent sunset.

Mom, what happened to you and your beautiful family? Did you watch sunsets together?

The questions trigger a thundering in my chest. It feels as if I might burst.

"Your heart is racing again," Aunt Melina whispers.

"Sorry," I mumble, ashamed of my internal turmoil.

The contentment on her face is extraordinary. She seems entirely at home in this moment, a part of this place—the palm trees, the ocean, the sky.

"How is your search going?" she inquires softly.

"My search?

"Oh, dear boy, you don't even know what you're searching for."

I sigh. She sighs too.

"Tell me what's on your mind right now," she says.

She is chattier today. I extend my legs on the soft grass and support my body from behind with my hands. "I thought I had pieced together my life's puzzle." My tone is heavy with resentment. "But lately, everything I thought was settled has been turned completely on its head."

Her glance falls on me.

"I don't think I even introduced myself. I'm Roy. I'm from England."

"This is a small town, Roy. Everyone knows who you are." She smiles warmly. For some reason, I like that she knows who I am.

"What makes you from England?" she asks.

Okay, I guess Aunt Melina is driving the conversation here. "Hmm, I suppose because I was born there. My roots are there."

"My family comes from many different places. Different roots."

"Different places, huh? I thought roots were supposed to be in one place but where you belong could be somewhere else."

63

"Why limit yourself to one spot? You already have some roots here, by this palm tree."

I chuckle. "Nah, this palm tree thinks I'm a nuisance."

"Did you ask the palm tree, or is that your assumption?" she asks with a big grin.

"Well, I didn't ask, of course." This conversation is getting silly. "Did you know my grandparents?"

"This is a small town, Roy. Everyone knew your grandparents." Something in the ocean catches her attention. "That's a mom and a baby." She points at two whales blowing clouds of moisture into the air, and I wonder when the time will come to hear about my mother and her baby son.

I steal a glance at her. Her hair is pulled back in an intricate updo adorned with a single plumeria flower tucked just behind her left ear. She's wearing a long, colorful dress, and there's a shawl over her shoulders.

"Have you learned any Hawaiian words?" she asks.

"No, I haven't. I only arrived a few days ago, and I'm not planning to stay long."

"It's polite to learn a few words of the place you're visiting, regardless of the length of stay."

"Sure," I say respectfully, inhaling a deep breath.

"And you've Hawaiian blood in you," she continues. "Learning even a few words of our language will deepen your understanding and appreciation of the traditions that make our islands so special. And who knows, you may even find yourself connecting with your roots in ways you never thought possible."

Bloody hell. Those roots again. It's not like I had a choice.

"I know *aloha*," I say, and immediately regret it.

She blinks slowly, and I can almost hear the clicking of her eyelids.

"Sorry, yes, I should have learned some Hawaiian, but I didn't have a chance. I had to travel on such short notice."

"What's your plan with the land and the house?"

"I'm planning to sell it as soon as possible."

"What's the rush?"

"I want to return to my life and my travel plans," I say. I feel on edge now.

"Your grandparents were attached to their house, the land, and their ancestors," she says, gazing at the ocean. The sunset colors are spreading on the clouds, creating a canvas of oranges above us. "Even though your grandpa Ben wasn't Hawaiian, he greatly respected your grandmother's culture. They made their home sacred. Hina and Ben's love story impacted all of us, and their home was much more than just a piece of earth or a house. You've had many generations of family on that land that you can't wait to get rid of."

My family. Generations of my family.

I'm not going to get into how life didn't give me those roots from the start or how I felt like a leaf blown about during autumn storms while growing up. Aunt Melina speaks of many generations here, but regrettably, I had no part in that story.

She looks at me as if she's just read my mind then adjusts her posture, turning to face me fully. "Some people enter this life with a deep connection to their background and a sense of where their home is and then realize it's not where they belong. Others search for years for that sense until they unexpectedly find the right place or person."

She tilts her head slightly, her eyebrows raised.

"Ultimately, *roots* and *belonging* mean different things to different people, and they may even change during a life. But everyone writes a unique story, whether they start with strong foundations or they're a broken branch, a tiny bud, or a single seedling. We always have the choice to create our own story."

I give her a nod.

"Hina and I grew old together. But when we laughed, we grew younger. She used to sit where you sit right now, on my right, watching the ocean or sunset, waiting for her family until her last day. Her family was somewhere across this ocean. She knew they were over there, and here you are, sitting where she loved sitting."

I close my eyes and listen to the waves. I almost don't notice when Aunt Melina rises to leave.

"Can I ask a question, please?"

"Tomorrow, my child," she responds, slowly walking away from me.

Chapter Ten

As I walk around the garden, I examine my surroundings and shudder a little as the evening breeze brushes my face.

I think of what Frank told me about my grandparents. Hina, a young Hawaiian woman, fell for a young military man serving in O'ahu. At first, her family opposed their relationship, but their love eventually won the hearts of everyone. She inherited the land from her grandparents. The land beneath my feet, the very ground I touch. This ground, this dirt. The smell of it in the air.

I look at the house and its surroundings in awe but with a heavy feeling in my gut. The sun descended into the ocean an hour ago, and the sky is a deep pink.

I walk back to the house—this house they built in the sixties. "Hello," I whisper, caressing the door. Before stepping inside, I take off my flip-flops. Then I empty the bucket in the main bedroom and check the other bedrooms.

There's a pink bedspread in the third bedroom. Positioned beside it is an old wooden nightstand, with a drawer and a brass handle that invites me to pull it open. When I do, it reveals a world frozen in time.

A weathered book. A few photos of my mom. I gingerly lift the book: *The Little Prince*.

Leilani is inscribed on the first page. With a deep inhale, I flip a few worn pages.

"So this is your room, Mom," I say out loud, touching the pink material. And the room opposite must be Aunt Kalani's.

As I hold the book, I feel closer to my mother than I have in years. I now know her favorite book. Well, possibly one of her favorites, and I'm good with that.

"Mom," I say, sitting on the edge of her bed.

On Sunday morning, an intense headache grips my temples when I open my eyes. I only slept for a few hours because of a combination of jetlag and turning the pages of *The Little Prince* and imagining Mom reading it.

It feels as if a wire is tightening around my head, causing me to wince. I can practically hear my own pulse throbbing in my ears, and the pain makes it difficult to concentrate.

I rub my temples gently.

Doubts and uncertainty occupy my mind. I know that selling the property is the right path. I have my plans to travel around the world. I have my family in the UK. I didn't know I had roots in Hawai'i; no one can expect me to change everything now.

Even though I feel as if I'm forming new connections with my mom and her family, I need to push my heart aside and let my head take the lead.

What is this pain?

A couple of painkillers and a few hours of dozing on the couch later, I wake up feeling much better. It's a sunny afternoon.

I sense a pair of eyes watching me. "Hey, kitty cat, how are you?"

She runs away.

"I'm good too. Thanks for asking. I say enough of resting and catching up on sleep. It's time to be useful. What do you think?"

Outside, I fetch the rickety ladder from the back. The cat appears on the porch and I yell out, telling her to keep her distance. She moves closer to the ladder.

"You're a strange one all right," I say with a laugh. "But I like you just the way you are."

The afternoon sun beats down on my back as I ascend to check the leaking roof. As I climb, my skin tingles as if being beaten by a hundred tiny drumsticks. The ladder is old and worn, but I checked each rung a few days ago. All stable, waiting for me to step up.

It feels different today, though. More wobbly. Growing up, I loved climbing trees, ladders, and fences. I can tell if something feels stable or not. But I dismiss my concerns and decide it's safe enough to quickly attempt to stop the leak.

I carefully position myself next to the roof. With tools in hand, I began inspecting the damaged area, pinpointing the source of the leak.

I enjoy mending things, and there's always something to fix at my coffee shop.

Easy. Until it's not.

The ladder beneath me shifts ever so slightly.

A sudden crack echoes through the air. Before I can react, the ladder gives way, collapsing under my weight. I plummet toward the ground without time to brace myself for the impact.

The world spins as I crash onto the hard earth. Pain radiates through my body. I lie there for a moment, disoriented and in shock. Slowly, I try to assess the damage, gingerly moving my limbs to ensure nothing is broken.

Realization strikes as the pain intensifies. My right arm throbs. Frustration wells up. It's as if the very house itself resisted my attempts to mend its damage.

There's no way that I can reach my phone to call emergency services. I then see my next-door neighbor by the window, but she steps back, as usual. Oh, this place is a shitshow. Your neighbor won't even help when you're lying on the ground in pain.

The next thing I know, paramedics have arrived. They swiftly assess my condition, and with gentle precision, they prepare me for transportation to the hospital.

"Who called you?" I ask a paramedic.

"I don't know. Maybe a beach walker saw you fall."

"Okay." My voice is barely audible.

Everything is far from okay.

In the emergency room, a doctor conducts a thorough examination of my arm and orders an X-ray to assess the extent of the injury. A few hours later, I leave the hospital in a taxi with my right arm in a brace. Fortunately, it isn't broken or fractured, but the brace is required to immobilize the arm and provide support for the serious sprain.

I remind myself that in three days' time, I'll be leaving.

Back at the beach house, I grab a chair at the dinner table and lower myself into it, my mind wandering to thoughts of who might have occupied this exact seat. I envision my grandparents at the head of the table. As I stare at the tabletop, feeling somewhat alone, a sudden, intense pain creeps up into my shoulders and then descends into my chest.

I believed that I'd left my unhappy childhood behind. But a deep pain I haven't felt in years has returned. Is this the same hurt I used to feel when I was young? Can pain be dormant for years?

It sounds as if my grandparents were really good people. I'm sure I would have loved them if given the chance. But my mother never disclosed anything about them to my father. Why?

And is my aunt still alive, as my grandmother believed? If so, do I truly own this house, and is it my decision to sell? Where is she? She never sought me out. Why?

The questions pile up, and I wonder if I even want to know the answers.

Hell yes I do, I think, surprised at my eagerness. It surprises me further that thoughts of my grandmother bring me warmth rather than sadness or anger.

It's all right for me to like her even though I found out about her only a few weeks ago.

I try to ease my somewhat-guilty conscience by thinking about how I plan to donate much of the earnings from the sale of the house to charities supporting foster children. With the rest, I can spoil my mom and gift some to Luke and Dasia.

But what if my aunt is still alive?

I head to the kitchen and crack open a can of beer with my left hand. Easy . . .

Chapter Eleven

I'm up, standing on the back porch, admiring the sky, which is painted with the softest hues of lavender and pink. The sun, rising behind the mountain, is already touching everything in its path. It's 6:30 a.m.

It's a take-it-easy kind of Monday. My arm will dictate how I spend the day, as training my left arm to do my daily tasks is taking longer than anticipated. Frank canceled his visit. He needed to attend to important family matters. I hope he'll come tomorrow, as I'm leaving on Wednesday.

After showering and having breakfast, I walk into the bedroom with a green bedspread. This house is like a top-secret treasure trove. There's a diary with a rusty lock sitting on a small bedside table. Is it wrong to break open and read a teenage girl's diary if she's no longer around and I'm desperate for answers? The faded blue cover is marked by the wear and tear of decades.

"Sorry," I say out loud and use a big rock to break the lock, feeling guilty with each hit until it opens and falls apart. There's a name on the first page. *It's Kalani's!*

As I suspected, this room was Aunt Kalani's.

I gingerly turn to the next page, settling at the table outside. There it is— my aunt's scrawl from many decades ago. The ink has faded but the words are still legible.

"*Dear Diary,*" it begins.

As I read, I'm transported to a time when my aunt was a young girl, full of dreams. When she starts writing about her crush, Kimo, I yell, "Aha, there he is!"

She talks about the remarkable coincidence of her path crossing this boy's at the most unexpected place—an open-air concert, a community-support gathering.

Then their first date. I can't help but smile when I read about how he swept her off her feet. *Kimo sure knows how to show a girl a good time.* A love note given to her on the beach, a surprise picnic, a dip in a refreshing waterfall, stargazing after my aunt quietly sneaks out of her room . . .

"Whoa, whoa, whoa." I drop the diary on the table as if it burns my fingertips. *Dear Aunt, that's a tad too revealing to write in diary pages, lock or not!*

Leaving the diary on the table, I take out some cat food for the cat, my cheeks still aflame. Anything to avoid dwelling on the passage I just read.

Sinking back into the chair outside, I quickly flip pages, hoping to find out more about Kimo. But, nope, just more detailed pages about that night. It started on the beach, at their favorite corner, underneath a tree.

When everybody was on the beach watching the sunset, they sneaked into this very house, into her bedroom.

I turn the pages faster and faster. In her last entry, she finally moves away from that night.

I'm furious, I have to tell Kimo. I heard them. The man was saying things like Daddy would lose so much. And that he should give his family a better future. Daddy told him to get lost and that he wouldn't sell our house. He shouted, "There's nothing to sell here! Leave my ohana alone." But I know he's sad. He was quiet at dinner. I hate seeing him like this.

The man said he would use the documents and that would hurt our ohana even more. What are these documents? I'm angry, I must do something to help Daddy.

I told Leilani, but she said Daddy would deal with it, he wouldn't let anyone upset our mother, and he'd not let anyone disrespect her ancestors. But I see he's sad and worried. I'll talk to Kimo, he'll help Daddy and protect us. We're meant for each other, the serendipity. After all, since yesterday, I'm his girl now. And he's my man.

So my grandfather was being threatened.

Where are you, Kimo? Did you protect them?

As I stroll along the beach, the sand slides between my toes. The ocean stretches to far corners within my sight. Its vastness mirrors the emptiness I feel within. My thoughts drift to my mother.

Mom, I can't believe I'm taking steps on your beach. You must have taken your first steps here.

I slow down and watch my foot shaping the sand, leaving a footprint.

You must have chased your sister Kalani here, on this beach. Or Kalani chased you.

Catch me!

I start running. But moments later I sit as my arm starts throbbing.

"Okay, geez, it's only a sprain," I say, talking to my arm.

There are a few people scattered on the beach. A young woman on my right appears to be wholly engrossed in her book. My chest tightens, and my breath catches in my throat as a deluge of emotions comes over me. How is this even possible?

She's reading *The Little Prince*.

Chapter Twelve

I'm still shaken by seeing the woman reading *The Little Prince*. It's one of the most widely read books in the world, though, so it's possible that it was a mere coincidence. Clearly.

A knock on the door interrupts my solitude. I rush to answer it, wanting a distraction. I open the door to find Aunt Melina wearing a sympathetic smile and holding a small, intricately carved wooden box.

"Good morning," she says. "I've come to see how you're doing. I heard that you hurt your arm."

"I'm grateful, thank you. Come in. What may I offer you?"

"You're such a British gentleman. Nothing. But I've something for you. It's a special gift to protect you."

She takes off her shoes, walks in, settles herself in the armchair, and then looks around the room. A bittersweet smile graces her lips.

Curiosity fills me. She's also holding a mango—a very large one.

"What is it? And is that a mango?"

"Yes, do you like mangos?"

"I like them enough, but not my favorite fruit."

"Until this one." She hands over the mango.

I breathe in the sweet aroma, my fingers running over the smooth skin.

"It's from the tree in my garden. Hina's favorite tree. It's very tall. You should come and pick some yourself." Then she looks at my arm. "Once your arm is better."

I examine the mango as if it's an art piece. It's vibrant yellow with a hint of red on the peel. A masterpiece.

"Is it even mango season?" I ask.

"Some trees are not bound by seasons. They produce fruit three times a year."

Then she moves to the sofa and beckons me to sit beside her, tapping the seat. I join her. She opens the box, revealing a miniature turtle pendant made of green stone hanging from a black leather cord.

"This is a honu, a green sea turtle," she says.

Intrigued, I lean closer and pick up the necklace. The black leather is worn.

"I think you'll tell me more," I announce.

Her gaze becomes distant, as if she's delving into memories. I join the moment. I'm transported back to my early childhood in London, far away from the shores of Hawai'i. Despite the distance, the memory feels so vivid, as if it's imprinted in my brain.

I'm standing on a chair, peering out at the bustling streets of London below. Then I'm sitting on my small bed. There's a baby blanket. Is that a green turtle on the edge of it?

I snap back to the present, my heart racing with confusion and intrigue. What a vivid memory!

"This is an aumakua, your family's protector. This necklace was your grandma's. She inherited it from her grandma."

"I suppose the family's aumakua didn't stop my fall from the ladder," I joke. "Maybe it left the property with Grandma."

With a sad expression, she places a gentle hand on my shoulder.

"Oh, my dear child, you're bitter and sad. Aumakua never leaves us, and you'll realize this one day."

Time slides once again, this time to ten-year-old me. I'm sitting on the edge of a chair, meeting my new foster family. Once again, everything feels unfamiliar, from the furniture to the faces of the people around me. I clutch the one constant in my life: my yellow fire truck.

"How long will you stay, Roy?" my new foster mom asked me.

I was surprised that she'd asked me this. Usually, I didn't get to decide.

"I dunno," I said, my voice low. "As long as you let me stay."

"You're a funny boy. It's not my place to say how long you stay."

79

"Huh?" I mutter, as I hear Aunt Melina's voice.

"Roy?"

"Oh, I'm sorry about that. I was just thinking about my home. Home in the UK." I try to avoid her gaze. "Home, family, belonging—it's all uncertain right now." I give her a weak smile and look into her deep-blue eyes.

"Do you have anyone special in your life?"

I shake my head.

"That's a surprise, a kind and handsome young man like you. How come?"

I shrug and change the subject, then stand and walk to the table. "I assume you sat around this table often?" I ask.

She nods. "More times than you can imagine."

"Can you tell me who would sit where? Did they have specific chairs?"

A beaming smile spreads across her face as she approaches the table. While sitting, her hand gently covers mine, its palm radiating comforting warmth. The veins underneath the skin resemble small, meandering rivers.

"You're sitting in your grandma's chair."

"I like this spot. It's close to the kitchen and I can see the rest of the house." My vision blurs as I blink back tears.

Her grip on my hand tightens. "You're an ohana," she says, her voice strong and determined. "Ohana means family in Hawaiian, including close friends and people who matter. You're part of this land and its family. It's also in your DNA to protect your ohana, whether you like it or not."

With a slight nod, I find my voice. "I like it."

Somewhere deep in my chest I feel a faint sense of pride, a subtle acknowledgment of the connection to my ohana.

For a split second, I feel family. I remember what Frank said—"da family."

Letting out a resigned sigh, I say, "I'll extend my stay. You were absolutely right. There's no need to rush things. I need this arm to be a little better anyway. I'll find an appropriate buyer who will treat the property and the home respectfully. I promise you."

A radiant smile lights up her face.

"But," I continue, "I have a question I must ask."

"I know you do. Come and meet me at the sunset and ask as many questions as you want."

As soon as she leaves, I don't even bother to check the time before I video-call my mother. She answers immediately but sounds sleepy.

"Hey there, son."

"Did I wake you up? Sorry."

"No, it's only nine here. Not in bed yet. How are you doing?"

"I'm good." I hide my right arm, keeping the phone close to my face. "Mom, I've got a question. I have a hazy recollection of a baby blanket. Maybe it arrived with me. Do you remember it?"

She thinks for a beat and tucks a strand of her ash-blond hair behind her ear. "Yes, I think there was a blanket, but I don't think we kept it."

"I see, okay."

"You're sad. Why?"

"Don't you worry. I thought I remembered something maybe from this house, maybe that my grandmother knitted for me, some physical connection to this place? It's okay, though."

"I'm sorry, son."

"Do you happen to remember if there was a honu on the blanket?"

"A what?"

"A green turtle."

Her forehead creases as her brows knit closer. "Now you mention it, I believe so."

"Yes," I exclaim. So I did have a blanket with a turtle on it. But my joy fades fast as I realize it couldn't have come from this house. My grandmother didn't even know about me. My mother must have knit it in London.

After our call, I think about my mom, Elizabeth. She can always read me and see straight through to my sadness. I remember returning from school with bad teacher reports or having overheard kids speculating about me and my past.

My shame usually came out as rage at my mom. I'd shout, "See, I'm not good enough. You'll realize that too." I felt sad and ashamed, and I wanted her to be angry with me. Her anger would be proof that I was bad, that I wasn't good enough for her.

I'd run away into my bedroom, squirming and shriveling into a tiny ball at the back of my bed. I just didn't fit into my new family's normal world, so I wanted to be smaller and smaller.

Yet every time, she'd come into the room and sit in the chair by my bed with a book in hand. She'd read to me or tell me stories about her family or school. Each time, it became easier to lift my head and listen to her voice. She was the best foster mom. No, she is—and always will be— the best mom ever.

Who needs a physical connection to this house?
Not me.

Chapter Thirteen

Cradling my mug of coffee, I take another bite of the mango Aunt Melina brought me. I hum with appreciation, closing my eyes as I savor its sweet flavor. No other mango will ever taste quite like this one. It's quickly become my favorite fruit.

I think of Pages and Beans. The beginning of the week is especially busy—the commuters treat themselves to special coffees to help with the Monday blues. And here I am, sitting outside in February, watching the ocean and beach walkers. I need to call my travel agency back in the UK to reschedule my globe-trotting dates so I can stay another week here. One more week.

"Hiya."

I look up from my phone; it's the ball-throwing woman, Curly's Human Family. She's standing by the small gate between the sand and the garden. Curly appears to be excited to see me as his tail wags furiously.

"Well, hello." I rise from my chair and walk toward them.

"Oh, what's happened?" she asks, as she notices my injured arm.

"I got another injury to take over the ball pain," I say with a chuckle. My face tingles as I remember the incident, but I find the ball-thrower intriguing.

"I'm sorry about that." She tilts her head with an apologetic expression while I pet Curly.

"No worries. This was a mishap."

"Hope nothing serious."

"Nope, but each day is wonderfully eventful on this island."

"Yes, it's an exceptional place. Am I interrupting?"

"No, come over, please. Is the garden okay? I can fetch another chair. I just brewed coffee. Would you like some?"

"I'd love a cup. Black, please."

"Sorry, I don't have a treat for this fella."

"I do, no worries."

While she gets Curly settled by the table, I rush to get a chair first, then bring the coffee pot over and pour a cup for her.

"Here you go." I place the cup of coffee in front of her.

"Thank you," she says. "This is a very large yard; it doesn't look this big from a distance."

She takes a sip. Damn, she's mesmerizing. I order myself to stop staring at her.

"Oh, this is excellent." She remarks.

"Hmm, I hope I've nailed the whole coffee-brewing

game." I watch her expression as she takes another sip. "I own a coffee shop in London."

She beams and says, "That's awesome. We need more coffee shops around here."

"I might consider starting a Pages and Beans Café out here then."

"Pages and Beans Café—how adorable."

"I'm proud of it. But how did you throw the ball that fast? I'm curious." I'm curious about many things when it comes to this woman.

"Okay, confession time. I was a professional softball player in the past." She shrugs and gives me a shy smile.

"Were you? Then I guess it was my lucky day."

She holds up her hands in surrender and shakes her head. I notice the soft curves of her cheeks, her caramel-brown hair tied back in a casual beach style, her tanned skin, her easygoing summer clothing—a pair of shorts and a tank top. But what stands out most to me is her captivating smile.

"So, what brings you to this beautiful corner of the earth?" she asks.

I look back at the house. "Some family business." There's a sudden breeze, making me shiver a little.

"We have more dramatic weather here in the winter months, but mostly warm days." She takes a light top hanging around her waist, puts it on, and zips it up. "I assume you own this place?"

"Yes, but not for long, hopefully."

"Oh, you're selling. I know a great person who can help."

"I'm having my lawyer take care of that."

"No harm in speaking with real estate agents directly. You can even meet her this afternoon if you'd like. I hear that it's a good time to sell."

"Sure," I say. "Why not."

Petting Curly as he gets close to my legs, I ask, "What's your story? Do you live here?"

"Yes, I do." She smiles. "Have you had lunch yet?"

"Is it lunchtime already? Wow, no, I haven't."

"I can drive us to a food truck. I suppose with your injured arm, you're not driving around much. How about a poke bowl? We can bring it back here."

Her suggestion surprises me, but why not? She's a dazzling distraction from everything going on.

"Yeah, that would be great. Thanks."

"Okay, let's go." She stands.

"Do I continue calling you Curly's Human Family or should I call you the Professional Softball Player?

"Amy will do."

I find pure delight in every bite of my delicious lunch—cubed ahi tuna marinated in a flavorful blend of soy sauce, sesame oil, and other seasonings. The tuna is served on a bed of steamed rice.

Amy and I delve into our lunch bowls at the small

table. I'm mesmerized by the ease of her laughter and the sounds of the waves in the background.

"I became an official poke eater when I moved here seven years ago," she announces.

We laugh so much, and conversation with Amy is effortless. The time flies as we enjoy each other's company. I realize it's the first time I've wished time would slow down since I arrived almost a week ago.

"Life here isn't all that tropical for the locals," she says, as we finish up. "It can be pretty challenging too."

"How come?" I ask.

"I'll save that for another time. I need to be somewhere by three thirty. But let me call my friend who's a real estate agent before I go."

I eat the last of my poke bowl while she makes the call and arranges for her friend to meet me the next morning.

"She always tells me it's best not to have too many middlemen. It'll be better to deal with her directly. I know she'll help you to sell."

"Thanks for the advice," I say with a smile.

She fixes her eyes on mine for a long second. "I need to go."

"Oh, sure." I push back my chair and rise. "I'm not here long, but I'd love to return the lunch favor."

"Of course," she says. "Give me your phone and I'll add my number."

We stand, and she walks to my side of the table. I offer her my phone, but as she reaches out it slips from my grasp and onto the ground. We both lunge forward to our knees and our hands intertwine. Her breath is warm on my face.

Our lips meet. The currents between us are powerful, the moment so charged with desire that I can't discern who initiated the kiss.

The chemistry is undeniable.

I pull away first. "I apologize sincerely," I sputter, rising while grabbing my phone. "I'm not sure what came over me." I hold her hand to help her up and keep babbling. "I genuinely didn't intend for this to happen. I'm truly sorry." I hand her my phone.

With a deep, intentional breath, she presses her slender fingers to the small keypad and dials in her number. Meanwhile, I wish I could be the air she just took in.

"Here it is." After giving me a tiny smile, she starts walking to the gate. "It was great to get to know you. Come on, Curly, let's go. This way."

My list of reasons for rushing the sale is getting longer by the minute.

I just kissed a stranger. Do I hear my own heart thumping?

My heart has learned to shield itself. If I don't let anyone in, then I don't have to worry about being abandoned.

My father left me with my stepmother.

My stepmother couldn't stand the sight of me.

Several foster families took me in, and my presence upset some.

My father agreed to give me up and, with one tiny signature, let me be adopted.

Because of my father, I've decided never to have children; the apple doesn't fall far from the tree. Although I'm not him, he's part of me.

I was twenty-eight when I proposed to my girlfriend of four years. I've strong legs—I cycle a lot. But when I got down on one knee in front of her, my legs were shaking. My hands were also trembling, my shoulders tense. The words barely came out.

"Will you marry me so I can dedicate every second of my life to making you smile?"

Her expression should have been a clue, but I took her silence and her eyebrows shooting up in an arc as a yes. Until she started crying, and not tears of joy.

"I'm really sorry, Roy. But I can't go through with this."

"What do you mean?"

"I want a child."

"But I thought neither of us wanted one."

"I changed my mind. I'm sorry. I love you, Roy."

And yet another person exited my life mere moments after uttering "I love you, Roy."

My heart shattered. It physically hurt. As much as it had hurt when I was abandoned at six years old.

Since then, I haven't let myself get close to anyone.

I think of Amy. She's so beautiful, like a sea goddess, with twinkling eyes and an enchanting smile—not to mention those cute dimples! And that was a hell of a kiss.

What have I done?

Chapter Fourteen

"**I**'ve never done anything like that before, kitty. That wasn't cool, you know." The cat no longer hides from me but still keeps her distance, staring at me from the kitchen.

"And honestly, I can't even be certain I initiated the kiss." The cat creeps closer to the sofa.

"Our lips connected. It was instant."

She meows. I swear she gets me.

"I don't do things like that. I'm a gentleman."

Mi-aw

I kneel, but she doesn't move. "I think we're getting closer, right, kitty?"

There's a knock on the door, and she flees. Opening it, I'm surprised to see the woman I've spotted in the window next door. She's with a man.

"Hello," I say, not releasing my grip on the door handle.

"Hello, we're your neighbors, the Johnsons. I'm Phil, this is Claire, my wife." His voice is unnecessarily loud. "We thought we'd introduce ourselves." He places his left hand on his wife's shoulder and extends his right hand. He's over six feet and has a large belly.

"Thank you, how nice of you. I'm Roy."

He pulls his hand back when he notices the black brace on my arm. "Oh, sorry about that. Is everything okay?"

"Yeah, a silly accident. I'll be fine in a few days."

"Here's a loaf of banana bread," says Claire, her voice soft.

Her hair is striking, with long pieces at the front and shorter locks at the back, all of which cascade around her face in beautiful ash-blond and gray ringlets, contrasting her lightly tanned skin.

"Oh, banana bread, thank you."

"Claire makes the best banana bread on the island," declares Phil.

Claire remains stoic, as though her name weren't even mentioned.

Intriguing dynamic, I muse. They don't even stand close to each other; Claire sidestepped away from her husband's hand when passing me the banana bread.

"Shall we sit outside? I'm afraid the house isn't in good-enough condition to accept guests."

"We won't be long, but let's do that," Phil says, his deep voice still louder than necessary.

I set the banana bread on the table in the kitchen. But as I prepare to step outside, I see the cat jump, that playful

94

little furball. She lands precisely on the spot where the freshly baked banana bread rests. The table teeters and, in the blink of an eye, chaos erupts.

The container hits the floor and the banana bread is done for. The cat, well, she makes a quick exit.

As I survey the wreckage, I shake my head.

"Guess I won't be having a slice of banana bread with my coffee tomorrow," I announce, when I join them on the porch.

"I'll bake you another one," Claire says.

"We must do something about those stray cats," says Phil, his voice even louder now. "They're nonsense. You shouldn't let them in."

"She was here when I arrived, so technically, she let me in. Not the other way around."

Neither of them comments. We settle around the table in the garden.

Phil asks, "How long are you here for?"

"Not long," I say, and notice Phil's smile.

"This isn't our permanent home, so we're not always here. But your grandparents were awesome neighbors. We loved them."

So he lies.

"What are your plans?" he asks.

I glance at Claire, who's staring at the beach house as if she's not with us.

With a sigh, I say, "I'm not sure yet." I won't give him the pleasure of knowing that I'll be selling.

"Let us know if you need any help with anything."

"Thank you, I will," I respond dryly.

He rests his elbows on the table, leaning in slightly. "Roy, I want you to know that I'm an open book and a good neighbor. If you ever consider selling, I'd be happy to have a chat. It would mean a lot to your grandparents as well if you were to speak with us first."

I steal a quick glimpse at Claire, who looks away from me. I nod, and they say their goodbyes. I continue to sit outside, thinking things through.

I want to sell the house. Phil wants to buy it. But I'd rather not sell to him. It's likely he'd tear it down and build another enormous monstrosity.

"What's happening, man?" I mutter to myself.

The cat steps out from underneath the porch.

"Let's continue our chat, little kitty. Was there a reason you jumped on the banana bread?"

Mi-aw

She takes a step closer.

"You don't like them, do you?"

She says nothing.

"Shall we give you a name?"

Mi-aw

"You're such a cutie. Shall we call you Cutie?"

No sound from her.

"Hmm, I see. How about Ginger?"

I'm still waiting for a response. I think for a moment.

"How about Cheddar? I know you like cheddar cheese."

Mi-aw

She takes a few steps closer and brushes against my leg.

"Oh dear, thank you for that, love. Okay, you're Cheddar."

I swear she understands me. She looks up and walks around my legs, her soft fur brushing against my skin and her tail gracefully following her movements, occasionally caressing my leg like a gentle whisper. It's as if she's saying, "I'm here, I'm listening, and I'm with you."

She sits and curls up next to my feet.

"I need to meet with Aunt Melina, Cheddar, but I'll come back and you can tell me your story—why you're at my grandparents' house. Okay?"

I make my way to the beach but am disappointed to find that Aunt Melina isn't there.

Chapter Fifteen

In the morning, Amy's friend Chelsea arrives.

"Amy tells me that you're after a fast sell."

"Yeah," I say.

"You're in luck, I actually have a potential buyer," she says, flashing her extremely white teeth. Her long blond hair is in a high ponytail, and to my surprise, she's wearing a formal gray dress, makeup, and even heels. Her look is very fancy compared to that of most of the other locals.

I wonder if Amy told her about our kiss.

Am I in high school or what? Stop it.

She tours the house and takes notes. As she makes her way back to the door to leave, she says, "I hear you're going back to the UK soon."

"I've extended my stay."

"That's awesome," she says, and shakes my hand for a little longer than necessary. "Give me a shout if you're up for grabbing a drink," she adds, with a flirtatious tone.

I respond with a smile and thank her.

Someone at Frank's office called me this morning informing me that he was unable to meet, so I'm free for the rest of the day.

It's been almost twenty-four hours since Amy and I shared that kiss, not that I'm counting or anything, and I've been looking for her on the beach but haven't seen her this morning. Maybe it's for the best.

I change my mind immediately when I see her graceful figure coming out of the ocean. With each step she takes toward her beach towel, time seems to slow.

You must check things on your phone! I make myself busy.

I bet she won't approach me after what I've done. Well, technically, it wasn't just me.

Her head tilts up, and our eyes lock. The seconds stretch. A smile tugs at the corners of her lips, making me smile in response. She's wearing shorts and a beach tank showing off her damp shoulders. I'm ready to break all my self-imposed rules and spend every second of my remaining time here with this woman. Seven days.

She turns around. "Come over here, you two." She beckons with her arm.

The distance between us narrows as she starts walking toward me. What did she mean, *you two*?

The waves crash against the shore, and then I hear a bark and a kid's voice.

"Wait up, Curly." Curly appears, sprinting toward me. A young boy chases him, and Amy follows closely behind.

The boy stops by the little gate.

"Aloha, I'm Sean."

"Very nice meeting you, young man. I'm Roy."

"You talk Brit." Strands of wavy dark-blond hair fall playfully onto his forehead, and his eyes sparkle with mischief. There's a dusting of cute freckles across his nose.

I look at Amy. Is she his aunt? Or his nanny?

"Meet my son." She smiles shyly.

I maintain a composed facade, concealing my surprise. She never mentioned having a son. Over lunch yesterday, she told me she moved from New York, left her career behind, and built an island life; she's a free diver and a snorkeling guide now and loves taking people to magical parts of the water. She even brought up her volunteering time for an education project.

Nope, she didn't mention a child. Although I'm not sure there are any rules about who should bring up what topics at what times when you've just met.

"My mom said that you're from London."

"Yes, I am."

"I love London. What do you do in London?"

"I have a coffee shop. It's called Pages and Beans Café. So you've been to London?"

"Not yet, but I will. You have a café? That's grand! Who's there now?"

Grand? Funny kid.

"My brother is running it for me for a few months. I meant to take off traveling but ended up here."

Just answer the questions, Roy.

"Isn't this traveling? Coming to Hawai'i?"

"I suppose. But it's a different type of traveling than I anticipated."

"What have you seen here? In Hawai'i?"

This kid is on fire. Amy tells him to slow down and not ask so many questions.

"I plan to travel to New York first," Sean says. "I'll visit my grandparents then go to London. I was a baby when I left New York. I'm partly Irish."

I look at Amy, who shrugs. "Come on, Sean, let's leave Roy in peace."

"No, no!" I open the little gate between the sand and the grass. "Come and join me. I have all sorts of drinks. Orange juice, maybe?"

"Can we, Mom? He talks Brit."

"Okay then. A short while, though."

We gather around the table in the garden.

"I took a dip in the water while Sean and Curly entertained themselves by running around."

"I can see that," I say.

I can see that! I scold myself in my thoughts.

"I'll be back with some orange juice." I hurry to the kitchen. As I step toward the house, a piercing hiss cuts through the tranquility. My head snaps toward the sound, and I see Curly running across the yard.

Then I see Cheddar perched on the fence next to the house with an air of superiority. Her fur stands on end, creating an intimidating silhouette against the bright blue sky. Her green eyes glint with annoyance and possessiveness, daring Curly to challenge her further.

The air crackles with tension as Curly's desperate bark merges with Cheddar's guttural growl. Suddenly, they erupt into a chaotic whirlwind of motion and color.

"Hey, hey, hey!" I shout. For a moment, I'm not sure who's chasing whom.

Curly darts through the grass, his nails tearing through the soil, desperate to put Cheddar in her place, but Cheddar leaps onto the fence again and assumes a warrior position.

Amy snatches up Curly from the ground, and then she and Sean walk off toward the beach to calm the dog. Meanwhile, Cheddar looks at me, her eyes blazing with fiery determination. She hops off the fence and takes confident steps into the house. A silent message hangs in the air: this land and home should forever be protected, cherished, and honored.

Once Curly has settled down and Cheddar is ensconced in the house, the three of us sit around the table with glasses of orange juice.

"Apologies on behalf of Cheddar," I say. "She needs to learn not to chase guests."

"Can I tell you a secret?" asks Sean, as Amy takes a phone call.

"Sure."

"I'm planning a secret birthday party for my mom. It's in a few months. I'm getting her a cake with three and seven on it. Do you want to come?"

"Thank you for the invitation. I'll join if I happen to be in town."

What did I just say? *Happen to be in town!* Yes, I rescheduled my flight, but her birthday is months away. Don't I know that I won't be in town?

"Okay," he says, and his attention turns to Curly.

I watch Sean and think about the time I left my first foster family. I was younger than Sean. The smiley woman sitting next to me in the car told me, "It's not your fault. They had issues. Adults do have issues sometimes. It's nothing to do with you that they argued a lot."

But I was sure it was because of me. People got upset when I was around, like my stepmother.

My next foster home was with a single woman. I liked her. She was the first person to ask me my thoughts on adult stuff.

"What do you think we should do this weekend?" or "What do you fancy for dinner today?"

"Dunno," I said a lot, initially. I thought it was a test or something. I wasn't used to adults asking me my opinion. But she never stopped asking.

After a few months I thought maybe her home was going to be my forever one. I'd have a loving and fun foster mom.

But that didn't happen.

She met someone. He was very nice at the beginning. He moved in with us, but I didn't like sharing her. So I gave him a hard time. We did fun things, though, the three of us. I started to like him.

Then he pushed me in the kitchen one day. He apologized, saying that it was an accident and that I shouldn't mention it to anyone. I didn't. Then it happened a few more times.

Another time, he whispered in my ear, "I wish you weren't here."

One day, he hit me, and I kicked him. Or maybe it was the other way around. They were expecting a baby, he'd been fired from his job, and he was drinking all day.

"You know when our baby arrives, she won't have any time for you," he said.

Okay, maybe I kicked him first, but he struck me so hard that I hit the kitchen cupboard. My face was cut and my shoulder was dislocated. I didn't tell anyone. I told the doctor I fell. But the hospital team reported the incident to social services.

Tears streamed down my foster mom's face as the man and woman took me away—again. I didn't cry until I got into the back seat of the car. On my lap I held a small black trash bag with my belongings in it, including my toy fire truck.

Chapter Sixteen

After Curly, Sean, and Amy leave, I feel an afternoon shower is in order. The sound of the water droplets makes me think of the drops on Amy's shoulders when she emerged from the ocean earlier.

So she has a child.

Before heading to the beach for sunset, I look at my reflection in the mirror—I have a cool beach-town look. This morning, I purchased some island clothes. There's a shopping center nearby, with stores scattered among swaying palm trees. Very cool.

I'm hoping Aunt Melina will be under the tree. My bare feet feel the coolness of the grass and soil first, and then the warmth of the sand. When it's time to leave Hawai'i, I'll miss these sensations.

Spotting Aunt Melina, I smile with relief then take confident steps toward her but pause to listen to the ocean for a beat.

"Aloha." I make myself comfortable next to her on the ground.

"Aloha," she responds, with a tiny smile. She's leaning back on the palm tree.

"I've extended my stay for another week," I blurt out.

Her smile grows. "I never doubted that you would. You're her grandson."

"What do you mean?"

"It's something you'll discover. I can't possibly attempt to tell you. Your grandmother was a special soul."

Another mystery to add to the mountains of mysteries, Aunt Melina?

She points at the sunset, and we watch the sun touch the ocean and slide in, spreading colors into the water and the sky. When I stand up to stretch my legs, I look away from the ocean and admire the brilliant colors of dusk on the mountain that towers in the middle of the island.

People on the beach start leaving as soon as the sun sinks below the horizon. Then it's only Aunt Melina and me.

"I need to find someone called Kimo."

"Kimo?" Her surprised tone tells me I'm on the right path.

"Yes."

"Why Kimo?"

"So you do know Kimo?"

"It's a small town, Roy. Of course I know Kimo. In fact, I know a few Kimos, but I think I know which Kimo you're looking for."

I explain that Kimo was my Aunt Kalani's boyfriend and that she wrote about him in her diary. I leave out the intimate details but tell her how Aunt Kalani was trying to help her father and that she planned on speaking to Kimo about it.

"Kimo might know something that will help me figure out what happened in the past," I say. "Even just speaking with someone who was close to my mom would be nice."

Aunt Melina listens intently, but her face is etched with sadness. "Okay, I'll ask Kimo, but you'll honor his wish if he doesn't want to talk to you."

I nod. Surely there's no reason he wouldn't want to.

Satisfied with my Kimo progress, I head home for dinner. I heat olive oil in a skillet and toss vegetables in. The colors brighten as the veggies sizzle in the hot pan. My left hand works diligently, and my injured right arm already feels much better.

I think about how much I love cooking for people. My mom still lives in Bristol, but she spends more time in London now, since Luke and I are both there. There's nothing like the delight of watching my close-knit family enjoying a meal I made with love.

Dasia recently stepped into our lives and quickly gained a place around our dinner table. My brother was immediately drawn into her orbit, and she fell for him before realizing it herself.

Luke and I met her in my café on the same day. I have to be honest—I had a minor crush on her too. But as time passed, I saw how she looked at my brother. My brother, who has always taken care of our mother and me, is now blissfully happy.

I vow to spend the evening concentrating on my family back in the UK instead of mourning the one I had in Hawai'i. I video-call Mom. I know she's an early riser.

"Hey, Mom."

"Hello, son," she answers, out of breath. "I was watering the plants and flowers and heard the phone ringing."

"Your indoor garden always looks lovely."

She chuckles; her voice is the most soothing and comforting sound in the world. "How are you doing over there? I'm happy that you extended your stay."

"So you don't miss me?"

"I miss you so much, but you know what I'm saying."

"I know. I'll get back to dinner now," I say. "Just wanted to say hi. I love you, Mom."

"I love you, son."

I prepare the dinner table, for one, and retreat to the time when I heard my mom whispering "I love you, son" into my ear for the first time. I was eleven years old. I panicked, but before I could run away, she held me so tight that I could hear her heart beating through her chest and feel the tears sliding down her cheeks. I stayed in her hold.

I can't wait to get on that plane in a week and see her.

Yet an unsettling, nagging question creeps into my mind, darkening the path I thought was well-lit.

What happened to my family here?

My phone dings. It's Aunt Melina.

Kimo will wait for you at the Aloha Brew Café, be there by 8 a.m.

Chapter Seventeen

I'm sitting at the café and it's not even 7:30 a.m. There's no table service; you order and then sit at a table outside, just off South Nalu Street. People are queuing to get their drinks. I feel my heart racing, but I'm not sure why I'm so anxious.

I see a man walking toward me. He's a big guy with broad shoulders. He's wearing a sleeveless shirt that reveals the tattoos on his arms; I recognize the triangular designs as well as some other shapes from the photos.

I rise, extending my hand. "You're early too."

He nods and takes my hand.

"Thank you for meeting me. I'm Roy. What can I get you?"

"Nothing, thanks." He sits down.

"I hope you'll be able to help me find out more about my family here."

"What do you want to know?" he asks, as he crosses his arms.

Okay, this is not going to be an easy conversation.

I get straight to the point. "I believe you were dating my Aunt Kalani, and I know she wanted to help her father and asked for your help. But I don't know what happened after that. Just that both my mom and my aunt left the island."

He looks toward the street, watching people. "How do you know all this?"

I ignore his question. "Do you know what happened to Kalani?"

He turns his eyes to me. "No good will come from this. Let it go."

I sip my coffee and take a breath. "Did you help Kalani? That's all I'm asking."

"You should leave the past where it belongs," Kimo says with a frown.

I remember my promise to Aunt Melina, to respect his wish. But I give one last gentle plea.

"I understand. But that past has become my present. I've discovered a family I never knew I had—aunts and grandparents. They're my reality today. I didn't know them in my past."

His eyes narrow, and three horizontal lines appear on his forehead. I listen to the silence between us, my expression pleading with him to say more.

"Are you staying at the beach house?" he asks as he stands, and a flicker of hope ignites in me.

"Yes, I am."

But he doesn't utter another word. With a heavy heart, I watch as he strides away, fading into the distance.

Well, that got me nowhere, and it seems I upset him.

Feeling down, I sit at the café a little longer. A friendly face would make my day better. A gorgeous smile would be a bonus. I take a chance and text Amy.

> I'm at the Aloha Brew Café. Care to join me for coffee?

> Sure, I just dropped Sean off at school. I'll be there in a few minutes.

My mood shifts as soon as I see her walking between the short palm trees around this cute café.

"Hello, sunshine," she says.

"Sunshine?"

"Yes, it suits you."

"A close friend calls me that too."

She sits and looks at me, her green eyes like emerald pools, they suck me in. I find myself staring back.

"What?" she asks.

"Nothing," I say. "So, you have a son."

She nods.

"He's a charmer."

"He surely is," she says, with a piercing gaze. "I'd love to be your island tour guide today. Can you spare the time?"

"You're in luck. I was supposed to fly home today, but since I've postponed leaving until next week, my calendar is completely open." I rise and present my left arm, offering her the chance to take hold of it. "Be my guide—I'd love that."

She laughs. "Great."

"Uh . . . the only thing is, I have a doctor's appointment in the afternoon to get my arm checked."

"That's fine, I'll drop you there before I pick up Sean."

We get in her car and venture along the stunning roads of the island. I'm entranced by the enchanting woman by my side. With her hands on the wheel, she navigates with an intimate knowledge of every inch of these roads. Her enthusiasm and deep connection to the island seem to breathe life into everything.

"I'm taking you to a beach on the north side today." She keeps her attention on the road. As we drive north, we pass through a delightful town that appears to have been plucked straight from the swinging sixties. It has bohemian vibes, with quirky boutiques and cozy cafés lining the narrow lanes. Here, it looks as if time decided to take a bit of a breather, and my worries melt away.

She parks by a beach.

"Prepare yourself. Something extraordinary is about to happen."

"Already happened," I say, stealing a glance at her.

As we approach the shoreline, my jaw drops in amazement. Soft, golden sand stretches for what seems like miles. Wind surfers are taking advantage of the strong wind, and Amy's hair flutters across her face.

"We'll soon see the famed inhabitants of this awesome place," she says, with a Sean-like spark in her eyes.

Then I see what she means. I'm in awe—utterly stunned—turtles on the beach.

A turtle basks on the sand close by, eyes closed. It's at least three feet in length, and its green shell bears a mosaic of patterns that shimmer under the sun.

She smiles. "Sea turtles. The honu. The majestic ocean creatures."

Time stops. We stand. I admire.

The turtle opens its eyes, deep and wise, and meets mine briefly, and it feels as if we share a secret connection across species.

"Sean is a honu advocate on this beach. He has the important duty of reminding people not to get close to the turtles."

"Not surprised he'd want to advocate for the turtles," I say, amazed by the sheer splendor of the scene. As I watch the magnificent creatures, my hand involuntarily touches the small turtle necklace I'm wearing.

We walk on the soft sand, leaving footprints behind. Then as if pulled by an invisible force, I stop and look at her, causing her to pause alongside me. Our eyes meet and hold. A silent understanding passes between us, and then, as if guided by an irresistible magnetic pull, our lips meet in a gentle kiss full of longing and surrender. Her hair falls onto my face, and I let it linger. Her lips taste like honey straight from the honeycomb—wild and sweet.

When we finally part, our eyes lock again in a silent acknowledgment of the moment. We turn to face the water and a turtle, basking in the sun, opens its eyes, joining our moment. We stand still, bathing in the warmth of the beach.

Another stolen kiss has been etched into my memory.

My left hand takes her right one, anchoring us together. It's as if nature has conspired to create a moment of pure bliss. What's going on with me? Did I initiate that kiss? I don't think so. Maybe I should stop asking myself questions and just go with it.

Enjoy this surreal experience, this moment.

We keep walking, and when we reach the end of the bay, we sit on the sand, still holding hands, keeping our distance from a group of turtles. Their shells, weathered and wise, glisten.

There's a huge splash—a whale breach! This place is overwhelmingly magical.

Amy examines our hands then tightens her grip on mine. She nestles her head into the crook of my neck.

My heart skips a few beats, and I can feel hers do the same. I can't say whether her heart or mine is beating faster.

We don't say much on the drive back, and when Amy drops me off at the doctor's office, I don't want to let her go.

Come on, man, you just met the woman, I think, as she drives away. *She has a child. And I'm leaving soon. She knows that. I know that.*

I take a deep breath, but my thoughts continue to move at a sprinter's pace as I walk into the clinic.

The doctor is pleased with my progress; my arm is doing better.

I walk back to the house, but just as I'm about to enter the gate I pause. I hear sounds coming from inside. Has someone broken in? A burglar? On a weekday afternoon? In Nalu Town?

The door is ajar. My heart thunders. I take a step closer. Every muscle in my body tenses. I can hear two voices and a strange clanking sound echoing off the walls. Pushing down the fear crawling into my throat, I sprint up the stairs onto the porch while shouting at the intruders, demanding they show themselves.

As I launch myself into the house, I lose my footing on the slick floor but manage to grab the door before face-planting.

My gaze meets Kimo's surprised face; he's kneeling on the floor next to towels and a bucket.

"What's going on?" I ask.

Kimo is the last person I anticipated finding here, let alone with towels and a bucket. Over by the kitchen sink, someone is engrossed in working on the plumbing.

"An hour ago, I came here to speak with you, but then I saw the pool of water coming from underneath the door. Good thing you left the key in the box, in its secret place.

Otherwise I would've had to break the door down to stop the flooding."

I look around. All the flooring is wet. "But everything was okay when I left this morning!"

"It's an old house." He squeezes water out of a towel and into the bucket, producing a splash.

Water. Everywhere.

"Hello," says the guy checking the pipes.

"I called my plumber friend, Tom."

"A pipe burst here, under the sink," Tom says.

The kitchen and living room have been transformed into a murky swamp. I exhale, irritated.

"Let's get the water out first," Kimo says. "Grab a bucket. Fast."

Next thing I know, I'm carrying the buckets with my left arm while Kimo fills them.

"It happens often around here," he explains. "These houses have old plumbing."

After a few minutes, Tom wipes his hands on a rag and turns to face us. His brow furrows, and his voice holds a hint of disbelief as he speaks. "This wasn't just a random plumbing failure, Kimo. The water pipe was deliberately cut."

A chill runs down my spine. *A deliberate cut?* Someone sabotaged the house? Sabotaged me? Questions flood my mind, but I struggle to find words. "Wha . . . what do you mean, deliberately?"

The plumber sighs; his expression is grim. "See these clean, precise cuts here?" He points. "It's not something that happens accidentally. Someone wanted this pipe to burst and flood the place. An act of vandalism."

Vandalism? The thought makes me furious. I clench my fists, trying to make sense of it all.

"What? I mean, what?" I yell, and then ask in a panic, "Where's Cheddar? Have you seen a cat?"

"Yes, there's a cat in one of the bedrooms," says Kimo.

I take a deep breath, trying to compose myself. "Can you fix it?" I ask Tom. "Can you repair the damage?"

He nods reassuringly. "Yes, I can fix the broken pipe and assess the extent of the damage. It'll take some time, but I'll do my best to restore everything to working order. But you should report this to the police. The station isn't far from here."

"Will do," I say.

I notice Kimo has been quiet. His knit brows form a sharp, thunderous line.

"What do you think?" I ask him.

"Water out first, then we talk."

"Okay."

After an hour Tom leaves and we're working with towels, although it's difficult because I'm operating with one arm.

"Tom will arrange for a couple of heaters tomorrow morning. It should speed up the drying process."

"Thanks, Kimo," I say gratefully.

"It's okay." Kimo says. "We talk, but let's get some dinner first."

I nod.

We talk. Those two simple words hit me like a sledgehammer. Am I finally going to get the answers I've been seeking?

Chapter Eighteen

Kimo calls his wife to inform her he won't be home for dinner.

"Let's drive to my friend's food truck. She has good food."

As we drive along the main street, I observe people. Some are coming back from a day at the beach, and others look as if they're just starting their evenings. A break-in and malicious damage to a home seem incompatible with this laid-back setting.

Kimo stares ahead.

"I'm completely stumped," I say, stealing a glance, trying to read the expression on his face. His brow is furrowed, and there's a tiredness in his face. His lips create a thin line, and he grips the steering wheel firmly. He has that unmistakable "something's up" look.

"Do you have any ideas?" he asks.

I shake my head.

The Johnsons? That's what I think for a few seconds, but it can't be. You don't bake banana bread for your neighbor and then vandalize their plumbing. Too bad I didn't get to try the bread before Cheddar turned it into crumbs.

We order from the food truck then take our meals back to the house to enjoy with a couple of beers. I feel one-hundred-percent better after taking a bite of the delicious food. We sit outside since the house is still quite wet.

A little grin forms on Kimo's face as he looks at his food: rice noodles with succulent shrimp, crunchy bean sprouts, and crushed peanuts. I appreciate people who take pleasure in their food. I've opted for the same dish.

Eyes on his plate, he says, "It'll dry in a few days, but you might have to check underneath the flooring."

I savor the explosion of savory and sweet in each mouthful. "This friend of yours, she's amazing. This is a culinary masterpiece."

As he munches on the tasty food, he nods proudly.

"I'm not going to worry too much about the floors," I say. "I'm selling the house anyway. I'm sure the new owners will knock this house down to build a new one." I'm surprised that my words sound bitter.

Kimo is quiet, but I sense sadness. He gazes at the house. "Your land, your house. Do whatever you want," he says, but irritation lingers in his tone. Why does everyone mention the land first when they talk about this house?

He sets down his fork. "What happened today has me very concerned. It's like going back in time. A sense of déjà vu. For the most part, I try to let the past stay in the past, but like I said, what happened today has me very worried."

"What do you mean, déjà vu?"

He leans back, and I hope to finally hear about what happened to my mother and aunt thirty-five years ago.

"Your aunt asked me to help her daddy. She and I had been dating for some time. She captured my heart like no other. She was like a waterfall. Daring. I was in love. She was fiery too. I used to tell her that she was my own waterfall and volcano."

He looks away for a few seconds. "Kalani's hair mimicked the waves. She was fluid like the ocean." He stares at me. "Your mom and aunt didn't resemble each other."

"Yeah. I guess I inherited my father's darker Mediterranean complexion."

"Don't get me wrong, no disrespect to my wife. I love her very much. But Kalani was my first love, you know, and I was a young man. And I never forgave myself for not being able to take care of her. And her family." He blinks back tears and looks away.

I keep quiet as Kimo takes a moment but give him all my attention.

He crosses his arms then pulls his T-shirt sleeve up. "This is her," he says, pointing at a tattoo. "You see, she's always with me. She was so happy when I showed it to her. I positioned it in the middle of my family tattoo design."

I look at the little waterfall nested within several triangles. The waterfall starts at the edge of a triangle and curves and flows downwards. I can almost see the movement of the cascading water.

I think of my aunt's diary but decide not to mention it to Kimo. No need to reopen old wounds.

"Your grandpa Ben got into trouble with some powerful people who wanted to buy this land. They were planning a big resort hotel and had already bought a lot of land from the neighbors. This land was the last piece of the puzzle for the developers to get their planning permission. Apparently, they held some documents against your grandpa."

He takes a sip of his beer. "Your aunt heard a lawyer who represented RLC threatening your grandpa."

"What's RLC?"

"We called them the Ruthless Land Corporation. It's a large conglomerate. They've gone under now; the lawyer was in prison for many years. He had a long list of crimes —forging documents, acquiring property illegally, intimidating and threatening property owners to sell. I followed his case closely."

"And my grandpa was one of those threatened property owners."

Kimo's chest rises and falls. "Yes, the lawyer turned up here. Kalani was at home, but her daddy didn't realize she could hear them from her room. Your grandpa told the lawyer never to come to his house again, and he was very sad afterward. He sat in the kitchen, his head in his hands."

126

"What made him so upset?" I ask, feeling a surge of frustration on his behalf.

"Yeah, I can remember how distressed Kalani was when she told me what the lawyer said to your grandpa. He said, 'Your loved ones, the army, the press, and the community you care about so much will all receive copies of these papers from me. When they do, everyone will know who you are.' She was in pieces."

"What did the lawyer mean? What sort of papers were they?"

"I dunno. But it didn't matter to me. What mattered was she was very sad and wanted to help her daddy. She never told him that she heard them arguing. She adored him."

"So you never found out."

"No, I didn't. She got upset whenever I asked her."

"He may have done something he wasn't proud of in the past."

"Nah, I knew Ben. This must have been something bigger."

Great, just what I need—more mysteries to solve and more truths to uncover concerning the suffering my ancestors endured long ago. My neck feels tight, so I try to loosen it by moving my head to the right and the left.

Kimo looks away. "I was young and daring and wanted to protect my girl and her family. So I agreed to help her. She was going to do something with or without me anyway. That's Kalani."

Kimo closes his chestnut-colored eyes. "We planned to

threaten the lawyer so he would give up those documents that he had against your grandpa. But things went bad, and your aunt had to run away."

"Threaten the lawyer? With what?"

"Yeah." He hesitates. "I still think no good will come from knowing the details. I'm not proud of what we did. Maybe it's best you leave the past in the past."

I squirm in my seat. "Kimo, like I said, it's not the past for me. Until a couple of days ago, I thought my mother had no family connections. This is my attempt to understand who my mom was. You owe this to me, and to my mother. To Kalani too."

"Okay, I'll tell you, but I'm not proud."

"No judgment, I promise."

The contrast between how stormy I feel inside and how calm I look on the outside is extreme. But I push the storm down.

"We had to come up with a plan that would force the lawyer to give us whatever he had against your grandpa. We needed to use intimidation, but we knew it wouldn't be easy because he was a tough one. Threatening him with violence wasn't going to do the trick."

Kimo rises from his chair. "Let's go for a walk on the beach."

"What, now? But you'll tell me, right?" I ask, worried that he might change his mind.

He puts on his sandals. "Yes, I will. Don't rush me, man."

"Sorry, okay."

We start walking.

Kimo sighs. "We made the plan on this beach, you see," he says, his tone filled with pain. "She made the plan. We decided to take his child."

"You what?" I stop walking.

"I told you I'm not proud of this." He stops too. His shoulders are slumped. "I've regretted it all my life."

"No more questions," I say, raising both my palms.

"Let's sit here."

We settle ourselves on the sand.

Kimo continues, but he's almost whispering now.

"There was an empty sugarcane warehouse where I'd done temporary jobs. The company had moved out of it, but I still had the key. It was perfect. Unused, in the middle of a field, waiting to be demolished."

The muscles in his forehead wrinkle with despair as his voice cracks. "I tried to talk her out of it, I really did. But it was no use."

He continues. "Your aunt picked the lawyer's kid up from school one day and told him that his dad had asked her to. He was happy to go with her. Eh, we didn't want to scare the keiki. We had toys for him to play with and even some malasadas to eat. He was eight years old."

"Keiki?"

"A young child." He plunges his hand into the sand and lets the grains run between his fingers. "She was determined. She said, 'I'm going to do this, and I don't need your help.' But I couldn't let her go alone—she was my girl, and I had to protect her."

129

His squinted eyes transform into wide, expansive ones. "The kid was excited to be with her, you know. She told him that this was a little adventure. A game. She spoke so gently to the child. She said, 'Can you stay here by yourself until we return? Show us that you're brave.' She was so calm."

He shakes his head, and when he speaks again, it's with a quivering voice. "We left him in one of the offices in the warehouse." He hugs himself with both arms.

Kimo's face is the picture of regret—sad eyes, lips pressed together in a tight line. His pain is vivid. His sigh joins the lapping of the ocean.

"Should we take a break?" I ask, as he visibly trembles.

"No, no. Now or never. Let me finish." He pauses. "We went to a phone booth close by. She made the call. I still remember her shaking voice. She told the lawyer to leave her daddy alone, to give her all the documents if he wanted to see his son again."

Kimo looks at the ocean as he continues. "She listened a little while and then started sobbing, losing all her cool."

"Why? What did the lawyer say?"

"He threatened to ruin her father because of what she'd done. We didn't expect this response. He was either bluffing or he knew that Kalani wouldn't hurt his son. But he certainly wasn't responding like a father who'd just found out his son had been kidnapped."

His gaze turns to the sand. "Her sobbing, it was like a steel blow to my gut. I panicked. You see, she made me promise that I'd stay in the background. The lawyer never knew I was there. We didn't realize we were dealing with an underground land mafia—scaring them was impossible."

I shake my head, looking at the ocean. "The land mafia," I mutter.

"Yeah, the land mafia. Forced evictions, bribing, land grabbing, money laundering. You name it. I told you before. I followed the court case against them years later."

Kimo extends his legs on the sand and leans back, resting on his hands. "Oh man, it was stupid. She started freakin' as soon as she put the phone down. She yelled, 'He's going to destroy my daddy. But he said if I tell him where his son is, he might not do it.'"

He quickly wipes away his tears. "She called the lawyer back immediately and told him where he'd find his kid. He told her to vanish if she didn't want her loved ones harmed."

I put my hands on my head to stop it from getting heavier.

"She insisted that we drive back to the warehouse. I didn't know what to do. She wanted to tell the kid that his father was picking him up."

"And the kid was in a warehouse, alone."

"I told you about the level of stupidity, right? But he was in a comfortable room, we left food with him, and he was alone only for fifteen to twenty minutes."

"Okay," I mutter, though I feel as if a volcano is

erupting in me. An eight-year-old kid abandoned in a warehouse. That's not okay.

"When we parked outside the warehouse, we could see a speeding car approaching from a distance. The lawyer was coming to get his kid. I told Kalani that we should leave, but before I could drive away, Kalani sprinted into the warehouse to tell the kid and make sure he was okay. I got out of my truck and ran after her."

The relentless crash of the waves is like a turbulent soundtrack to Kimo's story.

Continuing in almost a whisper, his gaze fixed on the sand, he says, "I still remember her scream piercing every fiber of my heart. 'Is he okay? He's okay, right?' she kept saying."

"What happened?" I ask, my heart splitting into pieces. "What happened to the child?" I swallow hard after the words force their way out of me.

"He was lying on the floor. There was blood on his head." Kimo struggles to contain his emotions.

"What on earth did you guys do?" I exclaim, springing up from the sand.

"We didn't do anything—I told you, we found him like that," he responds, his voice louder. And angry. "So I grabbed Kalani and pulled her out of the warehouse."

Kimo sinks his head into his hands. "We got in my truck and sped away in a cloud of dust and smoke."

His words hit me like a tidal wave of shock. I ask, "What happened to the kid, man?" My voice cracks.

Chapter Nineteen

All my limbs are tense. Kimo is silent.

"Will you tell me what happened to the kid?" I yell.

"He was fine!" he yells back. "Just sit down and let me tell you the rest of it."

"He was fine . . ."

Slowly I feel air entering my lungs. I drop back to the sand.

Kimo's voice is fractured and heavy with pain. "But we didn't know that the kid was okay. For a long time we thought he'd died. It broke our life to pieces." Each word is like a shard of the emotional wreckage he carries around with him.

We sit at the table in the kitchen—Kimo at one end and I at the other. He needed some time to compose himself, alone, before continuing. He was in the bathroom for a long time. His dark lids show a tint of red.

"We were terrified," he says. "So we ran and hid first. Then I helped her leave the island. Thirty some years ago, it wasn't like today. Not many people flew. But I had a cuz on the East Coast, and he helped me get her a ticket to New York first. She stayed there for a few weeks, and then she got on a ship that sailed to Ireland."

"But what about the kid?" I ask impatiently.

"I told you the kid was fine," he snaps. "Anyway, my cuz worked on the ships, and he happened to be on the same one she took. The journey lasted a couple of weeks. We planned to meet a year later in Ireland."

As I listen to the sad story, a weight settles on my chest like an enormous steel anchor from the very ship she once journeyed on.

Kimo continues. "I was also lying low, not knowing if the lawyer knew I'd been there too. I told my family that I needed to help a friend on a neighboring island and didn't return until I knew Kalani had reached Ireland. I lost my job because of my absence. But when I got back, I found out that the kid wasn't dead. He had diabetes. Eating so many malasadas rapidly increased his blood-sugar levels. When his blood sugar dropped, he got lightheaded and fell, and his face hit something. Not sure what, but there were desks and tables. When he opened his eyes in the hospital, he asked where the nice malasada lady was.

That's what my cuz who was a nurse in the hospital told me."

"Unbelievable. So Kalani didn't know this."

"No. I did go to find Kalani in Ireland, but I only managed to get there two years later. I couldn't make it any sooner. I waited for her at the meeting spot, but she never turned up." He looks down at the table.

"Where was she supposed to meet you?"

"At a small church in a village near the Port of Cork."

"How could she afford to leave and start over in Ireland? How did you afford to get there too?"

"I'm only a few years older than her, but I'd been working from age fifteen. I also borrowed from friends. My cuz told me that Kalani sold her necklace, which made me real sad. I used all my savings to buy that necklace. It was my first and last present for her."

"How about the lawyer? The kid's father? What happened with him?"

"He did trouble me for a while. He never knew I was with your aunt that day, but he knew I was dating her, so he targeted me. He told me that Kalani should never return. He continued to trouble your mom and grandparents too."

I stand up and walk around. Feels like I've got that massive lava rock on me once more. "I don't know what to say." I sigh.

"Nothing can be said."

"What about my mom, Kimo?"

"I dunno, she left a few months after Kalani. I

promised Kalani I'd protect her family and not tell them anything, but I had to tell your grandmother where Kalani was—she wouldn't leave me alone until I did. I told her everything. Your mom was with her. They both got very upset that I helped Kalani without telling them. And they were right to be upset, you know. I was so in love with Kalani that I thought I was protecting her and her family."

"I see," I say, although I'm unsure what I see.

"I was ready to tell Ben what was going on, but Leilani told me it would be better to stay away from her family because I'd already caused them enough damage. The lawyer claimed he knew where Kalani had gone and kept menacing your family, saying that she'd pay for what she'd done, though whether he actually knew she was in Ireland was a mystery. He just wouldn't let up. He was relentless. An evil person. He even turned up at my work one day and got me fired. I left the island after that."

"You did?"

"Yeah, I came back more than ten years later. I was engaged to Jenn at that point. My wife is from a neighboring island. I kept my distance from Ben and Hina."

"So my mom left the island to find her sister in Ireland?"

"Yeah. But neither of them returned."

We sit in silence. I take deep breaths and feel my throat tighten around my Adam's apple.

"Do you know any of my mom's friends?" I ask.

Kimo thinks for a few seconds. "Yeah, she had a pal

she was very close with. The last I heard, she'd moved to the Big Island. I believe she ran a bookstore there. Can't remember her name, but it will come to me."

His shoulders are slumped again, and his chest rises and falls unevenly. "I should get going."

I nod. By the door, slipping his sandals on, he says, "Your mom and aunt were my ohanas, and I failed to take care of them."

I sigh. "You tried."

He looks at me for a beat. "You'll come to my house for dinner soon."

"I'm leaving next week, but thanks for the invite."

"I'll let you know what day to come."

I stand by the door, thousands of questions running through my mind, the heavy lava rock pressing on my chest.

It's 3:00 a.m.

Tomorrow, I'll have to switch to one of the bedrooms. This couch isn't wide enough for tossing and turning.

I think of my aunt. A poor choice, a misguided judgment, and her entire life collapsed. I ponder what my grandfather didn't want exposed, what the lawyer had against him.

I step onto the porch and take a deep breath, smelling the salty ocean air.

By the light of the moon, I make my way to the water's

edge and stand on one of the lava rocks scattered on the beach.

My chest feels hot. My feet sink into the waves. With each step I take, the water rises higher until it reaches my knees. Then I sit down, letting the waves lap against my chest.

"Take it away, please," I whisper. "Take the lava rock away from my chest."

I'm not sure how long I sit in the water. Gradually, my breathing relaxes and my chest feels lighter.

Chapter Twenty

I get comfortable in my seat on the plane, my mind racing. Since Kimo's revelations, I've had an urge to see this lawyer who threatened my grandfather and led my mother and aunt to flee.

I've met with Chelsea, the real estate agent again, as well as Frank. There's a cash buyer if I want to sell, but the buyer wants to remain anonymous. A trust has been set up to conceal the person's identity.

"Hollywood stars own homes here," Chelsea told me, "so it's pretty normal to remain anonymous."

But I want to know who this buyer is. Why I care, I don't know.

For the past few days, I've been debating whether to call or visit this lawyer. It was stupid of Kimo and my aunt to kidnap his child—no one deserves that. But everything else I know about him makes it clear that he was not a decent human being.

It wasn't hard to track down his address since there's less of a premium on personal-information privacy here than back home. I called the care home yesterday, and the receptionist connected me to him.

His voice sounded thick when he picked up. "Hello."

"Hello, Mr. Devereux. Sorry to trouble you. I'm looking to uncover some details about my family, and I understand that you might be able to help."

"Your family, you say?" he rasped, his voice harsh like sandpaper.

"Ben and Hina Williamson."

The line fell so silent that I thought I'd been disconnected. But then I heard faint breathing.

"Can I come to speak to you?" I asked. "I won't take much of your time."

"Tomorrow," he croaked.

"Tomorrow is Sunday," I said, but he had already hung up.

A peculiar man. I shook my head and quickly booked my flight.

The flight to O'ahu is just half an hour—easy to go and return in one day.

I'm still unsure what I'll get from this visit, but I hope Carter Devereux will shed some light on what he was holding against my grandpa.

As the airplane climbs higher, I look out of the small

window and see the coastlines of the island and the ocean below. It's unbelievable that all the islands of Hawai'i are connected at the bottom of this ocean as part of a volcanic mountain chain.

Both excitement and nervousness are pressing heavily upon my chest. What happened to my family thirty-five years ago? Will Carter Devereux tell me more?

After landing, I exit the aircraft and make my way through the busy airport to grab a taxi.

My spine tingles uncomfortably as the taxi approaches the care facility where Mr. Devereux lives. It's a single-story structure with large windows.

I stop in the large entryway. *I should have just insisted he talk to me over the phone. It's okay to change my mind. This isn't a good idea. Turn around. It's okay.*

I force myself to step further into the building.

"Aloha, I'm here to see Mr. Carter Devereux."

The receptionist looks at me as if I've just announced I intend to disturb the Queen of England during her meal.

She lifts her eyebrows. "Mr. Devereux" is all she utters, but her curiosity doesn't require a full sentence or a question mark.

"Yes." I shift uncomfortably, leaning on the reception desk a little. *Turn around and leave the building*, my mind pleads. "He did agree to meet with me. I called yesterday." I smile, attempting to hide my nerves.

She looks at the potted plant in my hand. "It's just, hmm, he doesn't have visitors often. Much. I mean, kind of never." Placing her hand over her mouth, she says, "Sorry, I shouldn't have said that."

"It's okay." I chuckle. Her cheeks are getting rosy. "So, can I see him?"

"Rather you than me." She holds her mouth with both hands this time. It's comical. "I'm sorry, I don't know what got to me. Please fill this out."

She hands over a visitor form and says, "I'll prepare your visitor badge. Can I have your ID, please?"

I hand over my passport.

"That's a long way to come." She slightly lifts her right eyebrow, inspecting my British passport.

"Yes, a tad too long."

I continue filling out the visitor form.

Question 5: Are you a family member, friend, or other?

I'm not even *other* to him, but I tick it.

"Follow the corridor ahead, turn right at the end, and he's in room thirteen."

"Thirteen. Sure, thank you." Clipping the badge on my T-shirt, I stroll down the corridor, smiling at the residents I see as I pass.

I arrive at number thirteen. "Of course he's in room thirteen." I chuckle then take a deep breath and knock on the big white door.

"Come in," I hear a faint voice say.

When I open the door I see a frail and skinny old man, nearly invisible in the white sheets of his bed. The veins of his hands are thick and blue. With fingers slightly bent at the knuckles, he beckons me closer to his bedside. The smell of urine lingers in the air.

"Hello, sir." I set the potted plant on his small table by the window. "Is this okay here?"

He nods.

His room is bare, containing just his bed and a table with a chair.

"I'll grab the chair," I say, as I don't wish to tower over him.

"No need," he says. "Your visit won't be long." He looks up and locks his gaze with mine. Then he murmurs, "I never expected to see another Williamson family member in a million years."

I squirm uneasily. "I'm Roy Fernsby. I didn't know about my Williamson family until a few weeks ago. I'm Leilani's son."

"Leilani. I of course remember your mother."

Do I see a smirk on his wrinkled face?

He continues. "Your mom was a stubborn beauty."

I push aside the uneasiness spreading into my chest. "What do you mean?"

"I guess we'll get to that later."

Regret sweeps over me for being here. But I press, "Okay, I've got a few questions, and I was hoping you might be able to help." Though my tone remains polite, annoyance creeps into my voice.

"Sure thing." His lips curl into a half-smile and his eyes narrow slightly.

"I'm searching for my aunt, Kalani."

"Don't bother searching around here. I swore to ruin her loved ones and put her in jail if she ever returned. She cried like a little kitten."

My stomach knots as I try to contain my anger.

"So you spoke with her after she left."

"No, but I sent regular messages. I know she got them. I had strong connections in Ireland."

So he really did know that she was in Ireland. I take a few deep breaths to soothe the sourness rising from my gut.

"You have another question?"

"Why did you bully my grandfather? What did you have against him?"

"You know, your mother could have stopped all this. I promised to forgive her family and friends if she ran away with me. But, no, she wouldn't. I told you that she was stubborn. She should have taken my offer."

My hands form painful fists as I look at his miserable face. I won't give him the pleasure of seeing he has inflicted pain on another soul. Growing up, I learned to hide my emotions. I'm good at this.

"Give me a glass of water, will you?" he asks.

I pour him a glass from the pitcher on the table and pass it to him. His hand is aged and gnarled, the skin mottled and wrinkled. His nails are yellow and cracked.

"She came to my office demanding to know more about her sister and find out what I had against her father." He smiles a little. "She was the most beautiful woman on the island, so I offered her a deal—I'd leave the island and my wife if she ran away with me. And I'd leave her family alone."

I take a big breath, and my nostrils flare as I clench my fists again. The atmosphere is tinged with heaviness.

His lips curl into a satisfied smirk. A stark reminder of his vile nature. I see a few flecks of saliva on the corner of his mouth.

"I never knew a girl could slap that hard. The sting of it stays with me to this day."

This man is disturbed. He does not deserve my respect.

He looks me up and down. "Sounds like she had a good life."

"Yes." I can utter only the single syllable before I turn to leave. I will not say another word to him about my mother.

It's hard to understand how anyone can feel joy in causing someone else pain, and can feel no regret for their actions. It seems he wants me to hurt as well. Was his childhood difficult, or did something else happen to make him this way? Regardless, my empathy is limited. We all have the ability to make choices about how we live our lives.

"Your grandmother made it hell for me," he says, as I reach the door. "She and her friends. I handed over every document I had against your grandpa. And I'm certain she played a part in my imprisonment, even if I couldn't prove it."

I turn around, silently cheering on Grandma.

"I would have given my life for a family like yours,"

he admits with bitterness. "They'd do anything to protect their loved ones. "

I'm silent for a moment, taken aback by the revelation of this deeply troubled and angry person. "Don't you have a son?" I ask.

"It's been two decades since I heard his voice. He refuses to talk to me." He squints in anger. "Are you happy now? Leave me be!" He rolls onto his side, facing away from me.

Aunt Kalani might have made a mistake, but this man's actions were no accident—he made deliberate choices.

What information do those documents hold?

Thank goodness for that slap, Mother. He still remembers!

Chapter Twenty-One

I could get used to these kinds of Mondays. Here I am, in the front garden, taking in the beach walkers as I move my arm around in slow circles. After my trip to O'ahu yesterday, I need this: the gentle lap of the ocean, the blue, the swaying palms.

Then I see Amy and Curly getting off their stand-up paddleboard. My morning just got even brighter. I hope they'll drop by. I've been hit with longing to be around her. I've not seen her since our day with the turtles.

Could this be the sort of vacation romance people blabber on about? Did I have this in the back of my mind when I rescheduled my flight the second time?

Two more weeks. I can put off my globe-trotting for two more weeks.

I run a hand through my hair as she walks toward the house. *Just act natural. Stay cool . . .*

I grasp the handle of the small gate. "I'm not sure why this gate is even here," I say. "Even Sean can step over it."

She laughs. "I know."

"Do you need a hand?" I offer, gesturing to her board.

"No, thank you. This board and I are like one now."

I stop myself from saying "What a lucky board."

Curly heads toward the house and stops by the door.

"Keen to see his buddy," I say with a chuckle.

"So what's new?" she asks. Do I see a sparkle in her eyes?

"I rescheduled my flight again. I was supposed to leave this Wednesday, but I'm staying a little longer."

"How long?" she asks.

I'd hoped she'd ask. I smile. "Two more weeks."

"Your one week here extended to four weeks."

"Yeah," I say, stepping toward her. "Is someone counting the days?"

Our eyes lock. Was that what she'd wanted to hear? That I'm staying longer? I catch a minuscule smile on her lips. If I'd blinked, I would have missed it.

She looks at her board. "We just had a great paddle on the ocean. You should join us next time."

Oh, yeah, ocean, water, beautiful and all that. Can't get enough of it—from a distance. I don't know how to swim. It's a source of embarrassment for me. My biological family could barely provide meals for me, let alone enroll me in a swimming class, and moving from one foster family to another didn't give me a chance to learn.

She looks at me, smiling. Oh man, that smile. An ocean goddess.

"You're thoughtful," I say.

"So, there's something I wanted to invite you to. You don't have to come. Perhaps it's better not to anyway, but he'll be very happy if you do."

I frown a little. What is she talking about?

"Sean has a swimming competition and he insisted that I mention it to you."

"Oh! I'll be there. A swimming competition—I'm impressed."

"It's only a practice competition."

"Still. I'll be there." I'm chuffed that he invited me, but I shouldn't get too excited. *Don't get close to him. You won't be around for very long.*

I try to push my doubts and fears to a far corner of my head.

"Coffee?"

She nods.

I pour her a cup and we sit next to each other at the table in the garden. She casts her eyes downward then shyly meets my gaze.

Guided by instinct, I tilt her chin up and give her a little peck on her lips. She looks at me and then presses her lips to mine. Her taste mingled with the saltiness of the sea creates an intoxicating blend that leaves me yearning for more. We stand up and press our bodies against each other; the dampness of her swimsuit underneath her beach clothes becomes a silent promise. The fabric clings to her,

149

revealing the shape of her fit body. My hands discover her skin.

Hand in hand, we enter the house, our bodies buzzing with desire. We move with graceful urgency.

I pull her into the large bedroom, our lips locked. The air is charged with the electricity of our connection. I help her shed her sodden clothing, leaving a trail of droplets on the floor. She helps me remove my T-shirt.

Soft murmurs of pleasure escape our lips. Our hands explore, tracing invisible paths across each other's skin.

Words remain unspoken, as if any sound might shatter this moment we've been given. The world around us fades. The sensations become a language of their own, every touch, every kiss, every breath.

I pull away and stare into her eyes, asking, wondering, exploring. She responds by closing the gap between our bodies.

Moments later we lose ourselves in each other. Our bodies move as one. The knowledge that our time together is limited only fuels the intensity of our embrace.

Our shared passion intensifies, and we both climax.

Left breathless, damp bodies entwined, we cling to each other.

I know that our paths will inevitably diverge. However hard it is to accept, this is a short-lived lust.

A short-lived connection.

Chapter Twenty-Two

Friday night approaches. I have slept in the larger bedroom since Monday, having moved from the sofa. Good grief, I've crafted quite a memory in that room.

However, after a heavenly Monday, my week took a sudden plunge into chaos. I pace in the living room of the house.

It started with issues with the electrical system. It became impossible to know when the lights or outlets would work, and I worried about an electrical fire breaking out. I contacted an emergency contractor and had some repairs done, but the electricity just went out again. I was in the middle of preparing dinner. And the contractor now seems to be avoiding my calls.

On Wednesday, I received a notification from the town council. Apparently, the house doesn't adhere to the revised beach safety regulations. I called Frank immediately to look into it.

And yesterday, Kimo told me he could hear termites. He explained that these wood-boring beings could penetrate the base of a building, putting its structural soundness in jeopardy.

Then there were the plumbing issues last week. Too many coincidences are piling up.

"Okay, no one would deliberately inject termites into this house," I say to myself with a laugh.

I don't know why I'm so worried about these issues. I don't doubt that the new owner will demolish this house and build a brand new one. Nevertheless, I contacted a termite control company.

It's as if Grandma is whispering in my ear, "Take care of my house."

What exactly is going on?

Chelsea called yesterday to inform me that the buyer had increased their offer. She suggested selling quickly, as the market might not remain as favorable for sellers. But I want to sort out all these issues before the sale.

One step at a time. Food. *Get takeout.* Light. *Use candles.*

While the issues are being addressed, I'm hoping to find out more about Kalani and my mom. Also, I'd like to spend more time with Amy, Sean, and Cheddar.

It surprises me that Amy is now on my "Stay a bit longer" list. She used to be on the "Leave fast" list, but I'm enjoying this unexpected turn of events. This must be what people are talking about when they say traveling frees your heart and mind. *No kidding.* My mind is constantly flooded with memories of our time together, the way we kissed and touched.

When my food arrives, another poke bowl, I sit on the porch and indulge while watching the sunset—in shorts and a T-shirt in February.

As night takes over, I sense movement and look to my left. The large house next door stands tall over the beach.

I squint. What was that?

I thought I saw a figure in the window, but now the mansion appears to be completely dark.

Strange people.

Chapter Twenty-Three

On Saturday, I arrive at the open-air pool eager to see my little buddy. Still, nervousness trickles down my spine like a small waterfall. I know he understands I'm only here temporarily—that soon I'll be leaving Hawai'i behind. I'm just a visitor passing through his life.

With a deep breath, I steady my nerves and hope this fleeting joy can outweigh the worry. For now, I'll simply cherish the day. I head toward the crowd, taking in the warmth of the soft tropical breeze.

Laughter and chatter fill the air. Children and parents buzz excitedly, their eyes fixed on the pool, where young swimmers prepare to showcase their talents.

I spot Amy with a group of people. She sees me, too, and waves me over.

"Hey, everyone, this is Roy."

One by one, her friends introduce themselves. They're a friendly bunch.

"Aloha, I'm Susan," says a woman with sun-kissed skin and short bleached-blond hair. She shakes my hand, and her touch lingers. Her thumb lightly circles my skin. "Where have you been hiding this handsome face, Amy?"

Amy subtly touches my arm, and I discreetly break away from Susan's grip.

"Susan and I are both snorkeling guides," says Amy.

"Nice meeting you, Susan," I reply, and take a mini step closer to Amy. There's an underlying message behind my move: there's no one else for me while I'm on this island.

"You made it!" Sean shouts, as he sprints toward us with another boy around his age.

"Of course. I'd not miss it for the world."

"This is Liam, my friend," Sean says, pointing to the boy beside him.

"Hello, Liam. I'm Roy."

After I give Sean a big hug and wish him luck, he walks to his lane with determination.

"How come none of the rest of us got a hug?" complains Susan.

We all laugh.

Another friend says, "You'll be his best friend soon."

I turn my gaze to Sean. He's standing on the edge of the pool, his small frame radiating confidence. He looks at me for a beat. I give a firm thumbs-up. The anticipation grows. The race is about to begin.

The starting horn sounds, and with a boisterous cheer, the crowd erupts into a symphony of encouragement. I can't contain my excitement.

"Come on, lad! Show 'em what you're made of!"

Susan remarks, "I could listen to you holler in your British accent all day."

A chorus of laughs follows her words, and I laugh too, but my gaze drifts toward Amy, who's cheering for Sean and doesn't so much as glance in my direction.

As the race unfolds, I watch in awe as he glides effortlessly through the water. Every stroke and kick propels him closer to the finish line.

I realize that the true essence of this competition isn't the victory—it's about the effort, the commitment, and the sheer joy of participation. But I also want my buddy to do well, so I shout, my words blending with the collective cheer of the crowd. I clap, urging him forward and wishing I could swim too.

On Sean's final lap the excitement builds. The crowd's volume increases, and excitement crackles in the air. With one final, energetic surge, he reaches the wall, triumphant and breathless.

He emerges from the water with a beaming smile.

As the cheers subside, I turn and see Amy in tears. "Thank you for coming," she says. "He was so excited when I told him you would."

A grinning Sean runs toward us, and my chest is filled with the sound of his laughter like a joyous waterfall.

Amy and I sit on her balcony on a double-seater, side by side. Sean is asleep.

"I don't usually—" She clears her throat. "I mean, thanks for coming. He was very happy."

"Well, he insisted I join the after-party. So, please don't take this the wrong way, but I'm his guest here. I'll leave soon."

She laughs. "Thanks for making this easy."

"No worries. I'll go soon."

"You don't need to rush." She shifts in her seat. "Susan liked you a lot."

"Well, I'm only interested in one of the local snorkel guides." I place my hand gently on her arm. She grins, her smile as sweet as nectar.

"How did you end up free diving?"

"It happened gradually. I couldn't do my corporate work here in Hawai'i, so I looked for different opportunities and became a licensed snorkeling guide as well as a free diver. It's been almost seven years now."

"How do you train to become a free diver?"

"It begins with yoga and meditation."

"Really? I'd never guess."

She nods. "Many people don't. But the secret is to be still and relaxed. My heart rate drops so much when I dive that I feel like part of the ocean. That's the most tranquil state my body, mind, and spirit can ever achieve."

"Wow. It almost sounds impossible."

"It's not." She becomes more animated, clearly passionate about the topic. "Consider our connection to water. We start in liquid, in our mother's womb. The human body consists of approximately 60 percent water, and our planet is made up of about 70 percent water. Our relationship with water is embedded in our DNA. It's natural."

I'm genuinely intrigued despite the fact that I'm scared out of my wits in knee-high waters. Talk about coming from two totally different worlds.

By the time my adoptive mom arranged for me to take swimming lessons, I was already thirteen years old. I was the oldest participant in my initial lesson, and unfortunately, I didn't go back for more. Then during one of our beach outings, kids pushed me off a pier into the water.

I still remember the dread I felt when I fell in. The ocean is notoriously cold off the Devon coast. Someone showed up just in time to help me. That's when my terror of swimming peaked.

I may not know how to swim, but I can whip up one heck of a delicious meal.

"Would you like to come for dinner one evening with Sean? I'd love to cook for you guys." I'm surprised that I asked. The kitchen in the beach house is far from ideal for preparing a gourmet dinner. And we really shouldn't spend more time together.

"Don't get me wrong, but I don't think it's a good idea." She tilts her head and looks damn cute.

"I know." I nod.

I think it's best if Sean and I don't hang out. Amy seems to agree. It's not a good idea for him to get too attached. Or for me. But how do I keep my distance from Amy?

"It's hard to keep away," I remark, resisting the urge to pull her into my arms.

"I know."

"I better get going," I say, trying to swallow the lump in my throat.

Chapter Twenty-Four

It's Sunday evening, and Kimo and I are sitting on his and his wife's porch.

"Dinner was delicious," I say.

"Jenn is an amazing cook," he says.

"She is, and your children seem great."

Kimo's eyes glimmer. "Yeah, they are great kids. Kai should take you fishing. His friend has a boat, and they go most weekends. My boy is an excellent fisherman. I used to take him when he was this tiny." He moves his hand so it hovers just above the grass.

"And Pua seems to have found her British friend." He chuckles. "You've done well, patiently answering her thousands of questions. For a seventeen-year-old girl, she certainly knows what she wants to do in life, and living in London is one of those things."

"I'll talk about London as long as she wants," I say with a smile.

Kimo leans back, a warm smile lighting his face. His chin lifts with an air of pride. Then he frowns slightly. "But I'm worried about Kai. He's twenty-two and struggling to find his way. He dropped out of college and has been bouncing from job to job since then. It's been a real challenge for him—and me too."

"I completely understand your concern. You know, he reminds me of myself. I studied business in college and then pursued a career in that field, thinking it was the right path. But deep down, I always felt something wasn't connecting."

"So what happened?"

"Well, it took me a while to figure things out. I didn't know where I truly belonged. I felt a longing for something more fulfilling. I didn't want to work for 'the man,'" I say with a chuckle. "I ended up helping a friend who was setting up a restaurant, and I found I loved the thrill of entrepreneurship. So, with my brother's help, I followed my passion for food. I attended culinary school first, and that led to opening my own café in London. I've never been happier. My brother has a fifty percent stake in the business, but he hasn't been actively involved until recently. My plan is to buy out his share after I return from my globe-trotting."

"I'm sure your customers love you."

"Yeah, I love them too. To me, my café is much more than just a business. I love creating moments that touch people's lives, even in the simplest ways. When I realized I could make a difference with a cup of coffee or a delicious sandwich, bring a smile to someone's face on a busy Monday morning, that's when I knew—man, this is where I belong."

I realize how much I miss Pages and Beans. I miss watching people get lost in the pages of their books while sipping their drinks.

"I can see it in your eyes," Kimo says, nodding. "You love what you do. I hope Kai can find that same sense of purpose."

"I know he will. But it wasn't an easy process, you know. I had to do a lot of soul-searching and try different things. Give him time. He will."

His face softens. "I hope he finds a good girl to start a family with too."

Kai walks onto the patio. "I'm taking off."

He has the chiseled features of his Hawaiian ancestors, and from his maternal grandparents, who were Japanese, he inherited a confident nose and a strong jawline framed by wavy, dark hair that catches the sunlight. He also has the same triangle tattoos as Kimo, as well as tattoos of various shapes on his other arm.

"Okay, son. So I told Roy he should join your next fishing trip."

Kai looks at me with skepticism. "It's not a leisurely activity for tourists. Not sure if you would enjoy it."

I can understand why he wouldn't want to spend time with me. Why hang out with a tourist when you could have a good time with friends? But I'm too intrigued to back down. "I'd love to try it. Let me know when you go next."

There's a faint crinkle on Kai's face. He reluctantly tells me he'll be going next weekend, and that they set off early.

"Name the place and time."

After giving me the details, he takes off.

"He's a good kid," Kimo says. "But he's in the habit of opposing whatever I say or suggest."

"I see." So it was more about his dad and less about me.

"Your dad, is he around?" Kimo asks.

"Huh-uh. Growing up, I didn't see much of my biological father, but my adoptive father was wonderful. He's my dad. But he passed away when I was twelve years old."

"I can't even imagine what that must have been like for you. Losing a parent at such a young age."

"Yeah, it was hard. I only found a loving dad at the age of ten, so it was tough losing him a few years later."

Kimo's eyes widen, seemingly absorbing the weight of my words. He leans in, a mixture of curiosity and compassion evident in his expression. "I'm so grateful they adopted you. Your family here would have been devastated if they knew that you'd had to go from one foster home to another."

I don't have much to say about that. Not to Kimo, anyway.

"Kai will find his passion," I say, redirecting the conversation.

"You run a coffee shop. Maybe you have some ideas about what I should do with my coffee trees."

I blink. "Wait, you own coffee trees?" Some of the best beans in the world come from Hawai'i. "I buy beans from here, and my friend roasts them at his coffee roastery in London."

Kimo smiles. "That's great. The trees are on the Big Island, but they've been neglected since my parents passed away. All that's left is a field full of wilted coffee plants. I think Kai might have some ideas, but we get into an argument anytime we discuss it."

"I'd love to see them," I say.

"Kai would be a perfect guide for you. But that boy won't do it if I ask."

"I've actually been calling people on the Big Island to see if anyone knows my mom's friend Stephanie's whereabouts. I'll go there soon. Right now, I want to explore anything that connects me to my mom."

Kimo's eyes, the color of freshly brewed espresso, fix on me; their depth and intensity capture my attention. It's as if he pours a steaming cup of truth in that long beat.

"Give me a minute," he says, and vanishes into the house.

Jenn appears, an inviting grin on her face. She's holding a plate of doughnuts. Pua follows her. It's remarkable, the flow of the family. All evening, when one member steps away, another effortlessly steps in. They have a rhythm, a bond that ensures a guest is never left alone at their home. They're fantastic hosts.

165

"I love doughnuts!" I exclaim.

"These are not doughnuts—they're warm malasadas. And they're homemade."

I take one, and it dawns on me that this is what Kalani and Kimo gave the child when they abducted him. The malasada marked the beginning of the chain of unfortunate events.

I raise the warm, sugary malasada to my lips, my anticipation building. Pua and her mother are watching me with amusement and curiosity.

The scent of fried dough teases my taste buds and makes my mouth water. As I take that first bite, flavors explode on my tongue, sending waves of delight through my body. The delicate touch of cinnamon and sugar dances across my palate, creating a symphony of sweetness that's impossible to resist. The dough is pillowy soft, like a cloud, with just enough chewiness. It's as if the malasada is giving me a warm hug from the inside.

I let out a contented sigh, momentarily forgetting my surroundings. The world around me fades as I indulge in this delicious treat.

"Mom, your malasada hypnotized another person," Pua says with a giggle.

"If the world had more malasadas," I say, my mouth full, "I'm pretty sure we'd achieve world peace! Who can stay angry with this kind of bliss in their mouth?"

We all burst into laughter, the joyous sound echoing through the air. At this moment, with a mouthful of malasada magic, it's just me and this wonderful family.

Pua takes one. "My mom makes the best malasadas on earth."

Kimo returns. "Oh, malasada time. Let me get a couple."

"One only, Papa," says Pua, allowing him to take one pastry before returning the tray to the house.

"That girl runs a tight ship." He smiles with pride again. "Last year, I had a health scare, and it put a dent in my malasada consumption. She wants to go into the medical field."

Then with a deep sigh, he hands me the white scarf he's holding. "Your mother taught your aunt how to knit this scarf. I want you to have it."

"No, Kimo. I couldn't take this."

He gazes intensely. "Not asking, son. Take it before I change my mind."

I run my fingers over the wool.

"All right, thank you so much. I only have a few of my mother's possessions. This will be special to me."

"I thought so."

I feel someone's piercing stare and look up to find Kimo's wife standing in the doorway, her eyes locked onto the scarf. But instead of the warm look I've seen all night, her expression is cold. Shifting uncomfortably, trying not to make eye contact, I wonder what has caused the change.

Chapter Twenty-Five

I'm determined to have a better week. Spending the day with Kimo and his family yesterday was a great start.

Today, I've decided to be a tourist and drive to the other side of the island. After a bit of research, I settle for a lush rainforest and a valley just over 30 minutes' drive from the beach house. Apparently, Ulu Valley is the second wettest place in Hawai'i. I think the first one must have been Nalu Town the day I arrived. I chuckle as I drive and take in the scenery. The winding road is flanked by towering trees, their canopies forming a natural archway over the road.

In the heart of this valley lies a hiking trail. The beginning of the hike is uphill along wide steps. Families ascend and descend, taking pictures along the way. I start my climb too.

When I reach the top, the scenery is breathtaking: a

lush green valley. As I sit on a bench, debating whether to keep going, I spot a couple hopping over the short fence at one end of the path. Feeling encouraged, I jump over too.

The narrow trail opens up into a twisting path that winds through the thick rainforest. My ears pick up the sound of water nearby, there must be a stream ahead. As I finally arrive at the stream, I sink onto a smooth boulder by its edge. Closing my eyes, I drink in the sounds of rushing water, rustling leaves, and chirping birds all around me. *I could easily lose myself in all of this.*

An hour later, I set off on my return journey, but minutes in, a sheet of fog blankets everything. I come to a split in the path that I hadn't noticed before. I choose a direction and continue through the fog. Eventually, it's clear that this isn't the right route; I should have reached the top of the stairs by now. Retracing my steps proves difficult as visibility is greatly reduced. *Here it is, man. You got what you wished for. You're lost in it.*

"Is anybody out there?" I yell into the fog, becoming increasingly frustrated. I sit underneath a tree, leaning on its trunk.

My eyes examine its branches. *If I climb up, I'll see farther.*

However, I'm no longer eleven, and these trees are too tall and dense. I must find another way. I decide to wait for the mist to dissipate, although I'm sure the stairs are nearby. I won't risk wandering off again in such dense fog. I check my phone—one small bar of signal, which immediately disappears. The temperature has dropped, and I shiver.

I look around, taking in the various forms of vegetation around me. In the fog, they look mysterious. There are big monstera plants everywhere. Mom has indoor monstera plants. She would love this place.

It's getting even colder. I need to get moving, despite the fog. Just as I decide to take the path to my left, I detect something stirring close to my foot.

An iguana.

I freeze.

It moves slowly toward me. I remain still. It creeps up to my foot.

There's an iguana close to my foot.

Sweat runs down my back like the stream from earlier. It looks around and moves a little.

There's an iguana tail on my foot.

It doesn't move. I don't move. We sit motionless in the fog.

The grayish-green body is no longer than the size of my hand. It must be a baby. There are colorful red and orange markings around its eyes. Unlike the unfriendly, large, and grumpy image ingrained in my childhood visions, this one is almost cute.

My memory transports me back to a documentary I watched with Dad, Mom, and Luke when I was twelve. I can still hear the narrator's voice: "Survival and adaptability are what truly define iguanas."

It was a Saturday morning when I called my foster

father "Dad" for the first time—the day after I learned about the survival skills of iguanas.

"Can we go for a bike ride today, Dad?" I asked, as we all sat at the kitchen table eating breakfast.

The conversation stopped abruptly. Everyone in the room looked at me. Mom put down the food she was serving, and Luke stopped chewing. Dad tilted his head and stared at me with misty eyes. "Sure thing, son."

He told me that first he had to go to his horseback riding practice. That's what he did on Saturday mornings.

"But I'll be back around eleven thirty," he said. "Then we can go for a long ride."

"Why don't you and I go after breakfast?" Luke said, winking at me.

I checked my watch. "Nah, let's wait for Dad."

He was dead an hour later.

It was a freak accident. He fell from his horse and his head struck a large rock. And in that instant, life delivered another harsh blow to my young self.

I'm brought back to the present when the iguana begins to sway its tail and make its way into the forest. The fog is lifting, revealing the stairs in the distance, to my right. Good thing I stayed and waited.

Thank you, iguana.

I shake my head. I just thanked an iguana. Life is funny.

Chapter Twenty-Six

Over the past three weeks, Cheddar has been like a little ball of sunshine bringing joy and happiness to my life.

"What's your story, Cheddar?" I ask, as she hops onto my lap. I'm relaxing at the outdoor table the morning after my eventful hike.

She begins to purr, and her tiny paws start kneading.

"You're in a good mood, aren't you?" I gently stroke the white band of fur that encircles her throat.

"My aunt knitted this scarf," I say, gesturing to my neck. "And apparently, my mom helped her. It's like your white scarf. Maybe you're the one I was meant to find here. My white-scarf twin." I find it amusing, the idea of being the twin of a cat.

"I really like Amy," I tell my confidant. "Maybe a little too much. And I know you're eagerly waiting for your friend, Curly." I chuckle. "They'll be here soon." I invited them for breakfast after my hike yesterday.

With that, Cheddar runs off, and just then I see Amy and Curly getting off the stand-up paddleboard. Immediately, the little black bundle of excitement runs toward me.

"Hey there, little fella," I exclaim, bending down to play with Curly. His wagging tail and playful spirit never fail to make me smile.

"Spare me some attention too," Amy chimes in. I look up. There she is, holding her board. Oh boy, she's practically a sea goddess, and I'm about as aquatic as a potted plant.

I stand and pull her close, relishing the feeling of her body against mine. "I missed you," I say, leaning in for a kiss.

When we pull away from each other, she flashes a smile that makes my heart skip a beat. Oh, that smile. It's irresistible. Her shoulders glisten with ocean droplets.

I rush into the kitchen and attempt to pour the coffee, but a different kind of energy possesses my body and mind.

I linger in the kitchen for a moment to calm myself before heading back outside.

I hand her a cup then sit across from her. Curly's looking for Cheddar, but she's nowhere to be seen.

"What's that?" Amy asks, gesturing to my neck.

"My scarf."

A few lines appear on her forehead as her brows pull together. "It's not scarf weather."

"Sometimes the weather doesn't determine whether we need a scarf or not."

I sense her curiosity, but our connection is already so intimate that I'm hesitant to share more about my family history. I'm afraid of getting to a deeper level of intimacy with her.

I hold up the end of it. "Do you like it?"

"It complements your olive skin," she says.

I smile. "I always thought my skin tone came from my father—he's Mediterranean. Now I know it's from my Hawaiian grandmother."

She rises and stands right in front of me. Her skin makes me think of a golden-sand beach. She gently takes the scarf off my neck. "I wonder who you got your deep-brown eyes from."

She makes a loop in the scarf after folding it in half lengthwise. "Or your high cheekbones," she whispers.

Her eyes are locked on mine as she wraps the scarf around my neck. She smells like a honey macaron. She grabs one of the loose ends, still staring at me, and threads it through the loop. My thoughts and feelings spin.

Oh man, I can't take this anymore.

I pull her onto my lap and we kiss passionately, kindling a fire in me. With our bodies so tightly pressed together, we're like an unrelenting tide finally meeting its shore.

A while later, her head rests on my arm while her fingers play with the hairs on my chest.

"Let's have dinner, you, me, and Sean?" I suggest.

She moves slightly. "I thought we'd already decided that wasn't a good plan. You'll be leaving soon, and Sean is already attached to you."

"One more evening won't make much difference, but if that's what you think is best, then okay," I say, as she continues to twirl my chest hair.

I tuck a strand of her hair behind her ear. "Sorry that I mentioned it again. It's just, for me, cooking is my way of connecting. It goes beyond ingredients and recipes."

"Okay," she says.

"Okay what?"

"To dinner. Is tomorrow okay?"

"Sure, but I was just sharing my experience—"

She plants a kiss on my lips before I can finish my sentence.

Nothing else matters for the next couple of hours.

Chapter Twenty-Seven

It's bloody hard to prepare a gourmet Italian dinner on short notice in the middle of the Pacific Ocean. Luckily, the weekly farmers market was today, and every single ingredient seemed fresh. I love touching soil —that nourishing ground from which all life emerges—on vegetable roots and smelling each vegetable's distinct scent. That's how the preparation starts. Way before the kitchen.

Sean told me his favorite food is pasta, and I'm determined to cook him the best pasta he's ever had. I'm making a Tuscan-style pici with flour, salt, hot water, and olive oil. The egg is optional; I'll add it.

The flour . . . To me, flour is more than a simple ingredient. It's a portal to the heart of the culinary arts. I love how it takes in the water and integrates it. To me, it's like a metaphor for life. The Tuscan pici wants hot water, which differentiates it from other fresh pasta. A subtle difference, but it matters. I add a little hot water. Not too much nor too little. I feed the flour only when it gets thirsty. Every time I fold and press the dough, I think of the miraculous transformation of these simple ingredients.

Mi-aw

"Hey, girl, do you like fresh pasta?"

Cheddar stands close by, in a diva pose, as I call it. Head tall, all paws anchored with purpose.

I'm chuffed with how the dough has shaped up. I cover it with a damp cloth for thirty minutes. The next step is to flatten it with a rolling pin.

Cooking with fresh ingredients for someone you love. It changed my life. I wish it were easier to find our passions earlier. But it's never too late. Luke just realized his desire to publish his first novel. He's almost forty.

When it's time, I flatten the dough and cut thick, long pieces, much wider than spaghetti. I'm making a tomato sauce with fresh garlic—simple but delicious. Like food in Tuscany.

When everything is ready, I let out a long breath and step onto the porch. *What a perfect day!*

"Hello," I hear. The whisper comes from beyond the bushes between my yard and the Johnsons' house.

"Hello," I respond, peering at the bushes. Claire's hand appears through the green leaves holding a piece of paper. I frown and rush toward her. I rarely see her in her garden.

"Please take this," she says, waving the folded paper. "I must get back in."

"What is this? Are you okay, Claire?"

"Your grandma was very dear to me," she whispers. "Please take this, read it, and destroy it afterward."

I take the note, and her hand disappears. Peering through the hedge I see her retreating into the house. She wears a plain summer dress, and I can see the outline of her bones beneath her skin.

I clutch the paper for a few agonizing seconds. An overwhelming sense of dread comes over me. Something isn't right.

I reluctantly unfold the paper, which feels like an unbearable weight in my hand.

PLEASE destroy this after you read it. Everything is a setup. My husband is behind everything going wrong with your house. Everything!!! He wants to buy your land. He's the cash buyer.

Be careful with the contractors. Your girlfriend is in on it too. I heard her talking with my husband a few weeks ago. She agreed to help my husband persuade you to sell the house, and he said he'd give her quite a commission. She's not who she appears to be. Her friend, the real estate agent, works for my husband too.

I stare at the ocean as I struggle to catch my breath. A

million thoughts race through my mind before it goes blank. Empty.

The sound of the waves crashing nearby increases in volume. The salty air is suffocating.

I don't want to believe this, but no matter how hard I try to deny it, I sense some truth to it.

I sink into a chair in the kitchen, my fingers kneading the tension that's formed on my forehead. I read the note again. And again. I recall Amy asking a lot of questions about the beach house. I think about how her friend tried to pressure me into selling quickly.

I have to cancel dinner. My plan to make this week better crumbled by Wednesday. I'm defeated. I have a sinking feeling that my days won't improve anytime soon.

I can't bear to see Amy. Not now.

I splash water on my face in the bathroom then call her. She doesn't answer. I leave her a voicemail message:

"Hey, I'm sorry, but something came up. Can't do dinner tonight."

I feel as if I'm drowning in sadness as I sink into a chair at the dinner table, my hand reaching up to rub my forehead.

A few minutes later I hear voices approaching. "We thought we'd surprise you and come early," Amy says cheerfully as Sean runs into the house, startling me.

Gathering my composure, I crumple the paper into my pocket and force a grin onto my face.

"Hi there, buddy!"

"I told my friends at school that I'm having Italian pasta," Sean says.

There's no way that I can disappoint him—he deserves a delicious meal. I deliberately move my shoulders to shake off the tension that snakes underneath my skin.

As I present the meal, Amy watches without any idea of the battle waging inside me. I feel like a caged hummingbird.

You're a master at concealing your inner turmoil, I remind myself. It's a skill I honed through years of practice.

Still, this is quickly becoming one of the most difficult dinners of my life.

While we eat, Amy asks, "Everything okay?"

No, far from okay.

"I'm just a bit tired," I say, casting my eyes downward.

"Italian fresh pasta is my favorite," Sean gushes, his eyes lighting up.

"Sean, that's a lot of pasta in your mouth while talking," says Amy. "And since when?" she asks with a strained smile.

"Since now," Sean replies, still speaking with a mouthful of pasta.

"I'm glad you like it, buddy," I say. My heart hammers so fast I feel it in the pits of my gut.

A heavy silence settles around us. I feel Amy's eyes on me as I try to eat my own pasta, every swallow is a struggle, the food feeling like superglue in my throat.

"I need to check the dessert." I rush to the kitchen.

Amy follows me, and I feel her breath on my neck. "What's going on, Roy?"

I take a step away from her. "We'll talk later. Let's get through dinner first. Sean is enjoying the food."

I have to fight the impulse to yell at her. I have to hide my anger for Sean's sake.

"Don't scare me," she whispers. "What's going on?"

"Later, Amy," I snap, and she rushes back to the table.

With a grin, I present the mango dessert. My painted-on smile starts hurting my face, but at least joy is written all over Sean's face.

"What is this? I love the yellow color."

"It's called sunshine in a glass," I respond.

Amy takes a bite. "It's delicious."

I bob my head, yet all I can taste is bitterness.

Chapter Twenty-Eight

I splash water on my face and groan. What a terrible hangover. I stayed up too late and might have had one or two more beers than usual. I'm lying on the couch when the door swings open after a loud knock. Amy barges in, her brows knitted together.

I sit up and scowl at her.

"What's up? I've been calling all morning. I got your voicemail message. Why did you want to cancel? And why were you acting weird last night?" She sits beside me and places a comforting hand on my knee. The warmth of her touch jolts my nerves. I need to start locking my door.

"Stop all that," I say, as I push her hand away. My head throbs at the sight of her. "I just got up."

"I can see that. I dropped Sean off at school, and I wanted to come over immediately after, but I had to take a group on a snorkeling tour."

I rub my forehead. "This is messed up."

Her face takes on a puzzled expression. Her eyes are filled with worry.

"That dinner was one of the most painful evenings of my life," I say, rubbing my face. "If it weren't for Sean, I swear . . ."

"What are you talking about?" She tilts her head, and I turn away. I can't bear to look her in the eyes.

"Do you know how hard it was to pretend that everything was fine, to smile and laugh just for the sake of Sean? What sort of a mother are you?"

"Hey, don't bring my mothering into this!"

"Then talk!" I bark. My heart races. Is this really happening?

She swallows hard before responding. "Talk about what?" A single vein on her forehead is pulsing.

"Who are you, Amy?"

"I don't like your tone. You already know damn well who I am." Her eyes narrow.

"Why are you helping my neighbor, Phil?"

"Uh . . . Hmm." Her shoulders slump. "That."

"You're not even trying to deny it."

"I can explain."

"Explain what a deceitful person you are?"

"Again, stop with that tone, and please," she begs, "let me explain."

"Just leave. Please."

"I'm not going anywhere. Not like this." She gives a little shake of her head, and a tear rolls down her cheek.

"I'm begging you, Amy, I can't take this. My head feels like it's exploding. Please leave."

"I started to help him," she says, her voice trembling, "but—"

"But what, Amy? Was everything we had part of an act?" I look away from her again to avoid seeing her tears.

"Things changed. I was going to come clean, but I couldn't . . . I didn't know how you'd react."

"Here's my reaction. Happy?" I open my arms, palms up.

"You know, sometimes you make mistakes. Sometimes it's impossible to do the right thing. Sometimes you have to do whatever it takes to . . ." She trails off.

"Whatever it takes to what? Tell me! Whatever it takes to what?" I shout, but when I turn around, she's already stepping out of the door. And out of my life.

I think of Sean, and my intense fury transforms into a heaviness.

I'm sorry, buddy.

Chapter Twenty-Nine

Less than twenty-four hours later, I wake up to knocking on the door. Amy must be refusing to give up, but this time, I've locked the door.

"Okay, okay, I'm coming." I shake my head.

I open the door to find Sean there, out of breath, his cheeks red.

"You can't do that!" he yells, and pushes his way in.

"That's a hell of a greeting," I murmur, as he charges into the living room.

He whirls around. "You can't just fight and leave each other forever. What about me?" He wipes a tear on his arm.

"Whoa," I say, taken off guard. "Does your mom know you're here?"

He shrugs. "Dunno."

"How did you get here, Sean?"

He shrugs again. "I ran."

"That's a long way to run. It's Friday, don't you have school?"

He sits on the sofa, crossing his arms, a pout on his lips.

"Okay, let's call your mom first. She must be freaking out right now. And then we'll talk."

"No grown-up talks. Grown-ups are silly."

"Okay, young man. Stop the sulk and we'll have a heart-to-heart chat. Give me a minute."

I step outside to call Amy.

She answers on the first ring. "Oh, Roy."

"He's with me," I say curtly. "He's fine. A little upset but fine."

Amy starts crying and cursing. "I'm on my way."

"I don't think that's a good idea. Why don't you leave him with me for a while and I'll drop him off at your place in a few hours."

There's silence. "Please, Amy."

Time slows to a crawl while I wait for her response. I hear a sob. "Okay. But first, please tell me how he looks. It's pretty cold this morning. Can you check the color of his fingers and toes, please? Without him noticing?"

"Okay." Surely she's overreacting, but hey, she's his mother. I step inside. Sean is on the couch playing with Cheddar. I surreptitiously look at his fingers and toes. They seem normal.

"They're fine."

She exhales. "Thanks. I'll see you in a few hours."

I sit next to Sean on the sofa. Cheddar jumps on his lap.

"Wow, traitor," I say to Cheddar with a chuckle.

Sean's eyes brighten. "We like each other."

"Why don't you stay with Cheddar for a while and I'll make breakfast."

"Can we make pancakes?" His face lights up.

"I'm afraid not, young man. Simple cereal will have to do. You're still in trouble for running away from home."

"Are you also in trouble for leaving my mom?"

I pour two bowls of cereal and then sit back down on the sofa next to him. Cheddar takes off. "Buddy, let's have a man-to-man talk."

He nods.

"I didn't leave your mom. Sometimes grown-ups—" I stop midsentence when I see Sean squinting his watery eyes.

"I don't want grown-up talk."

"Okay, mate. We won't. Trust me, I know how you feel."

I used to squint like Sean when adults tried to justify their actions or behaviors. I wanted them to stop explaining why I was being moved from one foster family to another. They used words such as *safe*, *better*, *home*, and *bath time*, but nothing made sense. Grown-ups didn't make sense.

"Did you know there's a fish called humuhumunukunukuāpua'a in Hawai'i?" Sean asks.

It's fascinating how quickly a child can transition from intense drama to genuine enthusiasm.

"You're so making this up."

"No, I'm not," he says. "Check it on your phone." Then he mutters, "Typical grown-up."

"Okay, buddy, drop the grown-up bashing. Let's be Roy and Sean again."

As a gesture of friendship, I offer my right fist, which he bumps with his fist, and then we cross our arms to symbolize camaraderie. "So, is there really a fish called . . . what was that again?"

"Humu-humu-nuku-nuku-āpua'a" he says, slowly this time. "It has amazing colors. I've seen them while snorkeling with Mom."

I think of Amy's paddleboarding invitation. I never told her that I couldn't swim. I know it's nothing to be ashamed of. But I do feel some shame. And I should really learn.

The sound of our spoons clanking against our bowls fills the air. I added a banana to his cereal. He once told me he loved them. I look away, trying to avoid seeing the sadness in Sean's eyes—a sadness that only grows with each spoonful of cereal. My heart aches. I tried to keep my distance. Not get attached. I want to protect him from this pain, but I know it's too late.

"Can I tell you a secret?" I ask.

Sean nods.

"But it's between you and me only." I lock my eyes on his.

He's suddenly beaming. "Cross my heart and hope to die, stick a needle in my eye. I won't tell."

Okay, that's a little too dramatic. "I trust you. Here it goes, but again, this is only between you and me, all right? It's a big secret, and I've never told anyone here."

"Okay, okay," he says, getting impatient.

"Secret, okay?"

He nods furiously.

"I can't swim."

"Huh?"

"I don't know how to swim."

Sean sits quietly for a moment, cocking his head to one side, before he says, "I can help you out with that."

"I'd love that."

"Okay."

"Sean, can we also discuss what you did this morning?" I ask.

"I know, I wasn't supposed to run off. But this morning, she said I can't see you anymore."

Ouch. That hurts.

I look away. "Sorry."

"It's not fair." He's looking down, and the pout on his lips shoots pain straight into me. I groan quietly. "Look, it's not a big deal. You'll make new friends."

He looks up with such disappointment that I can't take it. I genuinely don't know what to do or say. So, I just tell him I'm sorry.

We sit in silence for a while.

Mi-aw

Cheddar is standing by the front door. There's something in her mouth.

"Oh no, no, no. What do you have in your mouth?" I ask, while Sean runs toward her.

"Yuck!" he yells. "It's half a mouse!"

So now I've got a disappointed runaway child and there's half a mouse in the cat's mouth. This morning just gets better and better.

"Umm, so do you want to know something interesting about cats?" I ask. I'm relieved to see a glimmer in his eyes again. "When they bring us mice, it's like a present. They're not being mean—they're actually showing love! Cats are way better at catching mice than us, so they're like, 'Hey, look what I got for you!' They don't know that we think it's yucky."

He chuckles. "A mouse present."

"Yeah."

His eyes grow sad again. "I wish grown-ups didn't change their minds so much."

The moment feels familiar, so I don't say anything. I just embrace him in a hug. He shuffles closer to me.

"I understand your reasoning, I really do. But it would be best if you weren't running away from home. It's dangerous."

"'Kay. I won't do it again. Can I share a secret with you too?" he asks, pulling away and tilting his head.

"Sure."

"Say, 'Cross my heart and hope to die, I won't tell.'"

"I'll keep your secret." I hope it's not something I can't keep from his mom. "Best-friend promise."

He beams before getting serious again. "My father is artificial."

"Your father is what?" I ask, not particularly eager to hear his response.

"My father is artificial. My mom told me once, but then she never wanted to talk about it again."

Once more, I don't know what to say. "Okay. Thanks for telling me. Shall we take a walk on the beach?"

An artificial father. Thousands of thoughts flood my mind as we walk, and not a single one makes any sense.

I drop Sean off at home in the afternoon. Amy hugs him tightly as if he's her lifeline. With a nod, I leave them in their embrace.

I might never see either of them again. Sorrow hangs like an anchor on my shoulders.

Chapter Thirty

I'm at the boat ramp in the predawn hours of Sunday. Darkness surrounds me. I stand in front of Kai's friend's fishing boat, which looks like a monument to the numerous journeys it has been on. Its aged facade reveals stories of battles fought with the mighty ocean. The once-bold paint on its hull has weathered over time, but traces of bright colors hint at the aquatic life beneath the surface. The smell of saltwater lingers in the air.

Kai arrives.

"Good morning," I say.

"Morning," he grunts.

"You're not a morning person, then?"

"I'll be better once we start cruising."

My stomach is churning with nerves. I'll be on a boat, on the water, for many hours. But I stand tall. "I'm eager to experience the beauty of Hawaiian fishing with the real experts."

He looks at me as if I'm from another planet. All right, we are from totally different ends of the world—but it's still the same, dear Earth.

I need to find out where the life jackets are. Just in case I need them later.

Kai proceeds to instruct me on the fundamentals of fishing in these waters. He radiates authority, experience, and enthusiasm, and he has an admirable knowledge of the marine life of Hawai'i. His friend arrives, and after we're introduced, the three of us climb into the boat. The sun is beginning to shine its warm rays from behind the mountain.

"Just wait until the sun rises," Kai says. "It's a sight like no other when its rays meet the soil and the ocean."

The merging of sun, soil, and ocean. Wow.

Kai's admiration oozes through his eyes as he stares at the mountain—An old volcano. Rising majestically above the island, it dominates the sky with its towering presence. I'm even more captivated by the sight of the mountain than by the ocean's vastness.

As Kai's friend starts the engine and sets us off, gently moving away from the shore, I take in the breathtaking beauty of the Hawaiian coastline—the incredible union of the sun, the earth, the mountain, and the ocean. Everything the light touches seems to come alive.

"This is a cool boat." I say, standing at the wider area at the back.

"Yeah, it sits low to the water, making it less prone to rocking and rolling."

This is less rocking?

"It's 25 feet, a perfect size too," he adds.

"Your grandfather Ben was a skilled fisherman," Kai says, standing next to me.

"Was he?"

"Yeah, I got to know him on the boats. He once caught a fish almost as big as him!" His eyes twinkle with mischief.

"Really?" I exclaim.

"Ah, but it's never about the catch," he continues, leaning in. "It's about respecting the ocean. There's a balance between taking and giving back."

I nod. "I see."

As we move farther, the shore becomes a distant presence on the horizon, and the ocean deepens its blue.

"You seem sad," he says. I hold the boat railing tighter as the engine roars into the waves.

"Yeah, I'm having a few challenges but happy to be here, fishing."

"I see that." He looks at my hands, gripping tight.

I release one hand. *Just stand firmly on the deck*, I tell myself.

"I expected you to be an annoying chatterbox," Kai says. "I kinda wish you were now."

"Sorry, man." I laugh shyly. "Let me know what I can do?"

"I certainly know what will take your mind off your

troubles." He hands me a fishing rod after his friend anchors the boat.

With focused determination, I firmly grip the rod, watching Kai and copying whatever he does. He's lost in the moment, and his arm looks like an extension of his rod. I cast my line and watch as the bait gracefully lands on the water's surface.

"Mahi-mahi love these waters," he remarks. "They're known for their vibrant colors and acrobatic displays. Keep an eye out!"

I nod and adjust my grip on the rod, ready to feel the strong tug of this sought-after fish.

Time slows. No one talks. The only sounds are the rhythmic crash of waves against the hull and the creaking of the boat as it rolls and dips with the tide.

A sudden tug on my fishing line breaks the idyll. "Whoa," I yell.

There's a powerful force pulling against my grip. Adrenaline rushes through my veins as I brace myself.

"Looks like you've got a lively one there!" Kai exclaims. "Hold on tight!"

With every ounce of strength I can muster, I begin reeling it in. The line cuts through the water, creating a trail of wonder.

"Look at the color," Kai says excitedly as he leans in closer, ready to assist if needed. "You've got a beauty on the line."

I tighten my grip as the fish nears the surface. A glimmer of silver breaks through the water. Its playful colors shimmer under the sunlight, a true marvel of nature's artistry.

"Nicely done." Kai's voice rings with admiration. "You've landed yourself a stunning mahi-mahi!"

With one last determined effort, I hoist the fish from the water. Swiftly, Kai helps me to remove the hook from its mouth and then I set it free into the embrace of the waves.

As the boat slices its way back to the shore a few hours later, a bucket filled with the day's catch rests on deck. Kai takes a seat next to me at the helm.

"You're troubled. I think it's heart trouble."

I look at him. "You could say that. I was careless, and it cost me. I let my guard down too quickly and got burned for it."

"Someone back home?" Kai asks.

"No, I met her here."

"Whoa, man. Didn't you arrive just a few weeks ago?"

"Almost a month ago."

"Sweet!" Kai chuckles.

"Not sure about sweet. Stupid for sure." I snort.

He briefly places his hand on my leg before saying, "It will pass. Time is the greatest healer. But to feel this way about someone in such a short span of time, that's special."

"Believe me, it's far from special."

"Give it some time."

"Is that experience talking?" I ask.

"You could say that."

"Someone from this island?"

"Yeah," he remarks. "But he left for a larger city. Instead of standing up for his true self, he chose to run away."

"I'm sorry to hear that," I respond. At twenty-two, he already carries the weight of a broken heart. Not that there's an age limit on such experiences.

I turn my face to the ocean. It stretches out in all directions, a vast expanse of serene blue in contrast to the dark storm inside me.

"How is your true self doing?" I ask, realizing that I'm pushing some boundaries.

"I still have a way to go, especially with my father," he admits.

A small smile plays on my lips. "He loves you. You know that, right?"

"Yeah, I know. But I also want his respect."

I nod in understanding.

I think of Amy and wonder who her true self is.

The boat glides effortlessly through the water, leaving a gentle wake. The smell of salt mingles with the breeze and wraps around me like a comforting embrace. I feel better. I'm also feeling more at ease with being on the water.

The ocean makes me better, regardless of whether I can swim.

I admire the trail behind the boat, the motion carving a

beautiful, distinct path. At this moment, clarity comes. A decision solidifies within me. I'll cancel my flight, which is scheduled for Wednesday.

I'm not prepared to depart. There are paths I want to explore here. The tighter I cling to my plans and timelines, the more I'm challenged to let go of them. I decide not to limit myself with time anymore.

"I'm going to go to the Big Island to meet my coffee supplier," I say. "Would you like to come with me?"

"You have a supplier in Hawai'i? You're full of surprises." Kai raises his eyebrows. "Why do you want me to come?"

"You're a local."

"I am that."

"So will you come along?"

He grins. "I'm busy."

"But I haven't told you when I'm going yet."

"I don't have a lot of free time. I work two jobs," he says, as he hops onto the dock and ties the boat.

I want to spend more time with this young man. Seemingly troubled and lost, he reminds me of someone.

I smile.

Chapter Thirty-One

The next day, Kai and I are seated side by side on a small airplane, on our way to the Big Island.

When I asked him what made him change his mind about joining me, he told me he wanted to see his family's coffee trees.

"So your dad didn't persuade you?" I asked.

"I can make up my own mind," he snapped. "I'll go see the trees while you visit your supplier."

"Do you mind if I come too?"

He hesitated but then agreed.

We're making progress.

After the plane lands, we head straight for the car rental kiosk and secure the keys to a white SUV. I get behind the wheel, and we set off on our journey to the coffee plantation. All the windows are down. I keep forgetting it's winter.

The asphalt is glistening from a recent rain shower.

This island is decidedly different from the others I've seen. There are lava formations on both sides of the road, their textures rugged and their hues earthy.

"Did you know I'm about to see coffee trees for the first time?" I say.

"Really?"

"It's not the sort of thing that grows in England."

"Well, if you're a first-timer, an abandoned plantation probably isn't the greatest place to start."

"On the contrary, it's perfect," I say, remembering the moments when I felt entirely abandoned—like a little tree in a large plantation.

As we drive further into the island, the road begins to climb. The air grows crisper as we ascend.

We continue along the winding road, and soon the scent of roasted coffee beans wafts through the open windows. I inhale the rich, comforting aroma. The driveway leading to the heart of the plantation is lined with coffee bushes, and an aged, weathered sign greets us at the entrance, welcoming us to a place that seems suspended in time. The plantation has been abandoned, but the atmosphere is still thick with the earthy fragrance of coffee beans.

As we step into the coffee field, the neglected, sad, and broken trees surround us with a melancholic feeling.

Kai touches a few of them. "I really want to do something about the trees, bring them back to health, but Dad never takes me seriously. I can't do it without his help."

I think about my conversation with Kimo—about how much Kimo wants to help his son.

I watch as Kai kneels and gently brushes the soil with his fingertips. His touch is respectful and caring, as if he's making a connection with something otherworldly, something that no one else can see.

Kai speaks in a tone I've not heard him use before; it's as if he's transformed into someone else. "These coffee trees hold the stories of our land."

I listen carefully, fascinated by the intensity of feeling conveyed in his words and the sound of his voice. His fingers graze the aged bark of a nearby tree. "Each tree has its own personality. They have seen the tides of time come and go. They have endured harsh storms and painful sunburns. But nothing disappoints them more than our lack of attention. They are unique living things, each one of them. And right now, they are sad and broken."

You are too, aren't you, Kai? That's why you feel connected to them.

We're all linked—he and I and the trees.

Kai stands and runs his fingers over the leaves. "Just imagine them thriving. All they need is a bit of love and care."

I notice the small tattoo nestled within the family design on his shoulder—two coffee beans.

He notices my gaze and touches the tattoo gently. "My family has a strong connection with coffee trees. They grew and harvested coffee until it became challenging. It

205

got to the point where small family businesses couldn't compete with the big corporations."

"What happened to the small plantations?"

"Bigger companies acquired them and used their resources to outcompete smaller farms. Most of the people we know had to sell their land. But not my family. We couldn't continue looking after the trees, though."

During the drive here, I envisioned learning about coffee trees. What I've experienced is much more than that. I observe Kai's connection with the trees, each yearning for the other's embrace. The trees tremble in the breeze, and I swear I see them speaking with Kai.

Man, this place is turning you into an overly sensitive, sentimental sap.

Kai digs his fingers into the dirt next to a tree, placing his other hand on the tree's bark. "There's something truly special about the lava soil here. It nurtures the trees and gives the coffee its unique flavor."

Intrigued, I also touch the soil. The rich, dark earth crumbles between my fingers. From this humble ground, life springs forth in abundance.

"I never thought anyone else would appreciate the dirt like I do," I say.

Kai laughs softly, then crumbles the earth through his hands.

"The volcanic soil is rich in minerals and nutrients. After lava cools, it breaks down over time and creates fertile ground. Our coffee trees thrive in it. The roots delve deep into this nutrient-rich soil, absorbing the goodness and translating it into the flavor profile of the coffee beans."

I examine the soil in my hand. "I admire your connection to nature, and your knowledge," I say.

"We're all part of the whole," he says, "with the ocean, the soil, the coffee trees."

Nice one, mate! Knew there was a reason I liked this fella.

"But the trees need help," he whispers, leaning on the tree and closing his eyes.

Kai is quiet on our drive into town. I tell him about Stephanie, my mom's best friend who used to own a bookstore. "She's no longer the owner," I explain. "I already called the store a few days ago. She sold it over ten years ago and moved off the island. But I still want to see if anyone is in touch with her."

"Sure, let's go and ask."

Unfortunately, we don't find out anything at the bookstore because the owners have changed a few times. I'm physically and mentally tired; maybe it's time to let go. I need to stop dwelling on the past, stop asking questions. I already know much more about my family than I did four weeks ago. So, maybe it's okay. Maybe now the pain in my chest will ease.

In the late afternoon, after meeting with my coffee

supplier, Kai was pleased to learn that it was a local, family-run business. Kai and I head back to the airport.

"How do you know so much about the trees and soil and all?" I ask as I drive.

"I just do. I watch, I listen."

Ever since we left the plantation, a thought has been brewing. "Kai, hear me out. I have a proposal." I flip on the turn signal and pull onto a side road.

"We'll miss our flight," he says, curiosity in his tone.

"What if we call your dad and tell him that we want to stay another day and make a plan to start taking care of those trees?"

Kai shakes his head. "He won't listen. He doesn't think I've got enough business experience."

"But I do, and I can support and help you. At least initially. Let's give it a try."

"Why do you want to help?" Kai asks.

"It's coffee, and I'm an entrepreneur. I'm also fascinated" *Also, you're lost and I empathize.*

"Dad won't agree." But I catch the spark of hope in Kai's dark eyes.

We get Kimo on speakerphone and relay what we witnessed. Occasionally, I put up my hand to stop Kai from saying too much or becoming irritated.

"Kimo, the potential here is huge," I say. "Can we investigate what's doable first? I'll help Kai."

After a pause, Kimo says, "All right, you two figure out the damage and devise a plan. But if we decide to proceed, remember, it's a marathon, not a sprint. Is everyone clear on this?"

"Yes!" Kai exclaims, his excitement echoing loudly through the car. It's clear that Kimo's question was directed at Kai.

"Let's find somewhere to stay for the night," I say with a grin. I turn and drive away from the airport.

The next morning, Kai and I are standing amid the coffee trees, our hands on our hips as we survey the work ahead of us. The plantation is overgrown and unkempt, but I can see the potential beneath the tangled mess.

"First things first," Kai declares. "Let's clear out the deadwood."

"Agreed." I grab a pair of pruning shears we bought earlier that morning.

We spend hours cutting away the dead branches, sweat pouring down our faces under the Hawaiian sun.

"Man, this is tough work," I admit, wiping my brow.

"You asked for it," Kai replies, tossing another branch onto the growing pile.

"You jumped on it."

Kai grins, clapping me on the back.

As we work, he tells me about his ancestors, the ancient Polynesians, who were adept at studying stars, birds, tides, rainbows, and whales. With their wa'a canoes, they sailed an astonishing two thousand miles and arrived in Hawai'i.

I observe Kai's connection with nature. He understands the soil, the roots, the bark, and the leaves. It's as if he's already on a journey with his ancestors.

When we've finished clearing the deadwood, we meet the coffee-tree expert my coffee supplier recommended. She teaches us about irrigation techniques and soil nutrition and shows us how to test the soil. She also recommends specific fertilizers to replenish the nutrients the trees need.

"Kai, you'll need to monitor the trees closely," she instructs.

He nods eagerly. "Got it."

After she leaves, we spend a bit of time walking the grounds. Soon, we'll have to leave to catch our evening flight.

"I think we made progress," I say.

"Thanks for speaking with my dad. I didn't think he wanted to do anything with these trees."

"Sometimes we assume the wrong thing for one reason or another."

Kai holds a branch. "I can't wait to see a cluster of healthy green leaves sprouting from this bare branch."

I swear I can see the green leaves in his irises.

Chapter Thirty-Two

I bought a new shirt this morning—I want to look presentable for dinner with Aunt Melina. Perched on a hill, Aunt Melina's home is a charming two-story wood house that blends into the lush landscape.

"Aloha, my dear!" she says, opening the door. "You clean up nicely. Come in."

"Thank you very much for your lovely invitation," I say, stepping inside.

"Ah, no need for thanks. It's the Hawaiian way. Hospitality is our culture. And you're family."

We walk into a large living area, taking center stage is a spacious u-shaped sectional sofa, its floral print fabric bursting with vibrant oranges, deep greens, and sky blues that mirror the colors of the surroundings. She introduces me to her large family—daughters and sons, their spouses, and Melina's grandchildren.

"Let me take you to my home before dinner."

"This isn't your home?"

"No, I have an ohana, my own place. Come, I'll show you."

We make our way to a small cottage next to the house.

"This is what we call the ohana, a small house for the family." She opens the unlocked door.

Stepping inside, I'm immediately greeted by a warm atmosphere. The interior exudes cozy charm; the essence of this island is in every corner. In the open-concept space, the living area is seamlessly connected to the modest yet well-equipped kitchen. My eyes are drawn to the rich reddish-brown dining table and chairs.

"This is made from the koa tree." Her fingers brush the table. "It's one of the most beautiful woods in the world."

"I can see that." My eyes follow the curved pattern in the wood. It looks almost three-dimensional. I've long believed the dinner table is the soul of a family home—it should be at the center of everything.

I stroke the table and recall fond memories of family gatherings: Mom serving, Dad pushing us to eat our vegetables, Luke and I making eye contact over the greens. Every night, without fail, we gathered around the heart of the house. The table. To me, it symbolized consistent love. From the moment I joined my adopted family, the dinner table was a place of comfort for me, as was the smell of home-cooked food.

"Koa tree grows nowhere else but Hawai'i," says Aunt Melina. "In the past, our ancestors used it to build canoes, spear handles, and ukuleles."

"It's stunning."

"Only somebody with expertise could make something like this." She smiles. "He put his heart and soul into it. My husband worked on this table for months. He actually had to wait to find a koa log from a fallen tree because it's not okay to take from healthy koa trees. This was a wedding gift to me, and we used the table for many family dinners until he departed this world."

As I look at her face, all I see is love. No sadness, only appreciation and love. What a sweet lady.

"Let's have a sit on the lanai for a few minutes."

"Lanai?"

"The patio, Roy. Learn some Hawaiian words, will you? You've Hawaiian blood in you."

Maybe not so sweet. She isn't one to mince words. Still, her voice radiates care, wisdom, and love.

"Your grandma dreamed of living in an ohana exactly like this next to her children and grandchildren," she says, as we settle on her lanai. "There's enough space on her land to build one, but it never happened. Hina never lost hope, though. She always said there would be an ohana next to her house one day."

"I'm sorry to hear that," I say sadly.

"You've been here for how long now?" she asks.

"Four weeks exactly," I respond. "The whole month of February."

"The whole month of February. So are you staying for a while?"

"Yeah, I think so."

A grin spreads across her face. "I knew you'd come to your senses."

"Not sure if it's anything to do with senses. I gave up on roots and answers a couple of days ago. I couldn't even find my mom's best friend. And I can't decide about the land and the house until I know Kalani's whereabouts. The least I can do is slow down, stop rushing to beat time."

Did I just use the two words together? *Land* and *house*?

"Let me show you something," Aunt Melina says, rising from her chair and gesturing for me to follow. We walk to the wooded side of the house. She points at an orchid plant growing from the bark of a tree.

I examine it closely. "This is extraordinary," I say. "There's no soil here."

"Not all roots are in the soil. There are so many types of roots. The beauty of orchids is that they cling to the bark without damaging it. Both exist in harmony."

I stare at the orchid in awe.

She touches a root. "We are all part of this incredible nature, and while you may feel shaken by all that you're discovering because of your strong roots with family in the UK, it's okay to allow some to grow here too. It's not an either-or matter. You can have it all. Roots can take hold in unexpected places. Roots look different in different environments."

I push the hovering emotions back.

She points at the trees at the bottom of the garden. "And look at those roots. They're above the ground."

214

"Yeah, I see them everywhere here. They look like gnarled fingers." I chuckle. "There's a tree like this in the front yard of the beach house too."

"That's a hala tree," she says, smiling. "Now, let's go back to the house and taste the flavors of the islands!"

I eagerly follow her to the dining room and sit at the table between two of her grandchildren.

"Hey, mister! Have you ever tried poi before?"

"Call me Roy, please. No, I haven't tried poi."

Aunt Melina chimes in. "You're in for a treat, love. Poi is made from taro root. It's a creamy paste, and it goes wonderfully with this pork dish."

As the dinner unfolds, in the midst of laughter and stories, I sense a familiarity, as if I've been part of these cherished gatherings all along. It's a strange feeling.

"Your grandmother, bless her heart, she loved this island," Aunt Melina says, pushing back a strand of long gray hair that fell out of her loose bun. "But because of some greedy people, she had to fight for her family and bury secrets."

"Secrets?" I ask, my curiosity heightened. *The same secrets I've already learned? Or different ones?*

"Oh, she mentioned some things, but that was so long ago," she says quickly.

What are you hiding, Aunt Melina?

Her eyes twinkle with mischief now. "Do you know why we say *ohana* instead of *family*?"

"Um, no," I admit.

"Because in our—and *your*—culture, family isn't just

made up of blood relatives. It's all the people who love and care for one another. And that includes you, Roy." She gives me a reassuring pat on the back.

"I have much to learn about my ohana," I say.

"Indeed, you do. But remember, sometimes we won't know all the answers."

But you do have some answers, Aunt Melina, I say in my mind, meeting her gaze.

"Anyway," she blurts, looking at her food and changing the subject, "are you free tomorrow evening? You've been invited to a private event by the mayor," she says, as if she's just invited me to have an informal cuppa at Pages and Beans.

"Me?" I ask. Why would the mayor invite me?

"Yes, you. Your grandfather worked closely with him, and I told him you're here."

"I see. Okay." *I'll have to check my jam-packed calendar*, I think with a laugh. "I'll be there."

Chapter Thirty-Three

S tanding on the mayor's porch, I ring the bell while removing my shoes.

"Hello," greets the woman opening the door. "Welcome. The guests are gathered at the back, and there's a path on the right leading to the back garden."

"Thank you," I reply, slipping my shoes back on. I then turn left and leisurely stroll through the side of the house into the garden. The path is adorned with smooth stones to tread on, and lush grass borders the edges of these stones. Tropical flowers line the wall opposite the house.

It's a modest gathering. There's a handful of individuals conversing in the garden. I scan the crowd in search of the mayor but can't identify anyone who fits what I expect. What should a mayoral figure look like, anyway?

While grabbing a drink, I see Amy walking into the

garden from the side of the house I had entered a few minutes earlier. My chest suddenly feels as if a heavy anchor just landed on it. She stops for a beat when she sees me then turns away.

Do I have an exit plan? Nope.

She hugs a guest tightly. A man.

"Hello, I'm Monica."

I turn slightly to see a woman approaching me. "Hi, I'm Roy."

"It's a pleasure to meet you. You know, I don't recall seeing you here before," she says.

"I'm visiting," I force a smile.

At the periphery of my vision, I see Amy and the man, still hugging. *That's one heck of an embrace. Who is he?*

I can hear Amy's sweet voice as she chats happily with the man while I attempt to converse with Monica.

I then see Aunt Melina walking in, and I silently thank her for saving the evening. As Aunt Melina and I greet each other, the man Amy was talking to approaches us.

"Daniel, let me introduce you to the trouble here." Daniel is an attractive man. He looks to be in his forties and has gray hair at his temples. "This is Roy. Roy, this is the mayor."

He smiles and extends his hand. "Nice meeting you, Roy."

"Pleasure is mine." I return the gesture. *He's the mayor!*

"How are you finding our beautiful island?"

"I've had my share of highs and lows here," I reply, sounding somewhat unfriendly. I'm not sure why I'm acting like this, but before I can change my tone, someone calls him and he hastily walks away. I grab a drink and take a seat next to Aunt Melina, who's perched on a bench.

"Aunt Melina, why am I here?"

"Your grandparents would have attended if they were still here."

Daniel calls for our attention and starts addressing everyone in a loud voice. Why is he standing next to Amy?

"Welcome, everyone," he says. "Thank you for your support in this important community project. Because of you, the Education Initiative will reach even more youths."

As Daniel—Mayor Daniel—wraps up his speech, he says, "Finally, allow me to introduce you to a special guest visiting our island. Roy, aloha. Welcome home."

I smile and nod.

"Roy is the grandson of Hina and Ben Williamson. They both worked tirelessly for this island and its community."

Okay, I wasn't expecting this.

After Mayor Daniel invites people to enjoy the food and drinks, several people introduce themselves to me and tell me about how my grandparents helped in various community projects. I find myself enjoying the conversations. I'm especially impressed by how much Grandpa Williamson became part of this community despite not being from the island originally.

Aunt Melina's sentiment comes to mind. For some, home is a never-ending search, and for others, it comes to an end when they finally find what they've been looking for and become part of somewhere or someone special.

I'm delighted to know that my grandpa discovered a sense of belonging and a place to call home.

I then notice the mayor and Amy making their way toward me. *Here goes.*

"Let me introduce you to Amy," Daniel says, "another person who loves this island and does so much for the community. She's one of the lead volunteers on this project, providing guidance and support for our youth."

I want the ground to open up and swallow me. I try not to look at her eyes.

"Amy, this is Roy."

She extends her hand and gently grips mine. "Lovely meeting you, Roy. Are you enjoying your visit?" Her voice drills into me.

I've loved every second with you. I can't stop thinking about you. "Yes, it's full of surprises," I say. *Daniel, can you quit looking at Amy like that?*

After the three of us exchange pleasantries, they walk off together while I busy myself pretending that everything is good, all is cool, and I'm not freaking out.

Looking this stunning in a simple summer dress should be a crime. I remind myself of her deceit. Even still, I'm oddly drawn to her. My chest knotted up. It's as if I'm in a play. The stage is set, she's here, but I can't find my lines.

Amy and I circle one another as the evening progresses, successfully keeping our distance. I spend every minute fighting the desire to be near her.

At one point, Monica brings me a drink and sits next to me. "I'll be in London this summer," she says with a playful smile. "I can't wait to explore—and who knows, maybe even catch up."

"That would have been amazing, but I'm gearing up for a six-month travel worldwide. However, you'll absolutely love London," I reply.

I'm not in the mood for conversation. I'd rather be on my porch at the beach house. Alone. I can feel a headache coming on.

I catch Amy glancing at us.

Moments later, after Monica excuses herself, I move to a quiet corner. Drawing in a sharp breath, I notice Amy heading toward me. She stands next to me, smells like hours of dawn, with promises of light and shine.

"Where's your sidekick?" I murmur.

Her long eyelashes flutter as she shakes her head very slightly.

"You're quite the puzzle," I continue.

"Puzzles can be interesting, can't they?" she answers steadily.

I sigh deeply. "Yes, but sometimes the pieces just don't fit together."

Amy's eyebrow arches. My breath catches for a moment. She's so beautiful.

"But you're still interested in the puzzle, aren't you? Maybe deep down, you want to find the missing piece."

"Maybe," I say, locking eyes with her. Her eyes. They pierce my soul.

She leans closer, her voice low and intimate. "Look deeper, Roy."

Chapter Thirty-Four

I've spent the last few days trying to find out more about my mother. With all the chatter about my grandparents at the mayor's event, I couldn't resist the urge to learn more about my mother.

The local library has become my second home. When I'm not poring over old newspapers and genealogy records, I'm at the beach, which is where I am now.

"There!" a child says. I look toward the voice. Several people are holding their phones up, capturing pictures of something in the water.

I squint at the horizon, shielding my eyes from the bright sun. Humpback whales breach the surface, and their massive bodies are momentarily suspended midair before crashing back into the water. It's a captivating sight.

"Wow," I say aloud.

I smile, thinking about what Sean once told me. "*You have to see a competition pod. Several male whales fight for the attention of a female whale! Usually in November or December."*

He went on to tell me about how male whales use their barnacles, flukes, pectoral fins, and sheer mass to fight each other. Sean, the future marine biologist.

I miss you, buddy.

I inhale a long breath and close my lids.

"Look deeper, Roy."

I don't think I can look any deeper. She's already shattered my soul. I'm not part of a competition pod. This fight is a solo one—me, myself, and I.

A shout goes up as another whale breaches. This one is very close to the shore and keeps breaching again and again.

"And this is with no food for months," I murmur. I've learned that mother whales don't eat while in Hawai'i as there isn't much food here, but they feed their babies until they're strong enough to travel to Alaska. I marvel at the selflessness.

Did you travel for safety, Mom? For me?

During a recent beachside conversation, Aunt Melina told me that my mom's favorite teacher is still on the island. I pulled a small notebook from my pocket and scribbled down the name.

"I see you have a detective's notebook now, keiki," she said with a chuckle.

The next day, I met with the teacher, Mrs. Donnelly.

"Your mother was a beautiful soul," she explained. "She would light up the room with her grace and energy. I remember your family had large dinners. Their food was always delicious. Famous, in fact, in the community."

I turn the pages of my notebook, look at all the notes about my mother.

I have a beautiful family. And I have another beautiful family.

But my patience continues to be tested. After spending a few hours on the beach, I return home only to discover my mailbox knocked over and letters scattered across the ground. Cheddar stands beside the letters, seemingly guarding them, alarmed and uneasy.

"Bloody hell!"

Surveying the mailbox, I can't help but ponder whether Phil's responsible for this too. Seems like a rather petty move.

My phone rings. It's Frank. I place the letters on the table and answer his call. After we exchange pleasantries, he explains, "I've been contacted by the trust again. You name the price and they'll consider it."

"Seriously? They'll pay whatever I ask?"

"That's what they said."

Looking at the enormous house next door, I notice there's one tiny light on.

"I'll think about it."

"And Roy, I have a feeling that Johnson is the buyer."

"How come?"

"I just have enough reasons to believe it's him. But this is not an official statement. Just my gut feeling."

"Okay, thanks for sharing that with me."

After hanging up, I walk toward the green hedge that separates the two houses and find an area where I can see into my neighbors' garden. It's dark and quiet, yet it doesn't feel peaceful.

Ever since Claire gave me the note, I've wanted to speak with her, but I haven't seen her. I hope she's okay. I make a mental note to check in on her.

Where are you, Claire?

The tiny light is coming from the first floor.

"Cheddar? What are you doing over there?" I whisper, spotting her at the side of the pool. The pool, expansive like the rest of their residence, is divided into a long lap pool, a larger main pool, and a hot tub nestled between their house and the beach.

I step toward her, but she darts off. "Cheddar! No, no, no."

Before I can stop her, she dashes into the house through a slightly ajar glass door, barely wide enough for a cat to slip through.

That's it. I rush to the Johnsons' front door and knock —hard. I don't stop until I hear footsteps.

Claire opens the door with a surprised expression. "Hello."

"Hiya, sorry, but I think my cat, Cheddar, is here," I blurt. "Apologies on her behalf."

"I don't mind her visits. She keeps me company now and then."

"Does she now?" I glance behind Claire into the dimly lit house.

"We both like it dark," she says, as if reading my thoughts. "Too much light hurts my eyes, and she only comes in when it's darker in the house."

"Huh. Sure."

"Did you say her name is Cheddar?"

"Yeah, I tried other names, but she responded to Cheddar. We agreed to be friends when I gave her a little piece of cheddar."

"That's so cute," she says with a smile. "Good to know. I tried a few names, but I love Cheddar."

Her posture is tense; I can tell she wants me to leave.

"Claire, thank you for warning me about Amy, but I'm confused—and curious. How did you find out, and why did you tell me?"

"Does it matter? I'll make sure Cheddar gets home later," she says, slowly closing the door.

I linger for a moment, hoping she'll open it again. She doesn't.

Chapter Thirty-Five

My mind is like an overly active beehive in the morning. While my coffee brews, I step out to check the damage properly as I've temporarily leaned the mailbox against the wall yesterday.

All right, this is strange. I glance around, half-expecting someone to be playing mind games with me. The mailbox was empty last night, and it's too early for the mailman to arrive. Yet there lies a slightly yellowed envelope inside. As I reach for it, the scent of aged paper hits me.

No more secrets, please.

I sit on the back porch, staring at the opened envelope. There is no return address. I swear under my breath and remove the letter from the envelope. There's a bank transfer receipt along with the letter. What on earth is going on?

The letter is dated eight years earlier.

Dear Mr. and Mrs. B. Williamson,
As discussed, our clients, Mr. and Mrs. Johnson,
are prepared to offer cash for your beach house at
236 South Nalu Street. Considering the conditions,
the proposed purchase price is fair and generous.

I scoff out loud. Fair and generous? That hardly matters. Eight years ago, and thirty before that, they didn't want to part with their land and home. No offer is generous when you don't want to sell.

Annoyance creeps into me as I read the rest of the letter.

The planning permission for the construction
project next door has uncovered that the current
boundary lines of your property do not align
accurately with the legal property boundaries. A
boundary adjustment will be necessary to ensure
that construction proceeds in compliance with
regulations.
The Johnsons are offering you an opportunity to
resolve this matter in an expeditious and mutually
beneficial way. Rather than proceeding with the
boundary adjustment, which may involve a portion
of your land being incorporated into the new
property, we recommend that you sell your
property. We're prepared to consider a price higher
than the market value.

I examine the bank transfer receipt. Who put this in my mailbox in the middle of the night? Claire? What does this eight-year-old letter even mean?

My frustration builds.

"You've got to lock your door, man. I swung by yesterday, and the door was unlocked. Yeah, it's a safe community and all, but still," announces Kai, joining me at the back.

"Hey, good morning to you too."

"I'm leaving both my jobs," Kai says, as he settles into a chair next to me.

"You are? Coffee?"

"Yes to both."

"Whoa, man. That grin is blinding me," I say.

He lets out a chuckle and I take in this new, joyful side of Kai.

"I'm all ears. Spill the beans."

Minutes later, cups of coffee in hand, we sit in the garden.

Before I can ask Kai to tell me about his news, Phil appears at the small gate.

"Roy, good morning!" He waves and walks into my yard.

Since my arrival, Phil has never come to say hello. I can detect a pretense of friendliness.

"Good morning," I say.

Kai acknowledges Mr. Johnson with a slight, cautious nod.

"Claire is preparing breakfast while I take a walk. We were talking about inviting you for dinner, but I guess you'll be leaving soon."

I tell myself to be polite despite what Claire told me. "Would you like some coffee?" I think about how Phil convinced Amy to work with him but I suppress a wave of anger.

"No, thank you. Listen, I heard about all the troubles and accidents you've had." His nostrils flare ever so slightly.

"Nothing that I can't handle."

"Very well," he replies. "But let me know if you need any help with anything. I must get going on my beach walk."

"Sure," I say.

As he leaves the yard, it feels as if I've just dodged a bullet.

"Well, that was strange," says Kai.

"Yeah." Something is off, but I turn my attention back to Kai. "Anyways, you were telling me you're leaving your jobs."

"Yeah, they were temporary anyway. I stayed because I didn't have a better alternative." His voice brims with excitement. "I can't wait to take care of the coffee trees, spend more time with them, nourish them, and turn the plantation into a business again."

"That's great, mate. I'm so happy for you. I know you'll do well."

He pushes some documents toward me. "I created a business plan. Would you look at it? I'm going to apply for a business loan."

"With pleasure, Kai. With absolute pleasure."

"And thank you for everything," he says, his tone sincere.

"Anytime." I smile at the young man discovering his true passion, and I can't help but feel that this could be something big.

Chapter Thirty-Six

At 7:00 p.m., I haven't seen Claire since yesterday evening. Cheddar turned up last night but wouldn't tell me what was happening.

"Can I join your game, kitty cat?"

She sits beside my chair and purrs as I pet her. The Johnsons' house is dark again. Only a tiny light emanates from inside.

"All right," I say, looking down at the cat. "Let's see if we can figure out what's going on with Claire. I might need your help."

I jump over the gate and wait for Cheddar, hoping she'll get ahead of me so I can follow her. Sure enough, she takes the lead, and we walk over the Johnsons' manicured lawn. I'm following a cat. Life is full of twists.

Cheddar slips through a slightly open door on the side

of the house and disappears. I stand there for a moment, not sure what to do.

It opens. "I knew you'd turn up," Claire says. "Come in."

An uneasiness creeps into my throat. "Are you sure?" I glance over her shoulder.

"Yes, it's his bridge night. He never returns before midnight."

I step into the house and follow her into a gigantic kitchen.

"So this is where Cheddar hangs out."

Claire smiles and looks at Cheddar lovingly. "She only comes inside when I turn the lights off. Let's keep it dim for her."

"Sure," I say, as I look around the kitchen, which is lit by only a small light underneath one of the cabinets. I sit on a modern-looking barstool. It's cold and smooth, like a polished stone.

This soulless kitchen could be a model in a magazine. It looks like a sterile laboratory. In contrast, Claire exudes warmth in her eyes and smile. There's a flicker of something I can't identify, though.

"What can I offer you?"

"A glass of water, please."

Her blue summer dress makes soft swishing sounds as she moves away to pour two glasses of water.

She hands me mine, and I take a large sip before I say, "Claire, I'm here to ask only one question. I've other questions, but right now, only one."

She pulls up a stool and takes a seat facing me.

"You want to know what I know about your family."

"No, not that." I shake my head firmly.

Her forehead subtly furrows.

I look at her directly and ask, "Are you safe here?"

When I was a kid, it didn't take me long to figure out when adults were hiding something. There were signs, gestures, and tones. I watch Claire with intensity.

She nods. "I can take care of myself."

So she doesn't feel safe.

She pushes a strand of hair behind her ear. "Your grandmother was a very dear friend of mine. When I saw you arrive, I sent a promise to Heaven that I'd watch over you."

"Thank you for that. But really, I'm only here to see if you're safe."

"You're just like your grandmother," she replies. "She'd go to any length, absolutely any length, to protect others."

It suddenly dawns on me. "You called the ambulance when I took that nosedive from the roof, didn't you?"

"Yes, I did."

Cheddar purrs while pacing slowly around us, and we both look at her. "What's the story with our kitty cat?"

"She appeared the day your grandmother passed. I was in my bedroom, by the window, and Cheddar was on the lawn, looking up at me. I used to think your grandmother sent her for me, but now I know she's here for you."

"That's super cool, Grandma," I say, starting to feel

more comfortable embracing the mysteries of the island. "I'm sure she sent her for both of us," I say to Claire.

Claire strokes the cat, and Cheddar soaks in all the love. What a significant change from the timid cat I first met.

"You know," Claire says, looking up at me, "Cheddar was the one who alerted me the day you had your fall."

"Did she?" I ask, a smile spreading across my face. "Wow, Cheddar, thank you."

"She only comes in when Phil isn't around, and when it's dark, but I saw her in my garden the day you fell, so I went out to see why."

"I met her in the dark on my first night here."

Claire smiles. "Cheddar and I both appreciate the sky, the beach, the ocean, and the garden more when it's dark. We don't like the interference of artificial lights." She studies me. "Are you wondering what my story is?"

I offer a nod and lean in.

She inhales deeply. "I fell in love with Phil when we were both very young. I can't be positive if the feeling was mutual, but I know for me it was instant. I was on vacation with my family then, and Phil worked at our hotel. My family's disapproval of our relationship only made me feel more deeply for him." She lowers her head, and there's a sad expression on her face.

"A charmer, but he changed over the years. He became obsessed with wealth. I thought living part-time in Hawai'i, would make a difference. I didn't appreciate how he handled our affairs with your grandparents, and we got into a lot of arguments. I didn't want a house this big, but he wanted to buy your land and make it even bigger." She shakes her head. "Nothing was enough for him, and it's still not. That's why he devised a detailed plan to force you to sell your land and house." Her voice wobbles. "I'm sorry. I know he's been making life difficult for you."

"Not your fault, please don't apologize. But why are you telling me all this?" I ask gently.

"Because I can't tell anyone else, and if anything happens to me, I know you'll help. You're Hina's grandson."

I raise my eyebrows, anxiety rising in my chest. I knew she wasn't safe. "What do you mean if anything happens to you? And if you're in danger, why don't you leave him?"

"He'll get what he deserves. I've got a private investigator, and I'll leave when the time is right. But I don't want my husband to suspect anything and take action. He doesn't even notice how quiet I've become. The more I look into his affairs, the more I see his dark side. A side that I never knew. Manipulations, wrongdoings. I left that letter in your mailbox. He fabricated the boundary issue. There was never a boundary issue. He bribed someone at the property survey office to pressure your grandparents. I didn't realize the extent of his greed. I tried to help your grandma here and there, thinking my husband would tire of his new focus. I told Hina about the height restriction after I heard Phil talking with an architect."

She sips her water, a solemn look on her face.

I wordlessly absorb the information.

"I'm sorry you're hurting," she continues, "but I had to tell you about Amy. I didn't anticipate you two getting close. I don't have proof, but I know he's behind many of the unfortunate things happening to you. We both saw you testing the ladder the day before you had a fall. He even joked about how old the ladder was."

My heart clenches, and I avert my eyes with a deep inhale. *Son of a—*

She exhales, and something in her demeanor shifts. "I recently found out he's been having an affair. It's been going on for a few years now. That's why I hired a private investigator. I'm taking my time, waiting for the perfect moment to leave him. I need to collect all the evidence I can. He purchased his mistress a condo recently." She swallows. "I thought he loved me. Maybe he did initially, but now I think he's been using me. I'm beyond angry and hurt. Nevertheless, I will not let him break me. Or you."

Her voice cracks a little, and glistening tears form, clinging to her lashes.

I take a deep breath. "I'm sorry, Claire. Tell me what I can do to help." I reach forward and grasp her hand lightly.

"Telling you is a great help. I know this must seem strange, but I feel like I know you. You're Hina's grandson, after all. So thanks for listening. You're a great listener. Tell me about you, your childhood. I'm so sad that Hina never had a chance to meet you."

I shift nervously in my chair, nearly knocking over my water glass. Claire reaches out and stabilizes it.

"That would take all night." I let out a nervous chuckle.

"I've got till midnight," she says encouragingly.

And so, I tell her. I summarize my early years, then relax as I describe my adopted family's love, my brother Luke's devotion and how he became my protector. I explain that I lost my dad shortly after he adopted me.

Claire listens intently, leaning forward, hanging on every word. "I'm so glad you found a place of belonging," she says, when I finish. "I know your grandma would be so happy to hear it. And your family, your brother—they sound amazing."

"Thank you. They are. And he is." I nod, warmth swelling within me as I think of my family back home in the UK.

I glance at my watch; it's getting late. "I should get going." As I stand, I ask, "May I give you my phone number, please?"

Claire smiles and fetches a notepad. As I jot down the digits, I repeat my earlier question, urgency in my tone. "Are you safe here? You're not being forced into anything against your will, right?"

"I appreciate your concern, Roy. But I'm fine. And I have Cheddar here. She'll let you know if I'm in trouble." Claire winks, though her smile seems strained.

I nod slowly, still hesitant to leave. But Phil will be

home soon. I head for the door, casting one last worried look at my gracious host.

She gives me a tiny nod, clutching the piece of paper with my phone number on it as if to say *I promise I'll call if I have to.*

Do I believe in telepathic conversations? No, but right now, whether I do or not is irrelevant. She just told me she would call me.

I hope she doesn't have to make that call, I think anxiously, as I step back toward my house. Cheddar is on my heels.

Chapter Thirty-Seven

I get up and make myself an espresso. I'm feeling pleased with my decision to spend the day alone in quiet reflection. Hawai'i is where I am, after all— the place of tranquility.

Then I hear tapping on the door reminiscent of a drummer rehearsing a symphony.

"Yes, yes," I say, walking toward the door. "Just chill out, okay?"

The door jerks back the moment I unlock the door. Result? Coffee sloshing all over the floor. A small body sprints inside, leaving me standing with an empty cup by the door.

"Hey, buddy, are you okay?"

"Curly has gone missing." Sean's large green eyes are streaked with red. "Have you seen him?"

"No, what happened?"

"Everything is horrible. I hate it. He was with us one minute then disappeared."

I step forward and embrace him, and he puts his head on my chest and wraps his arms around my back. When I look outside, I notice Amy standing by the fence.

"Let's go and talk to your mother."

"But can you help me find him?"

"Sure."

He sniffles. "What about the coffee on the floor?"

"Give me a second." I retrieve paper towels from the kitchen and wipe the floor quickly. "Done."

As we run outside, Sean exclaims, "I told you, Mom! He wants to help!"

"Okay, I'll go over there," she says, gesturing to a path. "You guys look in the other direction, okay?"

I jog behind Sean as he runs.

"He sometimes wanders away for a while, but he always finds his way back to me," Sean says in a frightened tone.

"We'll find him."

I remember a time I was told I was being transferred to a new foster home. I was probably seven or eight at the time. The years between the ages of six and ten are somewhat hazy for me, but this moment I recall perfectly. Before leaving for the new foster home, I realized that my yellow fire truck was missing. The only possession I've had all my life. I checked my black trash bag, but it wasn't there. The adults told me that it was okay, that I'd get another toy.

I grabbed onto the doors, yelled my lungs out, and refused to leave without it. It turned out someone had thrown my toy away, but a few hours later, it was recovered.

As I jog, I shake my head. *Adults. They really do make things more complicated than they need to be.*

After that incident, my fire truck was always with me. Luke informed me that it had been noted in my documents —the fire truck was to remain with me at all times.

"Sean, wait up." We pause at the sound of Amy's voice. "He's not over there," she says, approaching, "so I'll come with you."

"But Mom, our search party is fast," Sean declares.

Amy rushes ahead of us. "Don't challenge me."

Running behind Amy is the last thing I want to do. Her toned body threatens to overwhelm my senses and transport me back to moments we shared.

Avoid her at all costs, I tell myself.

"Hey guys, I think I'll search this way," I yell, and veer to the left into some bushes. I learned early on that sometimes it's better to stop fighting and to try a different path.

"Curly!" I hear Amy and Sean yell. "Curly!"

Then I hear a different kind of shout. I emerge from the bushes to find Amy sitting on the sand gripping her ankle.

Sean is kneeling by her side. "I'm sorry, Mom." Tears stream down his cheeks in torrents.

"What the heck happened?" I inquire, kneeling next to Amy.

"I slipped. Didn't see the rock buried under the sand."

Looking into one pair of tearful green eyes is excruciating. But two pairs? Unbearable.

"Yes, okay," I say. "First, we need to assess the damage. How about standing on it?"

She shakes her head while Sean continues to apologize.

I reach out and put my arm over his shoulder. "Hey, hey, not your fault, buddy."

I call 911 as passersby cluster around us. "Yes, I think we've got a badly twisted or broken ankle. Can we get an ambulance?" I give the operator our location then pay attention as she explains what to do. At least half a mile separates us from the nearest beach access.

"Of course," I say in response. "We'll start walking to the parking lot."

"I can't even stand on it, let alone walk," Amy shrieks as I hang up.

"Who says you have to walk?" I stand up. "I'm carrying you."

Her teary eyes widen.

"Hang on to me for dear life," I say, carefully cradling her in my arms. My left arm slips beneath her bent knees. She reaches out to put her arms around my neck. My arm is much better now, but pain still shoots from my wrist into my shoulder. I ignore the pain, holding her tight and running as fast as possible.

"Come on, buddy, help me get your mom to the ambulance." We hurry toward the parking lot. Some beach walkers offer to look for Curly as we were asking people if they saw him.

"Look," I say to Sean, "these friends will keep looking for him, okay?"

It's difficult to ignore the sound of Amy's heart. Her hair tickles my cheek with every step I take, and her breath mingles with mine. I wish I could take her pain away.

On a stretcher in the back of the ambulance, Amy has stopped crying. But Sean continues to cry and apologize.

"It's not your fault that she hurt herself," I say to Sean again.

Amy holds up her hand to me. "Let me, please." She extends her hand to Sean. "Come here, darling." Sean immediately takes it.

"Whatever you're apologizing for, it's okay. We'll talk about it later, all right?"

Sean nods and wipes his tears away. I watch them; I love these two. I shuffle uncomfortably. I mean, I love this kid.

At the hospital, Amy is taken to a treatment room, so Sean and I sit in the waiting room. The boy looks as if he's carrying the weight of the earth on his shoulders.

"Come here." I extend my arm, and he nestles into my side. He rests his tiny head on my chest, and after a while, his breathing becomes steadier and longer. He's drifted into a nap.

I remember sitting in the center of a dark wooded area when I was about eleven. Luke and I reclined under a tree, and I rested my head on his shoulder. He'd just tracked me down once again. I'd overheard my parents talking about adopting me and had decided that this promise was yet another adult fabrication. To me, promises made by adults were like snowflakes on a hot summer day.

I'd made sure to take my fire truck, a few of my favorite T-shirts, some homemade jam—I knew I'd miss it —some bread, and the rugby cards Luke had bought me. I felt accomplished.

I'd ditched school in the morning. The patch of woods on the outskirts of town was a suitable hiding area, a place where I could figure out my next move.

In the afternoon, hungry and exhausted, I nodded off, and when I woke up, Luke was seated next to me, a book open in his lap. There was a blanket draped over me. I thought it was a dream at first.

"Whoa, whoa, man," said Luke, when I stood up fast.

"I'm not coming back," I yelled.

"I'm not asking you to come back."

"What?"

"I'm not asking you to come back," he repeated.

My curious eyes interrogated him as he continued. "I want to run away with you. I've been thinking about it for a while but never had the courage, so here we are. Can I come with you?"

"Huh?" I blinked. "What?"

"What's the plan, man?"

"Dunno," I said, shrugging. "Are you serious?"

"Sure, why not."

"Okay then." I sat down next to Luke, and he put his arm around my shoulder.

Shaking off the memory, I cup Sean's small shoulder. I hope he meets his Luke one day. Amy is doing a great job, though—there's no doubt about that. Sean settles deeper against my chest.

"Have a rest, buddy," I say quietly. "We might be here for a while."

He places his hand on top of mine in a *don't take your hand off my shoulder* gesture.

I return to the memory of Luke running away with me. We sat under that tree for a few hours, until night fell.

"Maybe we should just go home?" Luke said. "It's getting cold, and Mom would be so happy to see both of us."

I nodded. I'd been waiting for him to ask me this. I learned years later that the school had called my foster family immediately. Luke had insisted on coming after me; he wouldn't let anyone else try.

My second chance in life manifested as my brother.

Sean gasps, abruptly awakening. He looks scared.

"It's okay, I'm here," I say, embracing him in a hug.

He starts crying.

"Your mom is okay," I whisper. "It's only a sprain."

But he continues to sob on my shoulder. I'm lost as to how to comfort him.

Chapter Thirty-Eight

I collapse onto the sofa, exhausted. What a day. Amy is finally home, her ankle wrapped in a bandage. She'll be on crutches for a while. Sean is at a friend's house, giving Amy some time to recover. He didn't talk to me after he stopped sobbing; I'm not sure why.

I think about how Sean fell asleep on me, his little head nuzzled against my chest. That boy has completely stolen my heart.

Then I think of Amy and am reminded of the constant battle between my head and my heart.

I let out a long sigh, running my hands through my hair. Man, this is messed up. My mind races with thoughts of Amy and Sean as I try to unwind. I want so badly to make things right for Sean, but I know deep down that walking away is the best thing for everyone—even if it breaks my heart to do it.

"Aloha."

I startle and sit up. Aunt Melina is standing in the doorway, an amused smile on her face. I must not have closed the door all the way.

"Aunt Melina, aloha," I say, feeling my cheeks flush. "I was just . . . lost in thought. Please, come in."

I make room for her on the sofa.

"I must tell you something," she says, as she settles next to me. Sadness radiates from her. "I understand you're searching for answers. Our past shapes us, and I know you want to fill in the gaps."

I nod slowly. Where's this going?

"But the past is only useful if it helps you enjoy the present," Aunt Melina continues gently.

I feel a lump rising in my throat.

She places a hand on my knee. "What good will the past bring if it disrupts the lives of others now?"

I furrow my brow. "Disrupt others? What do you mean?"

"Kimo worked so hard to build his family. He's proud of his kids, he loves Jenn."

My frown deepens. "I would never want to disrupt Kimo's life."

"I know your intentions are pure. But your presence here . . . it has upset the balance of their family."

I clench my jaw. That word again—*presence*.

I shove the flood of memories from my childhood aside. *My blimming presence. Again.*

"Don't get upset," she says, squeezing my leg. "It's not

you. Your aunt was Kimo's first love, and Jenn feels that bringing up the past may cause her husband's feelings for Kalani to resurface."

I let out a resigned sigh. "I understand. The last thing I want is to cause them any distress."

"I know, son." She offers an understanding smile. "Just thought you should know. Kimo's wife went to another island for a few days. Kimo will make it all right, don't you worry."

"I see. Okay."

It's as if the moment I arrived here, I ripped an old Band-Aid from my chest, exposing a wound. I've aggravated it, and it grows in size and intensity each day, hurtful and persistent. Now it feels as if the world is sprinkling salt into it.

After Aunt Melina leaves, I gently stroke the scarf that Kalani knitted for Kimo. I think about how Jenn looked upset when she saw it. With that in mind, I tie the scarf around my neck and head for the neighbors' place.

I know my presence tends to disturb people, to bring discomfort without intentional action on my part—to my stepmother, the bickering couple, the boyfriend of the solo foster woman, even the kids at school. And now I'm bringing discomfort to people on the island.

All because of my stupid presence. But this time, it's my decision. I'll remove myself from their world. I'll make my presence void. I'll leave.

I stride over to the Johnsons' and knock hard. They're both standing there when the door opens. Claire stands behind Phil and looks at me with eyes full of thousands of questions.

"Phil, do you have a few minutes?" I ask.

"Sure, come on in." He beckons me inside.

"This won't take long, so we can talk here. Would you like to buy my house?" I ask, knowing that he would. "If you offer a fast sell and a good price, it's yours."

As the words escape my lips, a searing pain grips the side of my neck.

Claire's face tightens while her husband's features light up with victory as a smile creeps across his face. I can feel his invisible sword in the air. I don't understand why he needs more land. But it's no longer my concern. I'll take my presence off this island.

"I'm sure we can get to an agreement," Phil says. "I'll call my lawyer immediately so we can start the proceedings." He glances at Claire. "We've another thing to celebrate, honey." A grin spreads over his face. "Claire and I are going for a sunset sail shortly."

I meet Claire's gaze. "One minute, Roy," she says, and disappears. Seconds later, she returns and hands me a cat toy. With a serious expression, she says, "This is for your cat, Lukas." Her eyes are as cold as steel, boring into mine.

"We must get going," Phil says. "Claire loves our sunset sails. Our friend has a small house on the small island, and we might stay over."

He closes the door. I stare at the toy fish.

"Who the heck is Lukas?" I murmur.

Chapter Thirty-Nine

I pace in the living room, squeezing the toy, trying to decode Claire's message. Surely it was a hidden message. The scent of catnip reaches my nostrils.

She said, "Your cat, Lukas." But she knows Cheddar's name.

Beads of sweat form on my forehead.

Cheddar will protect me . . . Your cat, Lukas . . . Lukas . . . My protector, Luke! Luke, cat, Lukas.

"Damn and crap and bloody hell!" I yell, speeding up my pace, my hand in my hair.

The next time I turn toward the door, I shout at the sight of Kimo standing there, watching me. "What are you doing here?"

"What's going on?" he asks, ignoring my question. "You look like you've just seen a ghost." He tilts his head, examining me.

"I think Claire is in danger."

"Claire who?"

"Mrs. Johnson,"

"Can you sit, please? You're making me dizzy."

We sit on the couch and I tell him everything. "My guess is that Phil must have found out what Claire was doing, gathering evidence and all."

"But that's his wife, Roy. He's not going to harm her."

I shake my head. "She insinuated that he's capable of many things, and if he thinks she's in his way, I'm certain that he'll take action." I rise abruptly. "This is messed up. She joked about Cheddar protecting her and then called Cheddar Lukas because I told her about my protective brother, Luke."

"What would Phil do?"

"I don't know, man, my mind doesn't work that way. Anyway, why are you here?"

"Aunt Melina told me that you were pretty upset. I didn't want her to tell you about my family affairs, but she did. I came here to say we'll be okay, Jenn and me."

I nod. I still feel bad, and I resolve to leave his life as soon as possible, but Claire's safety is more important than anything right now.

"Can we find out where the Johnsons' catamaran is?"

"Easy," he says, pulling his phone from his pocket. "But stop pacing. Stay still for a minute."

I listen as he talks to one of his captain friends, and a few minutes later, he announces, "Apparently, their catamaran is reaching the small island over there. Should we call the police?" Kimo asks.

"And tell them I have some suspicion based on my gut and a cat toy?" I sigh. "But I know something isn't right."

"Okay," Kimo says. "Let's go." He heads for the beach, and I follow. He points at some paddleboards. "Let's paddle into the ocean. I'll call Kai to pick us up. He's already on the boat."

Kimo sprints toward a couple, urgently conveying that we need to borrow their paddleboards. I wish people were not this kind here, but they are, so now we have the paddleboards.

"Can't we wait here for Kai to come and get us?" I ask, my stomach churning with dread.

"Boats can't get near the shore here. We must go to him. Roy?"

I'm staring at the paddleboards. I'm getting on a paddleboard. Swimming.

Paddling isn't really swimming, I tell myself. *You can't let fear control you.*

I laugh at myself for sounding like a self-help book, but it works. I pick up a board. The power of the mind never ceases to amaze me.

"All right, let's do this," I say, trying to sound braver than I feel.

We wade into the water. My breathing quickens and my throat tightens. It's as if the ocean is mocking me, daring me to overcome my fears. Damn it.

"Stay close to me," Kimo shouts over the crashing waves. He's lying on his stomach on a board, his strong strokes easily cutting through the water. "I'll guide you."

"Easy for you to say," I mutter, fighting the panic clawing its way up my throat.

Focus now. It's only an ocean.

Motivated by thoughts of what Phil might be planning, I propel myself forward with my arms. Kimo stays by my side, offering words of encouragement and guidance.

"Remember to breathe, Roy," he reminds me, as I gasp for air between waves.

"Breathing's overrated," I manage to sputter, trying to inject humor into the situation. It falls flat, and I curse myself for not knowing how to swim.

An immense sea turtle passes by, leisurely paddling through the water. In awe, I relax. The waves lift my board, and I stop fighting with them.

"Roy, look! That's Kai." Kimo points ahead, and I see a small boat in the distance.

When we finally reach the boat, or the boat reaches us, I haul myself onto the deck, my limbs trembling from exhaustion and a strange sense of ease.

Kai sets off into the evening, chasing the fading sun. As he steers the boat toward the shoreline of the small island, I grip the railing.

"Look!" Kimo shouts, pointing toward the dock ahead. My heart leaps at the sight of the Johnsons' catamaran.

"Kai, get us to the shore—fast," I say, through gritted teeth.

"Copy that," he replies, gunning the engine and navigating toward the dock with expert precision.

I nearly slip on the wet surface of the boat as I prepare to sprint up the dock, but Kimo grips my shoulders.

"Roy, we need a plan!" His face is right in front of mine. "We can't just turn up to their boat. They might be having a romantic evening."

"Look, there's a house on the shore," says Kai. "All the lights are on."

"She prefers the dark."

"What?" Kai and Kimo ask in unison.

"Claire would turn the lights off to watch the sunset. She likes natural light."

An idea takes hold. "Okay, I have a plan. Kai, can you take us to the other side of the island? See the hill there? There must be a way to access the house from that hill. We'll approach from the back, stay hidden, and check to see if she's okay. If all is well, we'll leave them in peace."

The engine roars again. Neither man questions how ridiculous my suggestion might be.

Once we reach the other side of the small island, Kai moors the boat at a small dock and we both sprint out. Kimo agrees to stay on the boat. We start running up the hill behind the house. I'm hoping there's a path down to a rear entrance.

"Damn, damn, damn!" I shout from the top. We're on a sharp cliff with lots of vegetation.

"Be quiet, man," says Kai.

"It's a cliff," I murmur, hopelessness settling on my ribcage.

Kai looks down, standing on the edge. "It's only a wannabe cliff."

Approaching the edge, my heart pounds as I peer over. Below, waves crash against the rocks with relentless force, but I also spot the path at the bottom of the cliff. Between me and the path, there's a very steep cliff side with lush and dense vegetation from halfway through to the bottom.

"Thanks to the courtesy of the Hawaiian richness." I murmur, looking down.

So, I could jump first, aiming for the vegetation, and then carefully climb down onto the path.

"We've got to get down there," I declare.

Kai hesitates, "Aim to grab branches or leaves, anything. It's just a few yards. But if you miss the vegetation, you'll fall fast. Are you sure about this?" His voice is barely audible.

"Of course I'm not bloody sure!" I snap as I kneel and grip the edge of the cliff. "But that's the only path to the back of the house, right?"

"We could swim from the boat."

"That'll take too long," I say. *If you only knew, Kai, how long it would take me to swim to the house. I'd need to start with some swimming lessons.*

Kai's expression is grim but determined. "All right then," he says, clapping me on the back. "I'll watch you first. You can do this."

"Wait," I say, hesitating. My palms sweat, and images of plunging into the ocean's dark depths flood my mind. "I . . . I don't know if I can do this."

"Hey," Kai says gently, touching my shoulder. "If you miss the vegetation, just aim for the water. It's deep enough to dive into. Avoid the rocks, okay?"

I take a deep breath, trying to steady myself. "Ha, thanks," I reply, rolling my eyes. "Your infinite wisdom truly knows no bounds."

With a deep breath, I back up and charge toward the edge, my heart hammering in my chest. Just as I'm about to jump, an image of sinking into the wild waves flashes through my mind, causing me to falter.

"Come on, Roy," I mutter. "You can do this. It's just like jumping off snow piles, except with more . . . death. And deep water."

I take another breath, feeling the salty air fill my lungs, and then, with a yelp of both courage and terror, I leap off the cliff with the hope of catching the branches on the way down.

My last thought is that if I endure this ordeal, I'll never take solid ground for granted again.

Chapter Forty

Water, water everywhere. I crane my neck slightly, but I still see water. My gaze darts around, only to be met with the relentless continuity of water. I'm lying on a small black rock surrounded by rippling blue vastness.

My eyes act like a 33 mm camera lens, scanning the area frantically. Still nothing but water. Ah, there's the sun, vanishing into the horizon and blending with the water.

I let out a sigh of exasperation. So, I really did jump off of that cliff.

A crab with beady eyes is scuttling toward me.

Looking around, the shore is over there, and the path is in that direction as well. This rock stands in the middle of the ocean. Oh, man. I can't swim, and there's so much water around me.

Something brushes past my neck, and I give a little

shriek. Looking down, I realize it's a necklace, not a creature.

Ah, it's a turtle-shaped necklace.

Why am I wearing a turtle necklace?

"Oh!" I say, remembering suddenly.

"Roy! Roy!" I hear his voice.

Kai appears, crawling on the rock. "We don't have time for a concussion, dude." He checks my head, arms, and legs. "Are you all right?"

"Define *all right*," I say, wincing.

"Can you move? That was a heck of a fall."

"Yep. But this rock is kinda small for both of us."

"No kidding. Remind me not to go along with your plans ever again," he grumbles. "Let's get to the house."

"But there's water between here and there."

Kai looks bewildered, as if I just stated the most obvious fact on earth.

I sigh. "We might have a small issue. I can't swim."

Now he looks thoroughly confused.

"Not everyone grew up by an ocean, you know." I sit up and punch the air with my fists then move my legs up and down to see if I injured myself.

"Wow, I love that you jumped into the ocean as a non-swimmer. Cool, man." He grins.

"You didn't offer many other options," I say, still moving my arms and legs.

"You were lucky." He shakes his head. "The vegetation did slow your fall, and this happens to be a smooth rock. But it looks like the fall impacted your brain—what are you doing with your arms and legs?"

"Just checking all my limbs."

Kai chuckles. "Here's what we'll do. We'll slide into the water and you'll lean on me, face up. Look into the sky, relax, and take steady breaths. The waves will help you. Don't resist them. Let them raise you. The shore is not far at all."

"Relax. Of course, I'll bloody relax. It's my natural habitat—water."

Next thing I know, we're in the water. I can taste the salt. I turn to face the sky and gradually lean on Kai. He's also facing upward, holding me tightly against his chest.

Just trust and let go.

"Great, you're doing great. I got you," Kai says reassuringly, as he swims to the shore. I don't panic, not even for a second. It feels odd to be so calm. I even note the hues in the colors of the sunset.

"Thanks," I whisper, as we reach dry land.

"For someone who can't swim, you did great," Kai whispers back.

"Yeah, I felt good actually."

I see the back of the house.

"Look," says Kai, gesturing, "we can peek inside if we walk into the water over there and use the steps to climb up to the small deck of the house."

"Sure, why not? The more water the better." I say.

Kai lets out a soft laugh.

We walk through the chest-high water to the steps connecting the ocean and the backyard.

The sheer number of lights on in the house is challenging to the pupils. As I approach one of the windows, I see Claire asleep on a sofa. I frown. It's odd that she'd be sleeping with all the lights on. And the sunset is still beautiful.

I hear Phil on the phone.

Dread swarms my mind. "Something seems off here," I hiss to Kai.

"Oh really? You think there's something odd about this evening?" he asks with a teasing tone.

I slide open the window. "Claire," I whisper. "Claire."

She doesn't move. I quickly climb into the room.

"Claire. Claire." She doesn't move. I touch her arm. Still no movement.

"Who's there?"

I look up. Phil is pointing a gun in our direction.

"Why isn't she responding?" I ask, my voice shaking with rage. "What did you do to her?"

"She took some pills for her headache," he says with a snarl. "They make her sleepy. Now why don't you explain what you're doing here? You know this is private property?"

"Yes, okay." I raise my hands in surrender. "Call the police if that's what you want. But I'm not going anywhere until she wakes up."

"Or what?" Phil laughs manically. "And what exactly

are you going to do, Roy? You're just like your grandpa—
Olympic-level stupid. I can get you locked up for this."

My voice is steady despite the danger. "You see,
there's something you didn't account for."

"And what's that?"

"You don't insult my grandpa."

"Ugh, spare me this sentimental nonsense," he says
with a scoff, tightening his grip on his gun. "I'm calling
the cops."

Kai sprints into the room and Phil quickly turns toward
him. Taking advantage of his temporary distraction, I
catapult into Phil with reckless abandon, throwing him to
the ground. The gun flies from his hand like a missile.
Cursing, Phil lies prone on the floor while Kai kicks the
gun away.

"This is private property!" he shouts impotently.

"I don't care about your property, man!" I shout.

As Kai restrains Phil, he firmly clasps his arms around
Phil's chest, locking him in a controlled hold. Phil
struggles against the grip, but Kai's strength keeps him
contained. I rush toward Claire. When I feel her breath on
my hand, I have a moment of pure relief. She's alive.

"She's breathing," I yell.

I look over at Phil and am shocked when I register that
Kimo is sitting on him.

"How did you get here?" I ask.

"I thought you might need help, so I brought the boat
back here."

"Good one, Kimo." I smile and hoist Claire's thin

frame into my arms. My injured arm screams in pain. "She's also ohana, Phil!" I yell, as I walk out the door, Kai on my heels.

Chapter Forty-One

A week has passed since the incident, not that I'm counting the days or anything, and I can't wait for my flight tomorrow. Finally, I'm ready to depart, and I'm departing as someone changed. I feel as if I've spent sixty years here, not six weeks.

After rescuing Claire, I called the police and Phil was taken into custody. Claire spent the night in the hospital, and then her family from California helped her leave the island. She video called a few days ago. I was so happy to see her smile.

"Hey, Claire, so lovely seeing your beautiful face," I said excitedly.

"You're such a charmer, Roy. Thank you for coming to rescue me. I knew he was up to something, and I knew you'd figure it out." Tears streamed down her cheeks. "I can't tell you how much I appreciate your help—I don't even want to think about what would have happened if you hadn't shown up."

"I'm so relieved that you're all right now, Claire. Using Cheddar and referring to my brother Luke in your secret code was a stroke of genius. I've never felt so relieved when I realized you were breathing." My voice breaks as I say this.

"I did have a terrible headache, but Phil has confessed to giving me strong painkillers and sleeping pills without my consent. He told the police I'd been restless and that he was just trying to help me sleep."

"The lowlife," I say with a sneer, wanting nothing less than justice for Claire's suffering.

"I think your offering to sell your house that evening; he drugged me to sleep so he could celebrate without me. But he also admitted that there were previous occasions of giving me sleeping pills without telling me. This time, he gave me so much that I might have died if I hadn't gotten to the hospital. So thank you."

"I can't believe you're so calm about all this."

"I've already gone through the shock, grief, and acceptance in the last few months, since I discovered his affair and other wrongdoings. The thought of finally being free from him brings so much relief. I still have lingering fear, but it's slowly fading. He's out of my life for good. That's what I want."

A sigh of relief escapes my lips.

"Also, I've been thinking about what to do with the

house, and my plan is to sell it and donate the proceeds to a good cause. Not sure what or how yet."

"That's so wonderful, Claire, but don't rush into any decision, please." Look who's talking.

We agree to keep in touch.

Since the phone call, I've had a quiet few days. I'm gathering my thoughts and packing. My arm is doing better. I had to go to the urgent care center, as the pain became excruciating after carrying Amy and then Claire. It's now in a brace again, and the doctor instructed me not to lift anything heavy, including humans.

I've gently declined to see anyone except Aunt Melina. She's popped around a few times. I gave power of attorney to Frank so he can proceed with the house sale. I hope someone will love this land as much as my grandparents did.

Things seem to be in order, but I can't shake a feeling of unease. Maybe I just need a peaceful last day here and a walk on the beach after my coffee. On the porch of the beach house, I inhale the warmth of the morning breeze. Just like the whales preparing to return home to Alaska, I'm preparing to return home to London.

Sipping my morning coffee, I jolt as I hear the gate creak. Amy walks through on her crutches. I look to the sky and murmur "Cut me some slack, will ya?" before slumping with defeat. I have no energy, desire, or capability to face her.

"I'm here, and you'll listen," she says, mirroring the turbulence of an ocean.

I look at her, but it's painful. "Please, Amy," I beg her.

Stop hurting my heart. Stop being this gorgeous. Stop being over there and not here.

"Look, I initially agreed to persuade you to sell, but I changed my mind after we spent time together. Sean is . . ." Her voice trails off. "What are you afraid of? Why don't you let me explain myself?"

More heartbreak.

I remain silent, trying to absorb the sight of her one last time.

She leans on the gate. "I told Phil I wouldn't go ahead with the plan, and he got upset with me. He even threatened me."

"He what?"

"Yes," she says with intensity, "but he couldn't scare me. I made a mistake, but can't you see that I'm genuinely sorry?"

I place my coffee on the table and walk up to her. *I need this. I need to inhale your skin one last time.* Our heated breaths mingle in the air.

"How could you make a deal with a monster like Johnson for your own selfish gain?"

"I can't believe what an evil man he is, but I didn't know that at the time, and I never thought he'd go this far. Ever since you rescued Claire I've wanted to come here, but I've battled the urge. I kept telling myself you're better off without me. I didn't want to hurt you. But let me explain, at least."

I cock my head. *Too late. I'm broken already.*

When Amy speaks again, her voice holds a mixture of anger and grief. "You think I did this out of selfishness? You have no idea what I've been through." Her words are laced with bitterness. "I had my reasons for making that deal. I'm now going to share them with you," she says, her voice getting louder. "And you're going to listen."

I scoff. "I'm sure your reasons are valid," I say, my voice thick with resentment and hurt. "We just met and had a few moments. You owe me no explanation."

"A few moments?" she yells. "That's it? What we had was just a few moments?"

"Look, you're making a scene," I say quietly. "Why don't you return to your world, and I'll continue my quiet morning. I'm leaving tomorrow anyway."

Tears gather on her trembling lashes. "You're leaving tomorrow?"

I look down so I can't see her eyes, her skin, her heart. My very heart is quivering.

Don't look up. Don't look up.

She abruptly turns around and, with the help of her crutches, steps out of the garden.

I stand motionless, staring at the open gate. That was it. The final moment.

I start walking toward the beach, but after only a few steps—before reaching the small gate—her voice pierces the air, catching me off guard.

"You will listen to me, sunshine."

I turn. She's leaning on the gate. "You know, some

things aren't so cut-and-dried. And you should know that better than anyone."

I move to stand right in front of her, looking at her in bewilderment.

"Don't. Don't you dare judge me without hearing me out." She takes a hobbling step forward. I take a step back. Then she takes another, and one more.

She's practically in my face.

I exhale sharply, struggling to keep a tight rein on my emotions. "Amy, please, just stop torturing us," I plead, my voice full of frustration and longing.

"Don't tell me what to do," she retorts, stepping even closer. Her proximity ignites thousands of sparks in my body.

I still crave her. The current running through every fiber of my being is nearly intolerable. It takes every ounce of willpower to resist the urge to reach out and pull her into my arms.

She presses her palm forcefully against my chest, and her eyes bore into mine.

"You will listen to what I have to say," she commands.

My jaw clenches in desperation. In a state of pure helplessness, I stare at her. She transforms my air, my oxygen. My world.

I close my eyes for a beat and feel her mouth crash into mine. The kiss releases something within me.

In a swift motion, she jumps into my arms. Her legs wind securely around my waist, holding on to me tightly. This is a familiar dance; I recognize every movement. I pull her tighter, encircling her tightly with my left arm and using my right arm as much as possible.

"Your arm," she murmurs.

No discomfort there. I no longer possess control over my body. It's as if I've transformed into a completely different being. Her breathing is fast and shallow, her lips parted. I stare at her. I could do this forever, look at her face. The only sounds are her breathing and my heart pounding.

Our lips meet again, and I carry her into the house. A moan slips out of her when my tongue sweeps her mouth. We're in the wild, the unstoppable. Her taste lingers on my tongue, a bittersweet nectar. I can't stop kissing her. I want to taste her again and again. We're lost in each other, starving for each other.

I lower her to the bed and she grabs my shirt and pulls it off, ripping buttons in the process. I slide her top off. My hand travels to her smooth bra. The turquoise complements her tanned skin. Taking a deep breath, I unclasp her bra to reveal the lighter skin underneath. I stop, taking in her eyes, her face, and appreciating every curve of her body. She is a world wonder, and every cell in her body demands worship.

I oblige.

I smother her neck in kisses, and she gasps in delight. Trembling slightly, my palm cups one of her breasts. It's intoxicating, a sweet danger. As I kiss her breasts, she groans with pleasure.

I move down to her stomach, and she arches into my

touch. The heat of her skin electrifies my lips and fingertips. My tongue takes a more daring journey, wanting to get to know every inch of her.

When our bodies eventually collide, my heart stops for just a second. Our connection is a raging volcano.

In that moment, I intend to spend the rest of my life exploring her.

Chapter Forty-Two

Am I under a spell? I ponder, fixated on her captivating face. She suggested we move to the sofa, and we did so carefully, hindered by the pulsating ache in my arm.

Now, the throbbing of my heart resonates in my ears. Her pupils are like stars twinkling in the night sky.

She's my brightness.

I'm doomed.

Then tears fill her eyes.

"No, no, no! Don't cry, or I'll scoop you up and carry you back to the bedroom!"

"I'm game," she says with a laugh, before growing serious again. "That's partly why I wanted to be on the sofa. Let's maintain some physical distance."

"Okay, let's wrestle with nature," I say, but I oblige and sit.

"Roy." Her voice is barely above a whisper. The

vulnerability in her eyes mirrors my own. "Please listen. Please let me explain."

"Let me have it," I reply helplessly, aware of her power over me.

"I need to take Sean to South Korea." She looks down. "For a treatment. I want him to have a normal life. It's his dream to go to New York, London, and Ireland." She looks up. I see the weight of her sadness in her eyes.

I squint at her in confusion.

"He has a rare chronic condition. He can't be in cold temperatures."

A lump forms in my throat. "A condition." My voice is a quiet rumble.

"It's called Raynaud's disease."

My little buddy Sean. My eyebrows knit.

"When exposed to cold, his blood vessels narrow, limiting blood flow to his extremities."

I feel as if I'm being pulled into the deepest part of a stormy ocean.

"In cold weather, parts of his body get numb or tingle painfully, especially his fingers and toes. But it can impact his nose, ears, and lips too. And it's not just painful—it's dangerous. It can be life-threatening if he gets an infection from it." A tear glides down her cheek. "He shudders uncontrollably. His body is simply unable to take the intense cold. It's heartbreaking to witness his suffering."

After a silence of many seconds, I rise. "This bloody life's got a right twisted sense of fairness, doesn't it?" My veins bulge with frustration and my muscles tense.

278

"Sorry, just give me a moment," I call out, before entering the bedroom and closing the door behind me. I kick and hit everything in sight then punch the pillow several times, spitting out curses with every blow.

When I step out of the bedroom, I try to appear calm.

"Feeling better?" she asks.

I shake my head. "Tell me about the treatment," I say, while I drop down next to her.

She sighs. "There's no cure so far, but there is medication that helps prevent and control the attacks. There's been a recent breakthrough in South Korea, though. A private clinic is having amazing success with its treatments. I've been following them closely for months. My neighbor travels there often to visit her family, and they helped me to research the clinic. It's very promising and hope is what I want for my little boy."

"So, he needs to go to South Korea."

She nods, looking more vulnerable than I've ever seen her. I lift her chin. There's a depth to her eyes that I can't fathom, yet I'm willing to dive in.

"Nothing matters more than my little buddy. He will get to South Korea."

I pull her close, and her words are muffled against my chest as she speaks. "I had a deal with Phil for only a few days, then I told him to go away and leave you alone. I even asked Chelsea not to take your call. The deal was foolish, and I regretted making it after our day at the beach."

"The beach with the turtles?" I ask.

"Yes."

"You needed the money to keep your baby safe," I say quietly.

She nods.

"How much does the treatment cost?"

She looks up. "I don't need you to worry about that."

"Amy, how much does it cost?" I press.

"Hundreds of thousands."

"Okay, we'll work it out. We'll get him there."

"I don't need your pity or help. I'm not here because I expect anything."

"I need you, though. And he's my best buddy." I get closer and hug her tight.

My life makes so much sense when she's in my arms. It's as if we're two parts of a finely carved sculpture. As if our bodies know how to be with each other; it's the most natural thing.

I close my eyes, listening to the waves outside and the tides in my chest.

"I married my first love," she says softly, "and our connection was undeniable, but the children we hoped for never came. After years of heartbreak, I suggested adoption and he proposed artificial insemination with a sperm donor—a last attempt to have our own child. Well, with my egg, as there was an issue with his sperm count. I thought he was doing it for me, for us. I admired him for doing this extraordinary thing for our family. But before Sean was born, my ex-husband left me. I later learned that in a drunken conversation, he told a friend that Sean wasn't his."

I mutter a curse. "Apologies, keep going, I won't interrupt again, I promise."

"Our parents are of Irish descent, so we selected a donor from Ireland. Sean, your best friend, is an Irish lad," she says with a small smile. "My parents were upset by the divorce, and they never knew the truth behind it. They even accused me of not being a faithful wife. Because my ex-husband didn't want anything to do with Sean, they assumed he might be right, that Sean was the product of an affair. But I never told anyone the truth. Well, I actually told Sean once, when I was particularly sad. I said he had an 'artificial father.' I regret it so much."

I nod. "He mentioned his artificial father."

Panic fills Amy's face. "What? I thought he'd moved on from that. It happened a year ago, and we never talked about it."

"Well, I'm his best friend, remember?"

"That boy!" Amy chuckles. "From the moment he was born, Sean was the shining light in our family, the precious gem my parents adored. They forgot that they were upset with me. Their grandson stole their heart the moment he was born. But living in New York was slowly destroying his health. Like I said, his disorder leaves him vulnerable to the cold. So I chose to uproot our lives and bring him here to Hawai'i, praying the warmth would give him a better life. And it did."

She chokes back a sob. Once again, I want to take her pain away.

"He was such a fragile child when we arrived, but the move has helped tremendously. Still, his weakened immune system means an infectious illness could spiral into something life-threatening."

I struggle to keep my composure. Her face is nestled in my chest, and I can feel the dampness of her teary eyes.

"In short, he's highly susceptible to infections and heals slowly. Each infection chips away his defenses a little more. I can't bear to think what might happen next time."

I wipe away the moisture from my own glistening eyes.

"He's already been admitted to the hospital a few times over the last couple of years. Each visit leaves me terrified it could be the last. Sometimes I think I might lose my mind from the stress and heartache of it all."

I take a shuddering breath.

She sits up, her head held high. "But I'll do whatever it takes to give my son the best chance possible. I'll gladly shoulder all the worry and pain if it spares him even an ounce of suffering. He's everything to me—my whole world." I wipe her tears away as she continues. "He wants to travel," she says, her voice trembling, "and do the same things as his friends. And it's painful to know he may never explore the world or travel as his heart desires because he could catch an infection."

I kneel in front of her, looking into her eyes and grasping her hands.

"He will travel and do what he loves."

She nods then gives me a small smile. "By the way, Sean's grounded. Just an FYI."

"Yeah, why?"

"It's about Curly."

After that day on the beach, she texted me to let me know that Curly was okay, but she didn't tell me how she found him.

"All right, tell me."

"You remember Sean kept apologizing, which made me suspicious. He eventually confessed that he'd planned the whole thing. He'd asked his friend to take Curly from the beach so that we would go and search for him and you could be part of it."

I gasp in shock before bursting into laughter. "No way! He knew where Curly was all that time." I shake my head in disbelief, still laughing. "I admire him for not giving up on us."

Amy gives me a mischievous scowl. "Well, he's still grounded. He scared us and lied to me."

"Why do you think he did it?"

Amy shrugs. "Because he's a pain."

"Nope, because he was fighting for his best friend."

"I suppose," she says with a subtle curl at the corners of her lips.

"I'm impressed by his determination. He's only eight, you know."

"Oh dear, don't encourage him! What he did was wrong on so many levels."

"Yes, but adults don't always make the best choices either. He figured out how to get our attention—and succeeded."

I kiss her forehead.

"I suppose, but he's still grounded." Then she crawls into my arms. "And you're as calming as the ocean."

Warmth floods into my veins as she rests her head onto my chest. I think of my flight tomorrow and embrace her tighter.

"Time to go," she announces. She kisses me, her eyes welling up with tears. "Have a safe journey."

I open my mouth, but she silences me with her index finger against my lips.

"Say nothing." Her words cut through the air like a fiery arrow. "When you get to London, if you want us both in your life, let me know. We'll be here, waiting for you. No rush. We're not going anywhere. Only if you want, though."

She plants a small peck on my lips, and then she's gone without a backward glance.

Chapter Forty-Three

Its a crisp evening. I mean Hawaiian crisp, not London crisp. I stand outside in a pair of lounging shorts and a snuggly sweatshirt.

Mi-aw

Cheddar and I have grown close, and we even have a morning ritual: petting, food, and a little treat—then some more petting.

"You love my undivided attention, don't you? I'm knackered, kitty cat. It's just you and me tonight."

She purrs as she circles my legs.

"All right, I'll give you some food. Let's go inside. But I must tell you that I'm leaving tomorrow."

My head hurts. Apparently, leaving is a painful subject.

"But Pua will take care of you. She'll pop round."

Before we can go inside, I see Kimo walking through the gate.

"Hey," he says. "I need to talk to you."

"Let me get us some drinks."

"Nah, no need. Let's sit." He's already by the table, beckoning.

I join him.

"Jenn and I had a bit of a tough time with the past bubbling up, and I don't think I handled it well."

"I'm really sorry about that."

"Not your fault. It's my doing. I'm her husband of almost twenty-five years." He looks determined, like a husband who's not prepared to lose his family. "Anyway, we argued and she went away. First time in our marriage. But I followed her, and we talked and talked. We're really good now."

I sigh with relief. "I can't tell you how happy I am to hear that."

"But she told me something very troublin'." He looks at me as if he's just revealed a classified national document and is waiting for my reaction.

My heart rate kicks up.

"About your mom." He shakes his head. "Jenn took a call from your mom once but never told me about it. We weren't even dating at that time, but she was at my house. The phone rang and my mom asked her to answer it."

My throat gets dry, and I feel as if I just swallowed a cactus.

"She didn't mean harm. She was in love with me."

I blink for a long second. "So, what did my mom say?"

"She said, 'Tell Kimo to find Marie Galway.'"

I blink. "Tell Kimo to find Marie Galway."

"Yeah, it was a short call. It wasn't easy to make long-distance calls then."

"Who's Marie Galway?"

"I dunno, never heard the name before. It must be your aunt's friend in Ireland. I wish I knew this when I was looking for her."

I can feel a tightness in my jaw. "All right, Marie Galway from Ireland. It sounds like a simple answer after three decades," I say, with an irritated tone. I immediately regret it. "Sorry."

"No worries, you've been through a lot." The wooden chair creaks as Kimo pushes himself up, and then I feel the weight of his palm pressing down on my shoulder. "I'm sorry," he says, his voice barely above a whisper.

I meet his eyes and bring my hand up to grasp his hand. A gentle breeze rustles the palm fronds overhead.

After Kimo leaves, I settle on the sofa for a long night with my laptop. There are hundreds of Marie Galways to research.

Mi-aw

Cheddar purrs, and then, for the first time, she jumps onto my lap, wedging herself between the laptop and my stomach.

"You want all the attention, don't you?" I stroke her head.

She settles in and closes her eyes.

"I see. You want to help while I search Marie Galway."

Her tail moves back and forth, brushing my arm.

"Sure, you stay right there. I like it very much too."

Chapter Forty-Four

I'm in my rental car driving away from the beach house. I got very little sleep, and after my fruitless research, I decided to hire a private investigator to find Marie Galway. But first thing first.

I park in front of Amy's house.

She opens her front door as I'm getting out of the car. "You missed your plane," she says. Her body looks as if it's made of delicate glass, and her tired eyes suggest that she was up all night too.

I rush over to her, and she leaps into my arms. Tears stream down her face. I cup her cheeks in my hands.

"You missed your plane," she says again.

Our noses touch. Her lips are a hair's breadth away from mine. "I didn't miss my flight—my destination changed," I say, before sealing our mouths together.

❀

Back home in the afternoon. I've canceled my trip around the world. Whatever happens between Amy and me, Sean's treatment is my primary focus now.

"Time to grab the helm," I say aloud, as if hearing my words will give me strength to confront the new path ahead. I might face storms or wild waves, but my ancestors never gave up. They crossed thousands of miles of ocean to reach the Hawaiian Islands.

I have it in me. I'll learn how to adjust the sails and read the wind and the stars. I'll talk to the turtles, the whales . . .

Well, I might have to learn to swim first.

My friend Sean will help me. The thought makes me grin.

I head inside to get myself a drink. The craft beer here is something else. It can make a person tearful. While in the kitchen, I catch a glimpse of a photo of my grandma and grandpa and their daughters. I've decided to get it framed.

Picking it up, I chuckle. "You have got an abundance of families, man."

I drink to that then head back outside to settle in the garden and listen to the soothing waves.

I text Luke and Dasia.

> Hey guys, didn't take the flight—again—but no more digging into what happened in the past. I'm going to focus on now and the future. I've met some extraordinary people here.

There's a ping almost immediately. They're up early, likely getting ready to open the café.

> Hey sunshine, I want to hear more about who makes you this happy. ;)

Dasia never misses anything.

> You'll meet her soon.

I'm surprised at how soon I want to introduce Amy to them.

> I'm proud of you.

I smile at the text from my brother. I'm proud of myself too. I've so much to look forward to. Enough searching for happiness in the past.

We send a few more text messages, and then, out of the corner of my eye, I spot something moving. It's Cheddar carrying something in her jaws.

"What have you got there? Please tell me you didn't kill anything!"

She drops a small yellow object at my feet and trots away.

"A present for me?" I bend down to look.

I take the yellow plastic ladder in my hands, and my blood races through my body so fast that I feel lightheaded. My heart races; my vision blurs.

I grip the ladder tightly and take a gulp of beer. And

then, cursing wildly, I storm back into the house.

Chapter Forty-Five

I sit on the couch holding the ladder in one hand and my phone in the other. Cheddar rests her tail on my feet.

"Hey man, I'm getting ready to leave for work soon," Luke says, by way of greeting. He's moving around his house.

"I know, but listen up—I need you to go to my place."

Luke sighs. "I need to run your café, remember? The one you asked me to take care of? I'll go to your place this evening."

"I can't wait that long."

I hear Dasia in the background. "Hey, sunshine, I'll go. What do you need?" She takes the phone from Luke.

"Can you find the toy fire truck in my living room and call me from there?"

Luke reappears on the screen. "Did you say the toy fire

truck? Okay, I'll call and ask Michaela to open the café without us. We'll go to your place now."

"Thank you, guys."

Time feels as if it's moving as slow as molasses as I wait for them to call me back. The thirty-minute drive that separates my apartment from their house stretches into an eternity in my restless mind. The clock, a merciless reminder of the crawling seconds, is my relentless obsession.

MI-AW. Cheddar.

CHIRP, CHIRP, CHIRP. Birds.

SPLUS-SHHH. Waves colliding with the shore.

TAP TAP TAP. The wind whispering through the palm trees.

LUB-DUB. My racing heart.

When the phone finally rings, I startle slightly. I answer and see Dasia and Luke standing in my living room.

"We're at your place, and we found the fire truck," says Luke.

"Okay, what are you waiting for? Show me, man."

Luke holds it up to the screen.

"Can you turn it around?" I ask.

He obliges, and there it is—the tiny ladder with wooden sticks that Luke and I built.

I raise my hand and show Luke the yellow ladder that Cheddar brought me. His eyes get wider, and he smiles. "Is that the original ladder?"

I nod.

"I think you found your missing puzzle piece," says Luke.

My emotions start stirring my stomach, so I quickly end the call to sprint to the bathroom. The gagging noises of my vomiting fill the room.

The fire truck I took everywhere and held as if my life depended on it as a boy came from this house. I don't know how, but it journeyed from this house into my hand. How is this even possible? My hand shakes as I continue to grip the ladder tight.

I lose track of time as I lie curled up in a tight ball on the cold tile.

My whole life, I've been holding on to something from this house. I didn't know I needed this so badly. The jumble of sadness and relief has hit me like a tornado. I'm tearing up for my mom, my grandparents, and the childhood I left behind. It's like a gut punch of emotions taking over my abdomen.

You always had it in your hand. You always had a connection to your family here.

I have no idea how long I've been lying on the floor when the bathroom door opens wide and Amy hobbles in.

She sits on the floor and embraces me.

"I'm here. Everything is okay. I'm right here. Whatever it is, you're not alone. We'll deal with it together. I'm here."

I lean my head on her shoulder, allowing myself to be vulnerable and open in the safety of her embrace.

"I found my missing piece," I say shakily.

A while later, we're sitting on the sofa.

"Who's with Sean?" I ask. "It's almost midnight."

"He's sleeping. I asked my neighbor's daughter to stay over."

"Why did you come here? How did you know I was upset?"

"Claire called. She was walking in her front yard and could hear you getting sick in the bathroom."

"Claire? Next-door Claire?"

"Yes."

"Why is she back already? She didn't tell me she was coming!"

"I don't know, but I'm pleased she is." Then she smiles at me. The smile that lifts my heart, the earth.

"So." I clear my throat. "I felt, uhm, I found out—"

Amy leans into my chest. "Let's sleep now. Here. You'll tell me later. I'll stay with you and get home before Sean wakes up."

"Thank you."

"What are girlfriends for?"

"Hmm, I like the sound of that—girlfriend."

"Me too," she says, before she leans in for a kiss.

It's the first time I sleep next to Amy for the whole night. It feels good. She makes the couch seem like the most comfortable place on earth.

But then the dawn comes, and she's up.

"Isn't it too early?" I ask groggily.

"I want to be at home when Sean wakes up. But I was thinking of coming here after school. With Sean."

"That sounds perfect," I say. "I miss my little buddy."

As I prepare after-school snacks for Sean and Amy that afternoon, I ask Cheddar, "Are you excited to see Curly?"

Mi-aw

Hearing shuffling feet, I walk to the door and open it to see Claire. A big smile spreads on my face.

"Come in, please."

She hands me a small plate covered with a cloth napkin and says, "I made another batch of banana bread for you."

"Thank you, that's what I need right now," I reply as I reach for the plate. "And it's still warm from the oven," I note.

"Always," she responds.

Claire pulls me into a tight hug as we prepare to sit down.

"How are you?" she asks, sounding concerned.

"I'm good, thank you." But her eyes are still full of concern. "Thanks for calling Amy. I appreciate it. I'm good now. Had a bit of a tough time. But how are you?"

"The pair of us, right." She chuckles. "I'm good too. I'm here with my sister. And I'm pleased to tell you that Phil will be my ex-husband soon—very soon."

"I'm so happy to hear that, and you look great." I place my hand on top of hers.

"I'm thankful he's finally going to be out of my life." I can see the determined glint in her eyes; her voice is fierce.

Just as Claire leaves, Sean runs into the house.

"Hey, buddy, the shoes, please!"

"Sorry, I'm just so excited," he shouts happily. "Mom told me that we're all going on a sunset cruise."

"Oh really?" I ask.

His head bobs, and then he suddenly yells, "Wait, is that banana bread over there?"

Chapter Forty-Six

The three of us huddle together. Sean sits between Amy and me on the steps at the back of the catamaran watching the wake. The sunset is creating mesmerizing colors. Amy's friend, who runs the cruise, had told her there'd been a last-minute cancellation, so Amy booked us tickets. Since finding the yellow ladder yesterday, I'm back to wondering where Aunt Kalani is. She somehow feels closer on the ocean, as if she's just beyond the horizon. But where? It's maddening not to know.

"Are you okay?" Amy asks, her brow furrowing with concern.

"I'm just thinking about Aunt Kalani. I thought I'd given up, but I need to find her, Amy. I feel it in my heart. Not because I need the key to my past or anything, just because she's Aunt Kalani. She's my family."

"We should try to find Aunt Kalani," Sean announces. "The ocean will guide us."

"Really, Sean? The ocean?" I ask teasingly, my arms crossed over my chest.

"It's a game," he says.

"All right, Captain Ahab, lead the way," Amy teases, her lips curling into a playful grin.

"So, do you have any clues?" asks Sean.

"Hmm, my mom had a friend called Marie Galway."

He peers at me. "Who's Marie Galway?"

"I wish I knew. My mom called Kimo's house and left a message with Jenn, who answered the call. She asked for Kimo to find Marie Galway. I searched social media and contacted all the Marie Galways I found. I'm still waiting for some of them to write back. I even hired a private investigator."

Sean asks, "Mom, can I have your phone for a second?"

Amy hands him her phone. I'm a little disappointed that Sean has already moved on from the Marie Galway conversation.

I stand and try to just enjoy the view.

Sean and Amy murmur in the background, both looking at the phone screen. Then Sean starts jumping up and down.

"Guys, guys, what's going on?" I ask, as Sean and Amy both throw their arms around me and jump up and down. "Are you going to tell me or what?"

"It's not a person, it's a place!" Sean says.

"What is?"

"Roy, look here." Amy shows me a map on her phone. "This is the county Galway. Because Sean is partly Irish and loves maps, he's memorized all the counties there."

Sean nods and beams.

"Look here, this village."

I stare at the screen. "Marie Galway isn't a person!" I yell. "It's a place!"

Sean confirms, pointing to the village called Maree.

Amy raises both her hands to her face. "Oh my . . . Wow, I can't believe this."

I grab Sean, lifting him in the air. His laughter is one of the best sounds on earth. It's contagious. "It's a place, not a person!" I say with a giggle. "Hey, buddy! You did it."

I look at Amy. Tears well in her eyes.

I pull them back to our seats. "Okay, let's think this over. She probably said 'Maree in Galway,' but Kimo's wife didn't hear it properly. It might still be a wild goose chase, but this is big."

"Are you going?" Amy asks.

"Oh yes, immediately—but I'll definitely get a return ticket," I say, pulling her close to me.

After we get off the boat, Amy and Sean help me book a flight to Ireland and make sure I have everything ready for the next day. As I pack my suitcase, I feel a mix of nerves and excitement.

"Hey, sunshine," Amy says, peeking into the bedroom. "Are you ready to go?"

"Born ready," I reply with a grin.

"Good, because you're staying with us tonight."

"I'd love that."

In the morning, I get up first and make coffee and breakfast. Sean stayed up later than usual the previous night to help me investigate further, and I now know more about Ireland and Galway than any other place. Witnessing his enthusiasm for Ireland, I made him a silent promise that I would take him there one day.

"Sean has never seen anyone else sleeping in my bedroom before," Amy said, when we finally snuggled into bed. "I was nervous when I invited you, but he's so happy to have you here."

"This is huge," I said, kissing her gently. "Thank you for including me in your small but perfect family."

When the alarm chimes, Amy and Sean both walk into the kitchen with sleepy eyes.

"Smells wonderful," Amy says. Sean gives me a hug from behind as I crack eggs into the frying pan.

When Amy leaves the kitchen, Sean says, "A quick chat, please."

"Uh-huh, okay. What's up?" I turn around, facing him.

"If you ever upset my mom, I'll really, really hurt you."

"Oh," I say, trying not to grin. "Thanks for letting me know."

Then the Sean I know comes back—big smile, wide eyes.

After breakfast, I head to Amy's room and zip up my suitcase. "Guess it's time to chase the Irish winds then."

Sean runs to the car ahead of us. "Roy," Amy begins, her voice catching, "You've been such a positive influence on Sean and . . . and on me too. You've shown us that family can be found in unexpected places."

"Hey, now," I say. "I'm just a guy who accidentally sailed into a wild family adventure. But I wouldn't trade any of it for the world because it brought me here—to both of you."

At the airport, the three of us hold each other tightly in a group hug, savoring the connection we've forged over these past few weeks.

"Take care of yourselves," I whisper, releasing them and stepping back.

"Likewise," Amy responds, wiping away tears from her eyes, which hold millions of promises.

"Go find your aunt," Sean says, giving me a thumbs-up.

"Will do," I promise, turning to walk away.

"Roy!" Sean calls out, catching my attention. "You can do this!"

His words soothe my anxious mind, and as the aircraft ascends, I close my eyes and imagine what awaits me in Ireland.

Chapter Forty-Seven

Three planes, four airports, many layovers, and over thirty hours later, I'm approaching Dublin Airport. I left Hawai'i in the afternoon and it's now morning. I'm not sure what day it is.

I'm on my way to find *da family*!

I look out the window, my forehead pressing lightly against the cool glass, to see a canvas of grays and misty whites. Rivulets of rainwater race each other down the windowpane. It reminds me of arriving in Hawai'i in a torrential downpour. I wonder if this is a sign of some sort.

With a jolt, the plane touches down, and the cabin fills with the sound of rain pounding on the roof. I can't help but smile. *Torrential rain might be my lucky charm.*

After grabbing my small bag, I eagerly make my way through the long corridors of the airport, excited to see Dasia and Luke. They wanted to be here, and my team at Pages and Beans is terrific so Luke doesn't need to be there every day. As soon as I step out of the arrivals door, they envelop me in their arms.

"How are you, mate?"

"How was your journey, sunshine?"

"Long but good," I reply.

I look at my big brother, who came through for me over and over when I felt utterly alone in this world, and then embrace him tightly again.

"Okay, are we ready to find this aunt of mine?"

"Absolutely!" says Dasia. "This is so exciting."

"Let's find something to eat first," Luke says. "I'm sure you could do with a meal, and the rain might also lighten up."

We have a two-hour drive ahead of us, so I agree. We find a restaurant in the airport, and as soon as we sit, Dasia says, "Tell us about her, Roy!"

A wide grin spreads across my face.

"Oh dear, you're in love." Her smile matches mine.

"I sure am."

"You're not even denying it," says Luke. Their expressions are comical. "That's fast," he continues, and I sense a bit of cautiousness.

"Love and time are independent variables," Dasia says with a scoff. Her excitement is so sweet. "Tell us more about her, please, Roy."

"She's a beautiful person, a stunning woman, and a great mother."

"And she's your girlfriend—so she's a smart and lucky woman too."

"Thank you, Dasia."

"I mean it." She chuckles. "Who would have thought you'd find love on the other side of the world."

"I'm surprised too. I have a lot to tell you guys about."

We eat, chat, and laugh—my family and I.

"Did you bring it?" I ask Luke, as we're finishing up. He knows what I'm talking about. He leans into his bag and takes out the fire truck. My yellow fire truck.

After removing the ladder already on the toy, I take the yellow ladder out of my pocket and inhale a long breath. It easily snaps into place on the truck.

"It fits."

Luke picks up the other ladder, the one he and I made. "You found the original."

"I'm keeping both. One is as significant as the other."

I avoid Dasia's eyes as a few drops of tears trickle down her face.

"Let's go and find your aunt," says Luke.

Dasia insists on sitting in the back, so I can clearly see the roads and the village. Luke drives.

The rain is heavy, and the windshield wipers are fast and loud, matching my heartbeats. What if Kalani doesn't want to be found? What if she doesn't want to talk with me? So many what-ifs.

One hundred and thirty miles to go. One hundred and

thirty miles to my aunt? To *da family*. Hopefully. What if she isn't there? What if she isn't even alive?

I cling to the hope that she is. Hope is good.

Dasia asks millions of questions, and I happily respond—anything to occupy my mind. But as we approach Galway, I become quieter. Rolling green hills and rugged coastline are dotted with traditional cottages and farms.

As Luke drives into a country lane, I give them an update.

"The village is situated on a peninsula, with a bay on one side and a lagoon on the other. Many different bird species live on the extensive salt marshes and mudflats."

Luke navigates into Maree. The place looks so peaceful. There's a mix of old and new homes and a few shops.

We park outside a small store. "Shall we stop here and ask about your aunt?"

The three of us proceed into the shop stocked with foodstuffs, beverages, stationery, tools, cards, and various other items.

A woman at the counter smiles warmly at us. She has a fair complexion, red hair tied neatly in a bun, and bright, sparkling green eyes. She looks like an extra in a movie set in Ireland. "Hello there, dears. What can I do for you today?"

I step forward. "Hello, ma'am. I wonder if you could help." I pause to take a deep breath. "I'm looking for my aunt, who may have lived here some time ago."

"Oh, you're in luck! I was born and raised around these parts, so I know everyone in town."

I glance back at Dasia and Luke, and both smile encouragingly. "That's fantastic. Her name is Kalani. She's from Hawai'i and was possibly around seventeen or eighteen when she arrived. She's fifty-one now."

She shifts, and the once-friendly woman now appears unfriendly, but she forces a smile. "Let me think." I can tell that she doesn't need to think. "I don't know anyone from Hawai'i. I'd have known if someone from Hawai'i lived here."

She stares at me for a beat then looks at Dasia and Luke. Man, I'm so glad that they insisted on joining me.

"It's possible she doesn't know she has a nephew," I say.

"As I said, young man, I don't know anyone called Kalani around here." Her uneasiness oozes out of her.

"Okay, sorry to bother you."

"No worries," she says, her friendly vibe returning. "Have a grand day, darling."

We hastily pile into the car.

"She knows something," says Luke.

"Yeah, she knows where my aunt is."

"Did you notice how well she pronounced Kalani's name?" Dasia says, leaning forward from the back seat. "She knows. She's a friend. What do we do now?"

"Let's follow her. I bet she'll close her store soon to rush to her friend."

The road curves up ahead, and Luke stops behind a

bend in the road. I get out of the car and spot the storefront in the distance.

I have a pounding headache.

Just then, I see the woman coming out of her store. "There you are!" I run back to the car. "She just locked her store. Let's go, let's go!"

"We'll follow her but that's it," Luke says. "After we see where she goes, we'll find a place to stay and have a rest. Then we'll decide what to do."

"Okay, Mr. Logical. I've waited thirty-four years and didn't even know I was waiting. Another day isn't going to hurt me."

The woman gets into a small white car and starts driving. We follow.

"Get closer, man," I utter anxiously. "We're on the verge of losing her."

"Don't get too close," says Dasia. "She'll notice us, Luke."

"If you two don't calm down, I'll leave you both here and go after her alone. I won't lose her. Promise."

"Okay," Dasia and I chime in unison.

"She drives like a race-car driver," he says with a laugh.

The white car signals and turns right, into a driveway.

Luke slows down.

There are tall bushes on both sides of the road. "I'll stop here for a while," says Luke. "We'll be concealed. This could be her house."

We wait silently for a few seconds. Then the engine roars to life.

"What are you doing?" I ask, startled.

Luke drives slowly, and a small two-story house appears in our view. The shop lady is walking into the house. Another woman holds the door open.

"Is that her?" Dasia asks, as she places her hand on my shoulder.

"That is my aunt, one-hundred-percent."

Chapter Forty-Eight

We settle into a lodge for the evening, but I feel restless.

I can't wait until tomorrow.

"I have to go—now," I announce, as we're finishing dinner in the restaurant in the lodge. "Can I have the car keys?"

Luke and Dasia look at each other.

"How about we come with you?" Luke suggests. "We can wait in the car if that's what you prefer."

"Sure," I say ignoring the burning discomfort in my upper abdomen.

Fifteen minutes later, I'm standing in front of the door of the house we passed earlier. I knock before I can change my mind.

313

The same woman I saw before opens the door. She stands there without a word.

"Are you Kalani?" I ask, knowing very well that it's her—dark eyes, high cheekbones, and brown hair streaked with waves of gray. I know. She's Kalani.

If she says no, you turn around and go.

If she says no, you turn around and go.

She inspects me from head to toe, her eyes piercing. Then her gaze meets mine.

I force out a strained "Hello," blinking more than usual as I fight the overwhelming urge to run back to the car.

Her hands cover her face as she steps back. A loud cry escapes her lips. "You're alive."

Then she steps forward and hugs me tightly. I can feel the tears on her cheeks. Time seems to stretch. I sense a strange familiarity, and the overwhelming sensation of comfort and belonging. Of love.

Luke and Dasia approach, their eyes misty.

"Please," Kalani says, beckoning to all of us. "Come in."

We cozy up to the fireplace in the corner of the living room.

"Uh, this is my brother, Luke, and his fiancée, Dasia, who's also my close friend," I announce.

Kalani stares at Luke then turns to me. "Your adoptive brother."

With a bitter smile, I say, "Yes." She doesn't need to know about the first ten years of my life. Not yet, anyway.

"Please have a seat. Can I offer you a drink? I certainly need something strong."

"That would be great," says Luke, sitting beside Dasia.

"No thank you for me," says Dasia.

Kalani looks at me, and I nod.

Standing, I watch as Kalani serves us bourbon, and I down it in one go. Kalani and Luke do the same.

"But we tracked down Leilani's husband," Kalani says, standing next to me. I love her accent, a mixture of Irish and Hawaiian. "I even went to London with Ian. You would have been seven years old.

"Who's Ian?" I ask.

"My late husband."

"Sorry to hear that."

She continues. "I thought Leilani was upset with me or something because she didn't get in touch. But her husband told us that she passed, and that you had been adopted. He was not a friendly man."

"You must have been devastated. About all of it," I say.

Tears stream down her face like two waterfalls flowing side by side. She doesn't attempt to wipe them away. I can feel my own tears rolling down my cheeks as well. I let them be.

"Yes, I was devastated. Each day I battled the inner torment that threatened to swallow me whole. The first few years were agonizing. I was in utter despair. I didn't even want to live anymore. But Ian and this community helped me to deal with the trauma. I also stayed in the hospital a few times."

I shake my head. Why would my father say that I had been adopted? I was between foster families. And how come he never told me I had an aunt?

"But it doesn't end there."

So, there is more. "Hit me."

"Once I was feeling more like myself again, we tried to access the adoption records but couldn't find anything."

I blink, not sure how to tell her that I hadn't been adopted at that point.

"We tried talking to her husband again, years later, and . . ." She chokes up. "And he told us that you'd passed. You would have been eleven." She starts sobbing uncontrollably.

I shake my head. *I'm gonna call that son of a—*

I have the urge to get up, scream, yell, kick things, but I compose myself and take her hands.

"I'm here. Look at me. I'm here."

The air between us becomes still. It's as though she's yearned for this very moment her entire life. She caresses my face, her eyes swollen and brimming with emotion, peering directly into my heart.

An hour later, we're sitting around Kalani's table. She prepared some snacks, not that any of us can eat, but I truly appreciate the glass of wine in my hand.

Kalani keeps gripping my face tightly. I feel as if I'm an eight-year-old. I suppose this is her way of showing belated affection. Connecting with her is worth the sore face.

"I can't wait to learn more about you and about my mother," I say.

Her eyes sadden. She must still feel the pain of losing her sister. She looks at me then glances at Dasia and Luke before focusing on me again. "If I don't say this now, it'll be buried with me for eternity."

"Please, no more secrets. I'm turning into Hercule Poirot trying to figure it all out. And I don't think a thin mustache will suit me."

We all chuckle.

"That's the Belgian detective, right?" Kalani asks.

"Yeah. I like reading detective books."

"Me too," she says, then looks around. "Can we all hold hands?"

"Sure."

Luke takes one of my hands and Kalani takes the other. Dasia is across the table, between Luke and Kalani.

"I have loved you unconditionally since you took your first breath," Kalani says.

I nod and close my eyes. So she's known me from the get-go. That's nice. She must have been present when my mom gave birth to me.

"I'm your birth mother."

I startle and open my eyes. Is my mind playing a trick on me? Kalani's eyes are closed, but Luke and Dasia both look as though they've just witnessed a flying pig performing aerial gymnastics. Dasia's jaw appears to have lost its functionality. It isn't firmly attached.

I'm at a loss for words. It's a loss that echoes in my mind too. Luke's grip on my hand becomes even tighter.

"What?" I whisper, my own voice foreign to me.

Tears trickle down Kalani's eyelashes. She opens her eyes. "I'm your mother." Her voice shakes. "I was afraid for your safety, and for Leilani's. I'm very sorry."

Kalani's trembling hands go to her face. I get up, in shock, then collapse on the sofa by the fireplace.

No one moves for a while—a few seconds or a few hours. I've no idea. And then, my body moving of its own volition, I get up and envelop Kalani in a big hug.

Noticing that Dasia and Luke are watching us, I nod, and they join us. Dasia presses her hand against my shoulder while Luke leans close to me. Kalani is now seated at the center of the three of us.

"So," I whisper, "that means the man I thought was my father isn't related to me?"

Kalani nods.

I pump my fist into the air, yelling, "Yes, yes, yes!"

I'm so relieved to know that the man who left me with a cruel stepmother, who didn't worry about my well-being, who deceived Kalani and sabotaged any possibility of my family finding me during my childhood is not my father.

He's nothing to me.

I need time to soak it all in. I rush outside, my heart fighting to get out of my ribs.

I sit down on the steps. It's a cold winter night, but I don't feel it.

A thought hits me.

Blimey!

A few long minutes later, Luke sits next to me. He throws my jacket over my shoulders.

"Oh man. It's like I'm witnessing my birth at thirty-four."

Luke squeezes my shoulder. "Too much to take in, I get it."

"No, no, no, you don't get it. I think I just figured out who my biological father is, but I need more proof. Let's go back in."

I head into the house, with Luke right behind me.

I walk right up to Kalani and say a word, a four-letter word loaded with thousands of questions. "Kimo."

Kalani gives the tiniest nod.

Kimo is my biological father!

All my emotions feel as if they've been poured into an enormous mixer. They're being vigorously stirred into an intense, tumultuous blend.

Kimo is my father. Kai is my half-brother. Pua is my half-sister.

Oh my . . . I'm mostly Hawaiian.

But the more I learn, the more questions I have.

Chapter Forty-Nine

I flop and roll around in bed at the lodge.

"I bet it was only a dream," I say out loud.

As quickly as I sit up, I'm overcome with vertigo from the sudden motion.

"Nope, it wasn't, and it's 5:30 a.m." I mutter, falling back to the pillow.

It's only been an hour since I closed my eyes. We stayed with Kalani until 10:00 p.m. It feels as if heavy rocks are pulling down my eyelids, and my eyes sting when I close them. Before we left, she told me to come for breakfast as early as I wanted.

I'm ready to step out by 6:00 a.m.

I watch Kalani as she prepares breakfast in her modest kitchen. Her cottage is old, but the interior is modern.

When I turned up, she was already sitting in front of her fireplace, sipping coffee and looking out of the window. Dasia and Luke will join us in the evening.

Observing her, I can't help but feel an unusual closeness. It's evident from our eyes that neither of us got much sleep.

"What do I call you?" I blurt.

Her long hair is pinned up. My aunt is a beautiful woman. I mean, my biological mom is. I'm having breakfast with the woman who gave birth to me. "Life is twisted in some wonderfully fucked up ways, right?" I whisper to myself.

Geez, I need to watch my language. I wonder how each of my mothers would respond to my profanity. I can't help but laugh at the absurdity of this situation.

"Kalani," she says, with a shy smile.

"Kalani?"

"Call me Kalani."

"Sure. That works." I pause. "Do you have children?" I realize the ridiculousness of my question. "I mean, any other children?"

"I was only eighteen when I moved here after meeting up with Leilani and giving her my baby—you." She looks away, out her kitchen window. "I knew you'd be safe with her."

"I'm sure I was."

"You see," she says, busying herself with slicing a loaf of bread, "it wasn't meant to be a long-term arrangement. I wasn't sure if my wrongdoings in Hawai'i would follow me here. As you know, I thought the lawyer's kid was dead. I didn't want to have a baby in prison." She looks outside again.

"We planned to reunite, Leilani and I, but we also agreed not to rush. Leilani called me a few months after she left, to share the news that she was getting married to a wonderful man. She sounded so happy and content with her new little family. Her tone gave me the sense that she had no plans to reunite with me. When she started calling less frequently and then stopped completely, I assumed she must have grown too attached to you. For a while, I told myself it was for the best. After all, I was barely getting by, living alone in a dingy room above the pub where I worked."

The sizzling sounds and mouth-watering scents of breakfast fill the air.

"At first, the ocean kept me going. I'd walk by it, swim in it, or sit by it. Then Ian came along."

No judgment, I tell myself. *Just listen.*

"I didn't want another child because I didn't think I deserved to be a mother, and I told him that. I'd harmed a young kid—well, I thought I had—and then gave my baby away. Leilani eventually told me that the kid was fine, that he hadn't died, but I still didn't forgive myself for what I'd done. The lawyer continued to threaten Leilani too."

Her eyes are downcast, but a warm smile appears on her face.

"It took five long years for me to trust that Ian loved me. And to love him. He didn't give up on me and never stopped loving me. He was twenty-four when we met, a newly graduated veterinarian who was from this village and worked at a clinic in a nearby town. He accepted my brokenness and fear. Five years later, he proposed in front of our entire village. We got married, but I was firm in my decision that I wouldn't have another child."

She sets our plates on the table. "Here's an Irish breakfast."

"Smells delicious. I had a college mate from Ireland— I've missed this breakfast."

"College." Her eyes sparkle.

"Yeah, we have a lot to catch up on, right." I take a bite of a tomato. "Like, I really love tomatoes."

She places her hand on my shoulder. "Thank you."

I tilt my head a little and ask mischievously, "Because I was born in Ireland, would that make me a tad Irish? Always liked the idea of a bit of Irish in me."

"I suppose so." She smiles.

I burst out in laughter. "Four weeks ago, I became a tiny bit Hawaiian then got myself an Irish American girlfriend. Then bam! I'm more Hawaiian than I originally thought, and it turns out that I'm actually from Ireland. Two places that I never even suspected I had a connection to. My mind is officially blown."

After breakfast, we sit in front of the sleek fireplace, which casts a warm glow across the room. Our coffee cups find places on the side tables. Kalani, comfortably nestled in the solitary armchair, cradles a small cushion against her chest. She finally asks, "How did you find out about Kimo?"

"I saw him in your photos then tracked him down to get some answers." I leave out the part about finding her diary, out of respect.

"How is he?" she asks, almost whispering.

"He's well, a happy family man. He has a son and a daughter. My half-siblings are pretty cool."

She beams.

"I'm not sure if I'll tell him that I found you, though."

"It's your decision," she says.

"You know he came to Ireland to look for you."

Kalani looks away while wiping away her tears. "I knew he would."

"But Kalani, I'm curious. Why didn't you contact him? You don't have to answer. I'm not questioning your decision. I'm just curious."

She takes a deep, shaky breath, and despair shadows her eyes.

"I was young and sad. And I was frightened too. When I realized that I was pregnant, the only thing in the world that mattered was your safety. Things probably felt worse than they were, but I was only seventeen. I had to stay in a safer place to give birth."

"Like the whales," I whisper.

"Yes, like the whales."

"And Leilani was like an escort whale."

Her voice rises slightly, revealing a fiery spirit behind

those sorrowful eyes. "What would I have said to Kimo while I was hiding from everything? Oh, by the way, I gave birth to a son and gave him to my sister." Her eyes glisten. "I found out that I was pregnant while staying with Kimo's cousin in New York. I got sick on the ferry so often but thought it was motion sickness. I wanted Kimo to forget about me and move on, have a life and follow his dreams. I was trying to protect him."

"You're not easily forgettable, though, are you?" I say, looking at her beautiful face and appreciating her graceful demeanor.

"I'll take that as a compliment, young man."

As we sip our coffee, we continue talking. She tells me she's teaching oceanography at a local college. What is it with the ocean and the people around me?

"You'll love Sean, my little buddy. He wants to be a marine biologist. He's my girlfriend's young son."

I love calling her my girlfriend.

"That's grand," she says. Then the cloud appears in her eyes again. "Kimo and I dreamed of having a family, but life had other plans for us." She looks at the fire as if she's searching for her soul, her land, and her home.

"I'm your ohana, Kalani."

She closes her eyes briefly. "Mahalo."

"Did you ever find out what the lawyer held against your dad?"

"No, never."

"Did you know he gave whatever he was holding to your mom?"

"Really? How do you know?"

"I visited him at a care home."

"Oh, did you?" Her eyes blaze with an intensity. All these years later, her dad's suffering clearly still shakes her to the core.

"Yeah." I tell her about my visit.

As I talk, it dawns on me that I think I know the details of the evening I was conceived. From her diary.

Good grief!

When I arrived in Hawai'i, I wanted to know more about my family. I've certainly received what I asked for —and then some. Losses were suffered. Decisions and choices were made. Now I have a choice: I can leave Kalani right now, be angry and bitter, or I can try to heal with her. I've already chosen the latter.

Kalani tells me more.

"Leilani came to find me in Ireland. Mom wouldn't leave Kimo alone until he spilled the beans about where I was. She told Leilani, 'Go and find your sister, do whatever is needed to protect her. Stay however long you need then bring her back.' She insisted we return only when it was safe."

She smiles widely. "I still remember when Leilani first saw my round belly. I was a lonely, desperate teenager, and Leilani gave me hope again. When she told me that the lawyer's kid was alive, I dropped to my knees and sobbed. I almost went into labor from the shock and relief."

She tilts her head, looking at the sky through the living room window. "But she also told me that the lawyer was frantic. He kept bothering my parents, and he told Leilani that he would dedicate his life to locking me up unless she agreed to run away with him. Even a decade after I left Hawai'i, he managed to contact me twice through people he knew. I was terrified, and I believed it was in the best interest of my parents' safety for me to keep my distance."

"I can tell you that he's a miserable old man nobody cares about. Not even his son."

She nods. "Anyway, Leilani stayed with me until I gave birth. Then she went to London with you and agreed to keep you until it was safe to go back to Hawai'i. You know the rest."

She looks at me with loving eyes and a tiny smile, and I go all shy on her, my cheeks burning a little.

"Like I said, when she took you, I thought you'd be safe." Her beautiful eyes glisten. "It took years for me to forgive myself. I was on thin ice for so long. I still wonder what would have happened if I had kept you. Would she still be breathing today?"

"Her book is still in her bedroom."

"*The Little Prince*?" Her face lights up as she asks.

"Yeah, it's next to her bed. You'll turn the pages when you get back."

I watch a deluge of emotions scatter over her face—a tumult of happiness, regret, pain, longing.

"How did you find the strength to overcome this?" I ask.

"Love. The ice gets thicker with love. And time. You

lean on love, and suddenly, the ice doesn't crack anymore beneath your feet."

She locks her eyes on mine. "I'm sorry." She stands and comes to sit next to me on the couch. "Please forgive me."

I nod before resting my head on her shoulder.

"Thank you," she whispers.

Chapter Fifty

I 'm amazed at how quickly a week has passed. During our visit on that first full day together, Kalani pleaded, "Can you please stay here for a few more days? Maybe even a week?"

Without a moment's hesitation, I agreed. It surprised me that I didn't even take a second to think. I'm following my gut, and it's urging me to stay.

Dasia and Luke had to go back to London, but I promised to fill them in on everything. Over the course of the week, Kalani introduced me to the whole village—all fifty-two people—and we spent hours getting to know each other.

On a phone call with Amy one day, Sean declared me the coolest adult he knew. That meant a lot.

"I still can't believe you were born in Ireland," said Amy. I love that the unfortunate events of my birth have transformed into something worthy of wonder.

"Who would've thought," I mused, "that I'd go from a kid with no family to having more family members than I can count on two hands?"

Amy's laughter was like summer on a cold day. I felt her sunshine in every fiber of my body.

"I miss my small family," I said, admiring my girlfriend. "I'll see you in a few days."

But before I leave Ireland, I need to call the man I thought was my biological father. I pace in Kalani's office before mustering the courage to make the call. He picks up promptly. The sound of his frail voice does little to alleviate my simmering anger.

"I know you met my aunt when I was a child. Why would you deny me my family?"

"Son."

"I'm not your son," I hiss.

He tells me that he doesn't even remember Kalani's first visit. But he remembers when she tried to find me again.

"I knew you'd been adopted by a nice family, and I knew you were happy. I was sad that you suffered and I wasn't around. Losing Leilani was hard on me too. So I worked hard as a way to cope. Your aunt was so determined, but I just didn't think it was best to disrupt your life, and the only way to stop her from tracking you down was to tell her that you'd passed."

Take a deep breath, Roy. A long, deep breath.

"When I called you a few weeks ago, I asked if you

knew about my mom being Hawaiian, and you said you didn't. But you met my aunt."

"I didn't know she was Hawaiian. She didn't tell me that. She came to London from Ireland. So I didn't lie to you."

I shake my head in disbelief.

"I'm really sorry," he continues. "I thought I did what was best for you. I thought I was helping you."

He sounds as sad as a hive with a lone bee.

"You know that your mother and I never asked each other questions about our families. I ran away from my past, and she did too. All I knew was that she had a son. Marrying your mother was the best thing I ever did. I loved her. I still do."

I decide against telling him that Leilani wasn't my biological mother. It's just a gut feeling, considering he's no longer family.

"Still, telling an aunt that her nephew passed when he's alive—man, I can't get my head round that. That's cruel."

"Yes. I see that now."

Despite the pain he caused, I feel sad for him. Nonetheless, I find relief in the fact that he isn't my biological father.

We say our goodbyes, and the end of the phone call marks the end of a chapter in my life.

Then there's the matter of my biological father. I've got maternal and paternal relatives popping up left, right, and center.

Smiling, I think of how I'll tell Kimo, but my joy swiftly deflates, much like a balloon punctured by a single sharp needle. He's not going to be happy. His wife won't be happy. My presence has already disrupted their marriage. And now I'm going to tell Kimo that I'm his son? No way.

One thing at a time, Roy. Focus on Kalani right now.

I grab a framed photo and join Kalani in the living room.

"When was this taken?" I ask. It's a graduation photo.

"Four years ago. It took me six years to get my degree because I went to school part time. Ian encouraged me to enroll because I was already working as a local tour guide for coastal hikes that explored how the ocean and earth existed in wonderful harmony. The coasts of Ireland are perfect for that. It was my dream to study marine science, and I enrolled in my forties."

"That's marvelous," I say, feeling proud.

"What did you dream of growing up?"

"Let me see . . . A few things. To have a family that loved me unconditionally. To travel, to fall in love, to have my own family. What did you dream of when you were little, in Hawai'i?"

She chuckles. "Kimo and I both wanted to become firefighters. Silly teenage dreams."

She notices my frozen face and asks, "What?"

"Wait here for a moment." I rush into her guest bedroom and return with the yellow fire truck. I place it and the small yellow ladder on the coffee table.

She stares at it for a few long seconds, looks at me, and then looks back at it as if it's too fragile to touch.

"Take it," I say.

She startles then gently picks it up. Streams of tears cascade down her face, and her shoulders shake.

Leaving her at the table, I open the door to let in a breath of fresh air. A gust of chilly wind sweeps into the room, and I fill my lungs with the cold and crisp air.

"Kimo got me this," she says, her voice trembling. "It was always with me, until Leilani left with you. I placed this in your blanket."

I close the door and sit beside her again, my hand on her knee. "It was always with me when I was growing up."

"That makes me really happy."

"Me too."

"I thought I lost the ladder when I fled to Ireland." She lifts the ladder up and examines it with admiration, as if she's discovered a hidden treasure. And for her, right now, it might be. She pushes the ladder into the fire truck.

SNAP

She grins with delight.

"Yeah, for many years it was a fire truck without a ladder, but Luke and I built a new ladder for it. Then a few weeks ago, I found the original ladder at your house—Grandma's house. Imagine my shock."

She exhales. "After we kidnapped the lawyer's son, Kimo and I returned to my house, but only for a few minutes. My parents weren't home. I threw a few items of clothing, my ID, and the fire truck in my small bag. The ladder must have broken off in the process."

"Or perhaps you unconsciously left it there for me to find thirty-four years later."

Her eyes glisten, and a big smile spreads across her face, much like the sunrise over the ocean. "I prefer that version."

Chapter Fifty-One

Eight weeks later, from my initial landing, I find myself once again touching down in Hawai'i.

"Home," I murmur, gazing out the small window as the plane taxis to its gate. The man who landed here eight weeks ago seems like a world away now.

I ponder what might have transpired if I'd chosen to stick to my original plans and depart Hawai'i after just a week.

Could it be that new paths show up when we don't stick to a plan?

My biological mother saw me off at Dublin Airport, and now, waiting for me in Hawai'i, is my girlfriend. Eight weeks ago, neither woman existed in my life. Let me tell you, life can take fascinating twists and turns.

In the terminal, I dash toward Amy and Sean. My buddy sprints ahead to hug me first.

On our drive home, we pass the café where I met Kimo

for the first time. Among all this joy is a tsunami of anxiety that threatens to drown me. I still don't know what to do about Kimo being my biological father. A significant part of me wants to tell him the truth. I like the idea of him being my father. But I'm just not sure if he has a space for me in his life. I'm not a product of an affair or anything, but my existence upset his wife, and this could be a big blow.

Perhaps Aunt Melina will have some guidance for me.

I focus on what Sean is telling me about his school project. The path forward will become clear with time. I don't have to have all the answers today. Today, I choose happiness.

The jetlag and anxiety made me desperate for sleep by 6:00 p.m., so I missed the sunset last night. Tonight, though, I'm determined to find Aunt Melina so we can talk.

I find her in her usual place.

"So you're back," Aunt Melina says, as she pulls me into a hug.

We lower ourselves to the ground.

"I have something big that I need help with," I say in one breath, feeling as if the words were waiting in a pressure cooker and I just opened the valve. As I look out at the ocean and watch the colors of the sunset deepen, somehow everything seems better. "Are the whales still around?"

"Mostly gone, but there's a chance you might spot one lagging behind, finishing up its packing before departing."

We both chuckle.

"I found out some important things in Ireland. It turns out that Kalani is my biological mother."

Aunt Melina looks at me with a smile. "Good that you're getting some answers."

Then I say it. Fast. "And Kimo is my biological father."

Rather than the shock I was anticipating, I see a smile on her face. "I gathered that."

Now I'm in shock. "What? What do you mean? Did you know? How?"

"There are many clues in life. We usually close our minds and eyes to them, though."

"I have thousands of questions, but what will I do? I don't want to upset anyone. I don't want to cause anyone pain. I'm lost, Aunt Melina."

"Give yourself time, child. A path will appear. Love will guide you."

"Please tell me what to do."

"I can't tell you what to do, my boy. But I think I know where you could start."

Chapter Fifty-Two

I approach Kimo's home with my insides churning. Jenn greets me with a small smile, and Kimo stands up from the sofa.

"Hello, Roy," he says uneasily, glancing at his wife. "I didn't know you were back. How are you?"

"I've invited Roy," Jenn says.

We all sit down in their living room, I'm on a small armchair, Jenn sits next to Kimo on a sofa.

"The kids aren't home," she says, which I take as my invitation to start speaking.

I inhale deeply but can fill my lungs with only a small amount of air. Feeling dizzy, I take a few moments to compose myself.

"So much happened in Ireland. I found Kalani."

I look at Kimo. He remains quiet, but I see the worry in his eyes.

"I'll get straight to the point. I also found out about my

biological father, who isn't the man I thought he was," I say, my heart pounding.

Kimo shifts his weight slightly, eyebrows furrowing. "That's big," he says quietly.

No one speaks. The silence hangs heavy in the air. Finally, Kimo breaks it. "So," he says, with uncertainty in his eyes, "who is your father?"

Jenn places her hand on his leg. "You are, dear," she says, gently but firmly.

Kimo pulls his leg away, his gaze darting between his wife and me. I can almost see the emotions swirling in his head—confusion, shock, fear.

"But that's not possible," he says, shaking his head. "I never had anything to do with your mom."

"I know this is confusing—"

"No, son, there's no confusion at all. You got it wrong. I never had any relationship with Leilani." His voice is strained.

Jenn says calmly, "That's correct, darling, because his mom isn't Leilani. It's Kalani."

The color drains from Kimo's face. His shoulders tense. The room feels compressed with unspoken emotions. I want to comfort him but don't know what to say.

Kimo puts his head in his hands. "No, no, this can't be," he murmurs. He looks up at me with eyes full of turmoil.

Jenn goes to the kitchen, and I hear her pouring liquid into a glass.

"Kalani and I . . . we were dating, but we got intimate just one time. How could this . . ."

I shrug.

When Jenn returns with a glass of water for Kimo, I say to her, "Thank you for helping me through this. I'm sorry to have caused you both pain."

She shakes her head gently. "There's been so much heartache in this story. But there's been so much love too. And it's time for the love to take over."

"What are you saying, love?" Kimo's voice holds a glimmer of hope.

"I fell for the man you became because of your youth, your devotion to your ohana, and your courage. Your past shaped you, and your past has Kalani in it. And I'm fine with that. You have a son. We welcome him into our ohana. I love what we've built together, our family. And this young man is part of you too." Her eyes shine with tears.

I swallow hard.

Kimo turns to me. "So you went to my wife first?"

I nod. "I told her everything. I was ready to wait or to never tell you, if that was her wish. But she urged me to do this now."

"I never forgave myself for not passing on Leilani's message after she called," Jenn says. "Now it's time for all of us to focus on what truly matters—not old pains, but new joy."

Kimo embraces her tightly. "Thank you, love. For still loving me."

Then he turns back to me. We share a vulnerable, searching look, both trying to absorb this truth.

"Go on," Jenn whispers. "Hug your son." She gently propels Kimo toward me.

He pulls me into a fierce, tearful embrace. Over his shoulder, I see Jenn. She's smiling.

Every fiber of my being joins her smile.

Chapter Fifty-Three

I've left it to Kimo and Jenn to tell Kai and Pua. Last night, I was able to get a good night's rest. The sound of Amy's gentle breaths as she sleeps is truly calming.

My focus now is on funding Sean's treatment. I'm on my computer this morning, researching the clinic in South Korea.

Mi-aw

She sounds different. And far away.

"What are you up to, Cheddar?" She gave me such a cold shoulder after I returned from Ireland, but now, on day three, she's been back to my lap.

I rush to Grandma's bedroom and see half of Cheddar's body beneath a broken floorboard. She's trying to escape.

"Here, here." I kneel and help her then cradle her. "You were supposed to stay out of Grandma's room while we're fixing the flooring. But, no, you're a curious little kitty cat."

I arranged for a contractor to repair the flooring, and the work started yesterday.

Purring, Cheddar playfully paws my arm.

"So much has changed since the day we met, right, sweetie?"

Noticing something shiny underneath the cracked floorboard, I take Cheddar into the living room before returning to investigate. I really don't want to find more secrets to uncover.

I reach in and pull out a little metal box. Before I open it, I check the time and then video-call Kalani.

"Look what I found." I show Kalani the box.

"Hmm . . . I recognize that. I think it's Mom's."

"It was under the floorboard," I say. "But I think we should throw it into the ocean."

She immediately objects to the idea. "It will pollute the water, and it might harm—"

"I'm joking, Kalani. Of course not. It's just that I've dealt with enough secrets. I'm a little worried about what we'll find."

"Whatever it is, we've each other now. You found love, and you have loving family all over the world. Whatever you find can't hurt you anymore. It might sadden you, but it can't hurt you."

"But this is your mother's box, so just know that I'm okay with whatever you decide to do with it. I'm more than happy with the answers I've found."

"I'm done hiding and being fearful," she says. "Open it, please."

Inside the metal box is another honu necklace, similar to the one I'm wearing.

She gasps. "Oh my. It's Dad's necklace."

Then I pull out some folded documents.

"Go on, Roy."

Entry to United States in November 1952.

The Immigration and Nationality Act of 1952 – McCarran-Walter Act

"Okay, looks like some immigration documents." I unfold another document. "I think this is a birth certificate, a Hungarian one."

"A Hungarian birth certificate?"

"Who's Benedek Vilmosson?" I ask.

Benedek Vilmosson.

There's an entry letter also for Benedek Vilmosson, no parents.

Kalani and I look at each other on our phone screens and shout out the name at the same time. "Ben Williamson!"

Grandpa's immigration document. He entered the United States when he was six years old. In 1952.

Kalani looks confused. "But many people arrived in Hawai'i from all over the world as immigrants. Why change his name? And never tell us?"

347

"Let's see what else is in here."

We inspect my grandfather's application for the army and learn that he applied as Ben Williamson at the age of seventeen.

We both know who can tell us more.

Hurrying to Aunt Melina's house, I learn from her son that she's at her ohana.

"May I come in?" I ask, finding her door already open.

She gestures for me to enter.

"Did you know anything about this?" I ask, showing Aunt Melina the documents.

"Yes."

I give her a disapproving look.

"It wasn't my place to say. Hina told me things in confidence."

"So what's the story here?"

"These are the documents from the lawyer who was threatening your grandparents. Hina found out the truth about Ben's past: he left Hungary when he was a young boy and changed his age on his new identity document, making him eligible to enlist in the military."

"So, he forged identity documents."

"Yes. Hina knew that Ben had been taken in by an aunt and uncle in the States, but Ben never told her about the false identification card. Maybe he wanted to leave a painful past behind—Hina never knew. Maybe he wasn't proud of what he did to survive and begin a new life as a young immigrant during that time."

"What happened after Grandma uncovered all this?"

"She didn't tell your grandpa. She knew he never wanted his past to overshadow his present or future. She hoped one day he would tell her about his past, and she was planning to give him all these documents when he did, birth certificate and all. I think he was worried that the army would disclaim his service because he'd lied about his age and his background. But he loved and served his country until he retired. He was a proud man, and your grandma respected his decision and never told him she knew his real background."

"It must have been tough to be an immigrant child in a new country. Sounds like he had to take care of himself. Would he really have been in trouble if the lawyer revealed everything?"

"Maybe not, but we don't know how scared he was. We don't know what he went through as a child. Also, that lawyer was a frightening man. Who knows what lies and manipulations he used against Ben."

"Wow, Grandpa," I say. He crossed the ocean at age six and arrived in the US with no parents, unable to speak the language, and he successfully built a new life.

"Humankind has moved from one place to another for one reason or another for thousands of years," Aunt Melina says. "It's natural for humans to migrate. Just like your Polynesian ancestors who crossed the ocean and settled in Hawai'i. But in the 1950s, it would have been tough to be an immigrant child with no parents after the war."

"How did these documents end up with Grandma?"

"Hina had her ways of dealing with bullies. When she found out that the lawyer was threatening Ben, she asked for assistance from her cousins. They helped her to retrieve the documents and somehow convinced the lawyer not to pursue it further."

"Did Grandpa know any of this?"

"No, Hina never mentioned any of this to Ben. As I said, he was a proud man. Things were different in those times."

"Well, Grandpa Benedek, I respect your courage, and I love that you took chances in life."

It suddenly dawns on me. I have Hungarian in me too.

What diverse and wonderful roots I have.

Chapter Fifty-Four

Eight months later

The raindrops fall. We stand in front of the old gate. I apply upward pressure, just enough to ease the latch out of its groove. The gate immediately slides back. It's as if the weight of the past has been replaced with hope, love, and endless possibilities.

After months of work, our beach home has been lovingly repaired and restored.

Amy squeezes my hand while Sean runs up to the house. Kalani is scanning the garden.

"Could you?" I ask Kalani. She smiles and retrieves the metal box from underneath the porch.

"Let's get this key out of this box forever," she says, handing the key to Amy.

Amy unlocks the front door, and it swings open as if eagerly welcoming us inside. She removes her shoes and gently touches the doorframe.

"I like our new home," Sean exclaims, sprinting inside with infectious enthusiasm. Curly follows, his tail wagging happily as he explores his new surroundings. Cheddar is already in the kitchen.

With careful planning, we kept many external facets but updated the interior for modern and comfortable living. Our renovated beach home contains many Hawaiian features.

A lump forms in my throat as I watch Amy and Sean. Amy's eyes well up with tears, and we exchange a knowing glance, silently acknowledging our shared journey and the strength we've found in each other.

"Can I live in your house, Aunt Kalani?" Sean's innocent plea makes us all smile.

"Of course. I need someone to look after my ohana when I'm back in Ireland."

We built a small cottage, an ohana, next to the house, just as my grandmother had always dreamed. Now, as we stand on the porch and look at the ohana, I place my arm around Kalani's shoulder.

I didn't need to sell the beach house or the land.

Pua, my sweet sister, started a private funding campaign for Sean, and so many people donated whatever they could—Amy's family, Luke and Dasia, my mom in Bristol, Kalani, and all the ohana here in Nalu Town. Once Sean's teachers found out, the whole community ended up chipping in. We suddenly had over two hundred thousand dollars in a few days.

I asked Luke if he'd be interested in purchasing Pages

and Beans to generate additional funds for the treatment, but he had a different idea: he suggested turning Pages and Beans Café into a franchise. We've been actively pursuing this and have already approved two international applications— one in Istanbul and the other in Tuscany. One of my regular customers is moving to Tuscany and is all set to open Pages and Beans Cafe´ there. I'm so excited for her.

The three of us spent a month in South Korea and are back home now. Sean is responding to the treatment well, and we're scheduled to return in a few months.

Amy and I applied to be a foster family, and Sean is excited to be a big brother. Additionally, he's dedicating some of the funds raised for his treatment to buying bags for the foster kids, ensuring they can keep their belongings in bags that are nicer and sturdier than garbage bags. I told him about my involvement in a cycling challenge in London—Ride for Smiles and Bags of Hope. Now, he's interested in organizing a similar event here, but with a swimming challenge.

I wrap my other arm around Sean's small frame, pulling him close. "I'll start my swimming lessons next week," I say to him.

His eyes sparkle. "Yay! Then we can go to snorkeling together."

"We will."

I look up to see Kai at the gate with Jay and Dasia. Jay is Dasia's best friend from London. He's a phenomenal calligraphy artist.

"There are so many people here from London," Sean says with a grin.

"I know, that's cool, right?"

Jay bursts with exhilaration. "Kai is the absolute best tour guide in town! I've learned so much about Hawai'i—the culture, the history, the nature. Mind-blowing!"

They lock eyes for a split second, and in that moment, I notice the unmistakable spark between them—Kai and Jay.

I glance at Dasia. She's looking at the pair, too, and then she sends me a wink. "Are you ready for tomorrow?" she asks.

I look at Amy, Sean, and Kalani standing on the porch —my ohana.

"I've never been this ready for anything in my life."

Chapter Fifty-Five

Among all the things I've learned since this adventure began, one piece of wisdom sticks with me: You can write your own story.

I've come to realize that not all roots are buried in the ground. Some are forged through love and shared experiences, and some thrive in unexpected places.

Kai looks dapper. He's one of my best men.

"I'm so happy for you, man," he says. "Who would think we'd be here today?"

I look at my brother, standing next to me on the porch of the beach house. My brother and I. This time round, I'm the older brother, helping a younger brother.

Kai has moved to the Big Island to take care of our coffee plantation business. I envelop him in a tight embrace, and we exchange pats on the back.

"You know what, you're like a big braddah to me," he says, his voice sincere with mischief.

"I am your big brother." I wink. "But thanks, Kai," I say, touched by his words. "I learned from the best."

"Speaking of the best, Luke is out there ensuring all the guests are looked after. He's so proud."

Mi-aw

"Are you joining us, sweetie?" I ask, looking down at Cheddar.

Mi-aw

"I know, you don't like getting close to the water. It's okay."

When it's time, Kai and I stroll toward the beach side by side. The leafy, green Hawaiian lei that I'm wearing drapes down on both sides over my white linen shirt and settles just above my knees. My feet are bare, and the sand warmly embraces my toes.

Wooden chairs are filled with guests who are chatting, laughing, and smiling. The vibrant hum fades to a hush as I step into the circle—a circle that embodies our life and our love. Every guest occupies a chair in the harmonious circle; each face is directed toward us; each presence is equally meaningful. In this gathering, we celebrate unity and love.

The simple bamboo arch is in the center of the circle, and Luke stands next to it. There's a big heart on the sand made of shells and pebbles. Pua and Sean collected them from this beach. Amy and I will stand in its center as we exchange vows.

As I look around, my heart tries to climb out and join

the guests. I'd easily trust any of these people with my heart.

My bride will be here soon. The bridal party is at Claire's house, next door.

I take my place next to Luke, who stands tall and proud. I'm wedged between Kai and Luke and the minister, who smiles at me. A shawl with traditional Hawaiian patterns is gracefully draped over one of her shoulders.

Luke whispers, "I can't believe you're cutting in line. I'm five years older and got engaged months before you."

"I asked your permission, man," I reply.

He chuckles.

I nod to Amy's parents; her mom smiles with tears of joy in her eyes. My mom sits next to her. She's the one who gave me a family. She's also the one who loved me unconditionally, as if I were her own flesh and blood, from the moment she welcomed me into her house when I was ten years old. She showed me how a mother's love feels, and I'm ever so grateful that I get to call her Mom. Her deep-blue eyes have been misty but happy since she arrived a week ago.

"I love you," I mouth.

She responds by blowing a kiss and then wipes her eyes.

Next to her is Kalani. Another pair of tearful eyes, deep and dark brown. She is my reminder of the power of forgiveness, courage, and love. Our eyes connect for a beat. *Mom*, I say in my mind. I know she can hear me.

My gaze darts to the other side of the aisle. Kimo gives me a warm nod, holding his wife's hand. *Not you, Kimo, please*, I think, when I see his eyes welling up.

Aunt Melina smiles as Claire sits down beside her. The circle of chairs is now full.

A local musician starts playing his ukulele. The notes of "Somewhere Over the Rainbow" fill the air, enveloping us in the magic of this moment.

My heart must have climbed out of my chest as I don't feel its beat anymore.

Dasia walks into the circle first. She's the perfect combination of intelligence, beauty, humility, and kindness: my future sister-in-law, my confidant, my friend. Luke stares at her as if she's a bright star in the sky. I hear his inhale, his heartbeat.

Pua comes next. My sister. Kimo's daughter. She was over the moon when she found out she had another older brother. She's constantly teasing Kai, saying that because he's no longer the only brother, she can pick a favorite now. She's like a butterfly. Happy and cheerful.

I can't take the wait anymore; I need to send some oxygen into my lungs. Luke's hand is suddenly on my arm.

Everyone rises, and the minister blows the pū, the conch shell horn. I blink rapidly, trying to banish the moisture gathering in my eyes.

Sean walks Amy down the aisle. I gasp as my dazzling bride smiles at me. She's my air. I inhale and my chest relaxes as soon as I see those green eyes and the accompanying smile.

Sean's dirty-blond hair is styled, and he's wearing a white linen shirt and cream trousers.

"You look handsome," I say, when he's in front of me.

"You don't look bad yourself," he says. We bump fists then cross our arms before hugging.

"I love you, buddy," I whisper into his ear. Then he transfers Amy's hand to mine.

At the sight of Amy's trembling lip, I can't stop a tear from falling. My Amy wears a simple white flowy dress. She's barefoot, and her hair is down. Plumeria flowers are tucked behind her ear. How can a human being look this radiant?

I place my hand on her round tummy.

"She's been kicking again," she whispers. "Nonstop."

"That's my girl," I say, my voice cracking. "She's not gonna miss her parents' wedding."

Sean is wiping his eyes, so I give him a tissue from my pocket. *I promise you, little man, I will always have your back and be there to wipe your tears. Same for your mom and your little sister.*

Yes, we're pregnant, and our daughter will join us in four months.

I hear Luke sniffle.

I look around the circle. Is every single person here weeping?

"You created more waterfalls here than there are on all of the islands of Hawai'i," Kai whispers.

Just as the minister starts the ceremony, Curly brings Amy a ball. Everyone bursts into laughter.

I grin, thinking of how it all began.

Amy throws the ball. Curly misses it. Ball hits my face. Eight weeks later, Hawai'i is home.

Minutes later, we're husband and wife.

I'm grateful for all the twists and turns that have led me to this moment, standing proudly next to my wife and son, among my ohana.

"My wife," I whisper to her. She smiles, her green eyes sparkling like emeralds in the fading light.

Our hands intertwined, I scan all the glistening eyes. "Da family," I whisper. It's a simple phrase, but it holds the weight of a thousand unspoken words.

Mi-aw

We all turn our heads. There she is, standing at the edge of the beach. *No way.* Cheddar doesn't normally step onto the sand.

Sean runs toward her, and they create a bundle of love and mischievousness.

Our first dance is on the beach, in our circle of love. A circle that never closes but expands. After a few moments with my girls, I scan the area for Sean and beckon him over.

"Roy," he says.

"Yes, buddy."

"You'll always be my best friend, even if I end up calling you Dad someday, okay?"

Oh my. He just claimed the deepest corner of my heart.

"That sounds perfect to me," I say, my voice shaky.

I inhale the salty taste in the air. I don't know whether

it's from the waves or the single tear running down
my face

The three—well, four—of us sway back and forth in
the sand.

Two sets of green eyes stare at me. And then, I feel a
strong kick against my hand, which rests on my bride's
round belly.

I've found what I've been searching for.

My home.

It's not a place. It's a person.

And then some.

Home is wherever my Amy, our son Sean, and our
daughter are.

Afterword & Bonus Chapter

Would you like to know what the characters are up to some years later? Here's a bonus chapter to give you a sneak peek.

https://GTLondonAuthor.com/RoyBonus

Thank you!

I'm so grateful that you've taken the time to read this book and joined Roy on his journey.

Thanks again, and I would greatly appreciate it if you could leave a review on Amazon or Goodreads—it would mean a lot.

More from G.T. London

Curious about what Roy was doing before the events of this book? Dive into my novel "Second Chances and Then Some" as well as my other books at:

https://www.amazon.com/author/gt.london

What's next?

Novella: A novella is on the way that will transport readers to Istanbul, where the East meets the West—introducing Ava and Lev. Prepare for a story filled with romance, mystery, secrets, and suspense with captivating characters. Summer 2024.

Tuscany Series: Additionally, I'm crafting a distinct three-book series set in Tuscany, featuring an incredible cast and an enthralling storyline. Stay tuned for updates.

A Note from The Author

How Roy became the protagonist of this book is a story in itself. I didn't plan for *Second Chances and Then Some* and *Eight Weeks Later* to be interlinked novels, but Roy insisted on his own story being told. And I'm glad he did.

I grew fond of him as he played a significant role in enhancing the lives of others in *Second Chances and Then Some*. Then he found his way into my heart and mind as the main focus of this book.

Home and a sense of belonging are unique concepts for every person. But discovering that home is a person, not a place, holds a special place in my heart.

And I am overjoyed to see Roy, a former foster child, find happiness.

Let's Stay Connected

Here are some great ways to stay connected and be the first to know about all things related to my writing journey.

1–The Newsletter: Join my newsletter family for updates on upcoming books, special deals, and events. Visit my website to join at GTLondonAuthor.com

2–Author Page: Follow my Amazon author page for the new release updates.

3–Facebook Reader Group: facebook.com/groups/GTLondonReaders

4–Email: gtlondonauthor@gmail.com

5–Social Media: Check the "About the Author" section for social media details.

6–Events: I love meeting the readers. Tell me about any literary events near you, maybe your book club. I might be able to attend—in person or virtually.

Special Thanks

Hawai'i!

My deep gratitude goes to the beautiful nature of Hawai'i: its rainbows, ocean, sand, people, turtles, whales, rain, sun, cats, friends, and more. As humans, we should be immensely thankful to these volcanic islands for allowing us to experience their wonders.

The Aloha spirit and the Hawaiian culture serve as a reminder of what truly matters: love, family, friendship, peace, and respect—especially respect for nature.

While the act of putting words on paper may be a solitary process, the journey of writing a novel becomes significantly enjoyable with the support of many people, both in professional and personal communities.

I am deeply thankful for the support of friends and family, both near and far, who cheer me on and provide daily inspiration.

A special acknowledgment goes to my insightful

editors, Jodi Warshaw and Rachel Small, for helping me become a better storyteller. I also thank Kelly Lamb for the meticulous proofreading work.

My heartfelt appreciation goes to my husband, my partner-in-adventure, Jason, whose constant support and belief in me drive me forward as a novelist.

I also recognize the invaluable contributions of the writing community and fellow authors, whose collective support makes the path smoother.

Last, but certainly not least, I am eternally grateful to YOU, the wonderful reader. Thank you for being an integral part of this journey with me.

About the Author

G.T. London writes love stories spiced with secrets, mystery, and some danger.

For most of her adult life, she lived in the bustling city of London and dedicated herself to making a difference as a business and leadership coach, consultant, and trainer in both the UK and Canada.

She holds an MBA from Warwick Business School in the UK and has served as a guest lecturer for MBA students. Now a full-time writer, she has published articles for *Entrepreneur* and *Training* magazines.

G.T. London mentors at business schools internationally and leads writing workshops.

She now lives in Hawai'i with her author husband and partner-in-adventure, Jason.

She's currently writing the next novel while also outlining the one that follows and plotting the one after that.

facebook.com/gtlondon.author

instagram.com/gt.london.author

goodreads.com/gtlondon

amazon.com/author/gt.london

bookbub.com/authors/g-t-london

tiktok.com/@gt.london.author

Printed in Great Britain
by Amazon

47676887R00215